THE ABANDONED ROOM

A Mystery Story

WADSWORTH CAMP

1st WORLD
LIBRARY
Literary Society

The Abandoned Room

Wadsworth Camp

© 1st World Library – Literary Society, 2006
PO Box 2211
Fairfield, IA 52556
www.1stworldlibrary.org
First Edition

LCCN: 2006930806

Softcover ISBN: 1-4218-2207-5
Hardcover ISBN: 1-4218-2107-9
eBook ISBN: 1-4218-2307-1

Purchase *"The Abandoned Room"*
as a traditional bound book at:
www.1stWorldLibrary.org/purchase.asp?ISBN=1-4218-2207-5

1st World Library Literary Society is a nonprofit
organization dedicated to promoting literacy by:

- Creating a free internet library accessible from any computer worldwide.
- Hosting writing competitions and offering book publishing scholarships.

The Abandoned Room
contributed by Tim, Ed & Rodney
in support of
1st World Library Literary Society

CONTENTS

CHAPTER I

KATHERINE HEARS THE SLY STEP OF
DEATH AT THE CEDARS

The night of his grandfather's mysterious death at the Cedars, Bobby Blackburn was, at least until midnight, in New York. He was held there by the unhealthy habits and companionships which recently had angered his grandfather to the point of threatening a disciplinary change in his will. As a consequence he drifted into that strange adventure which later was to surround him with dark shadows and overwhelming doubts.

Before following Bobby through his black experience, however, it is better to know what happened at the Cedars where his cousin, Katherine Perrine was, except for the servants, alone with old Silas Blackburn who seemed apprehensive of some sly approach of disaster.

At twenty Katherine was too young, too light-hearted for this care of her uncle in which she had persisted as an antidote for Bobby's shortcomings. She was never in harmony with the mouldy house or its surroundings, bleak, deserted, unfriendly to content.

Bobby and she had frequently urged the old man to give it up, to move, as it were, into the light. He had always answered angrily that his ancestors had lived there since before the Revolution, and that what had been good enough for them was good enough for him. So that night Katherine had to hear alone the sly stalking of death in the house. She told it all to Bobby the next day - what happened, her emotions, the impression made on her by the people who came when it was too late to save Silas Blackburn.

She said, then, that the old man had behaved oddly for several days, as if he were afraid. That night he ate practically no dinner. He couldn't keep still. He wandered from room to room, his tired eyes apparently seeking. Several times she spoke to him.

"What is the matter, Uncle? What worries you?"

He grumbled unintelligibly or failed to answer at all.

She went into the library and tried to read, but the late fall wind swirled mournfully about the house and beat down the chimney, causing the fire to cast disturbing shadows across the walls. Her loneliness, and her nervousness, grew sharper. The restless, shuffling footsteps stimulated her imagination. Perhaps a mental breakdown was responsible for this alteration. She was tempted to ring for Jenkins, the butler, to share her vigil; or for one of the two women servants, now far at the back of the house.

"And Bobby," she said to herself, "or somebody will have to come out here to-morrow to help."

But Silas Blackburn shuffled in just then, and she was a trifle ashamed as she studied him standing with his back to the fire, glaring around the room, fumbling with hands that shook in his pocket for his pipe and some loose tobacco. It was unjust to be afraid of him. There was no question. The man himself was afraid - terribly afraid.

His fingers trembled so much that he had difficulty lighting his pipe. His heavy brows, gray like his beard, contracted in a frown. His voice quavered unexpectedly. He spoke of his grandson:

"Bobby! Damned waster! God knows what he'll do next."

"He's young, Uncle Silas, and too popular."

He brushed aside her customary defence. As he continued speaking she noticed that always his voice shook as his fingers shook, as his stooped shoulders jerked spasmodically.

"I ordered Mr. Robert here to-night. Not a word from him. I'd made up my mind anyway. My lawyer's coming in the morning. My money goes to the Bedford Foundation - all except a little annuity for you, Katy. It's hard on you, but I've got no faith left in my flesh and blood."

His voice choked with a sentiment a little repulsive in view of his ruthless nature, his unbending egotism.

"It's sad, Katy, to grow old with nobody caring for you except to covet your money."

She arose and went close to him. He drew back, startled.

"You're not fair, Uncle."

With an unexpected movement, nearly savage, he pushed her aside and started for the door.

"Uncle!" she cried. "Tell me! You must tell me! What makes you afraid?"

He turned at the door. He didn't answer. She laughed feverishly.

"It - it's not Bobby you're afraid of?"

"You and Bobby," he grumbled, "are thicker than thieves."

She shook her head.

"Bobby and I," she said wistfully, "aren't very good friends, largely because of this life he's leading."

He went on out of the room, mumbling again incoherently.

She resumed her vigil, unable to read because of her misgivings, staring at the fire, starting at a harsher gust of wind or any unaccustomed sound. And for a long time there beat against her brain the shuffling, searching tread of her uncle. Its cessation about eleven o'clock increased her uneasiness. He had been so afraid! Suppose already the thing he had feared had overtaken him? She listened intently. Even then she seemed to sense the soundless footsteps of disaster straying in the decayed house, and searching, too.

A morbid desire to satisfy herself that her uncle's silence meant nothing evil drove her upstairs. She stood in the square main hall at the head of the stairs, listening. Her uncle's bedroom door lay straight ahead. To her right and left narrow corridors led to the wings. Her room and Bobby's and a spare room were in the right-hand wing. The opposite corridor was seldom used, for the left-hand wing was the oldest portion of the house, and in the march of years too many legends had gathered about it. The large bedroom was there with its private hall beyond, and a narrow, enclosed staircase, descending to the library. Originally it had been the custom for the head of the family to use that room. Its ancient furniture still faded within stained walls. For many years no one had slept in it, because it had sheltered too much suffering, because it had witnessed the reluctant spiritual departure of too many Blackburns.

Katherine shrank a little from the black entrance of the corridor, but her anxiety centred on the door ahead. She was about to call when a stirring beyond it momentarily reassured her.

The door opened and her uncle stepped out. He wore an

untidy dressing-gown. His hair was disordered. His face appeared grayer and more haggard than it had downstairs. A lighted candle shook in his right hand.

"What are you doing up here, Katy?" he quavered.

She broke down before the picture of his increased fear. He shuffled closer.

"What you crying for, Katy?"

She controlled herself. She begged him for an answer to her doubts.

"You make me afraid."

He laughed scornfully.

"You! What you got to be afraid of?"

"I'm afraid because you are," she urged. "You've got to tell me. I'm all alone. I can't stand it. What are you afraid of?"

He didn't answer. He shuffled on toward the disused wing. Her hand tightened on the banister.

"Where are you going?" she whispered.

He turned at the entrance to the corridor.

"I am going to the old bedroom."

"Why? Why?" she asked hysterically. "You can't sleep there. The bed isn't even made."

He lowered his voice to a hoarse whisper:

"Don't you mention I've gone there. If you want to know, I am afraid. I'm afraid to sleep in my own room any longer."

She nodded.

"And you don't think they'd look for you there. What is it? Tell me what it is. Why don't you send for some one - a man?"

"Leave me alone," he mumbled. "Nothing for you to be worried about, except Bobby."

"Yes, there is," she cried. "Yes, there is."

He paid no attention to her fright. He entered the corridor. She heard him shuffling between its narrow walls. She saw his candle disappear in its gloomy reaches.

She ran to her own room and locked the door. She hurried to the window and leaned out, her body shaking, her teeth chattering as if from a sudden chill. The quiet, assured tread of disaster came nearer.

The two wings, stretching at right angles from the main building, formed a narrow court. Clouds harrying the moon failed quite to destroy its power, so that she could see, across the court, the facade of the old wing and the two windows of the large room through whose curtains a spectral glow was diffused. She heard one of the windows opened with a grating noise. The court was a sounding board. It carried to her even the shuffling of the old man's feet as he must have approached the bed. The glow of his candle vanished. She heard a rustling as if he had stretched himself on the bed, a sound like a long-drawn sigh.

She tried to tell herself there was no danger - that these peculiar actions sprang from the old man's fancy - but the house, her surroundings, her loneliness, contradicted her. To her over-acute senses the thought of Blackburn in that room, so often consecrated to the formula of death, suggested a special and unaccountable menace. Under such a strain the supernatural assumed vague and singular shapes.

She slept for only a little while. Then she lay awake, listening with a growing expectancy for some message to slip across the court. The moon had ceased struggling. The wind cried. The baying of a dog echoed mournfully from a great distance. It was like a remote alarm bell which vibrates too perfectly, whose resonance is too prolonged.

She sat upright. She sprang from the bed and, her heart beating insufferably, felt her way to the window. From the wing opposite the message had come - a soft, shrouded sound, another long-drawn sigh.

She tried to call across the court. At first no response came from her tight throat. When it did at last, her voice was unfamiliar in her own ears, the voice of one who has to know a thing but shrinks from asking.

"Uncle!"

The wind mocked her.

"It is nothing," she told herself, "nothing."

But her vigil had been too long, her loneliness too complete. Her earlier impression of the presence of death in the decaying house tightened its hold. She had to assure herself that Silas Blackburn slept untroubled. The thing she had heard was peculiar, and he hadn't answered across the court. The dark, empty corridors at first were an impassable barrier, but while she put on her slippers and her dressing-gown she strengthened her courage. There was a bell rope in the upper hall. She might get Jenkins.

When she stood in the main hall she hesitated. It would probably be a long time, provided he heard at all, before Jenkins could answer her. Her candle outlined the entrance to the musty corridor. Just a few running steps down there, a quick rap at the door, and, perhaps, in an instant her uncle's voice, and the blessed power to return to her room and sleep!

While her fear grew she called on her pride to let her accomplish that brief, abhorrent journey.

Then for the first time a different doubt came to her. As she waited alone in this disturbing nocturnal intimacy of an old house, she shrank from no thought of human intrusion, and she wondered if her uncle had been afraid of that, too, of the sort of thing that might lurk in the ancient wing with its recollections of birth and suffering and death. But he had gone there as an escape. Surely he had been afraid of men. It shamed her that, in spite of that, her fear defined itself ever more clearly as something indefinable. With a passionate determination to strangle such thoughts she held her breath. She tried to close her mind. She entered the corridor. She ran its length. She knocked at the locked door of the old bedroom. She shrank as the echoes rattled from the dingy walls where her candle cast strange reflections. There was no other answer. A sense of an intolerable companionship made her want to cry out for brilliant light, for help. She screamed.

"Uncle Silas! Uncle Silas!"

Through the silence that crushed her voice she became aware finally of the accomplishment of its mission by death in this house. And she fled into the main hall. She jerked at the bell rope. The contact steadied her, stimulated her to reason. One slender hope remained. The oppressive bedroom might have driven Silas Blackburn through the private hall and down the enclosed staircase. Perhaps he slept on the lounge in the library.

She stumbled down, hoping to meet Jenkins. She crossed the hall and the dining room and entered the library. She bent over the lounge. It was empty. Her candle was reflected in the face of the clock on the mantel. Its hands pointed to half-past two.

She pulled at the bell cord by the fireplace. Why didn't the butler come? Alone she couldn't climb the enclosed staircase to try the other door. It seemed impossible to her that she should wait another instant alone -

The butler, as old and as gray as Silas Blackburn, faltered in. He started back when he saw her.

"My God, Miss Katherine! What's the matter? You look like death."

"There's death," she said.

She indicated the door of the enclosed staircase. She led the way with the candle. The panelled, narrow hall was empty. That door, too, was locked and the key, she knew, must be on the inside.

"Who - who is it?" Jenkins asked. "Who would be in that room? Has Mr. Bobby come back?"

She descended to the library before answering. She put the candle down and spread her hands.

"It's happened, Jenkins - whatever he feared."

"Not Mr. Silas?"

"We have to break in," she said with a shiver. "Get a hammer, a chisel, whatever is necessary."

"But if there's anything wrong," the butler objected, "if anybody's been there, the other door must be open."

She shook her head. Those two first of all faced that extraordinary puzzle. How had the murderer entered and left the room with both doors locked on the inside, with the windows too high for use? They went to the upper story. She urged the butler into the sombre corridor.

"We have to know," she whispered, "what's happened beyond

those locked doors."

She still vibrated to the feeling of unconformable forces in the old house. Jenkins, she saw, responded to the same superstitious misgivings. He inserted the chisel with maladroit hands. He forced the lock back and opened the door. Dust arose from the long-disused room, flecking the yellow candle flame. They hesitated on the threshold. They forced themselves to enter. Then they looked at each other and smiled with relief, for Silas Blackburn, in his dressing-gown, lay on the bed, his placid, unmarked face upturned, as if sleeping.

"Why, miss," Jenkins gasped. "He's all right."

Almost with confidence Katherine walked to the bed.

"Uncle Silas - " she began, and touched his hand.

She drew back until the wall supported her. Jenkins must have read everything in her face, for he whimpered:

"But he looks all right. He can't be -"

"Cold - already! If I hadn't touched -"

The horror of the thing descended upon her, stifling thought. Automatically she left the room and told Jenkins what to do. After he had telephoned police headquarters in the county seat and had summoned Doctor Groom, a country physician, she sat without words, huddled over the library fire.

The detective, a competent man named Howells, and Doctor Groom arrived at about the same time. The detective made Katherine accompany them upstairs while he questioned her. In the absence of the coroner he wouldn't let the doctor touch the body.

"I must repair this lock," he said, "the first thing, so nothing can be disturbed."

Doctor Groom, a grim and dark man, had grown silent on entering the room. For a long time he stared at the body in the candle light, making as much of an examination as he could, evidently, without physical contact.

"Why did he ever come here to sleep?" he asked in his rumbling bass voice. "Nasty room! Unhealthy room! Ten to one you're a formality, policeman. Coroner's a formality."

He sneered a little.

"I daresay he died what the hard-headed world will call a natural death. Wonder what the coroner'll say."

The detective didn't answer. He shot rapid, uneasy glances about the room in which a single candle burned. After a time he said with an accent of complete conviction:

"That man was murdered."

Perhaps the doctor's significant words, added to her earlier dread of the abnormal, made Katherine read in the detective's manner an apprehension of conditions unfamiliar to the brutal routine of his profession. Her glances were restless, too. She had a feeling that from the shadowed corners of the faded, musty room invisible faces mocked the man's stubbornness.

All this she recited to Bobby when, under extraordinary circumstances neither of them could have foreseen, he arrived at the Cedars many hours later.

Of the earlier portion of the night of his grandfather's death Bobby retained a minute recollection. The remainder was like a dim, appalling nightmare whose impulse remains hidden.

When he went to his apartment to dress for dinner he found the letter of which Silas Blackburn had spoken to Katherine. It mentioned the change in the will as an approaching fact nothing could alter. Bobby fancied that the old man merely craved the satisfaction of terrorizing him, of casting him out with all the ugly words at his command. Still a good deal more than a million isn't to be relinquished lightly as long as a chance remains. Bobby had an engagement for dinner. He would think the situation over until after dinner, then he might go.

It was, perhaps, unfortunate that at his club he met friends who drew him in a corner and offered him too many cocktails. As he drank his anger grew, and it wasn't all against his grandfather. He asked himself why during the last few months he had avoided the Cedars, why he had drifted into too vivid a life in New York. It increased his anger that he hesitated to give himself a frank answer. But always at such moments it was Katherine rather than his grandfather who entered his mind. He had cared too much for her, and lately, beyond question, the bond of their affection had weakened.

He raised his glass and drank. He set the glass down quickly as if he would have liked to hide it. A big man, clear-eyed and handsome, walked into the room and came straight to the little group in the corner. Bobby tried to carry it off.

"'Lo, Hartley, old preacher. You fellows all know Hartley Graham? Sit down. We're going to have a little cocktail."

Graham looked at the glasses, shaking his head.

"If you've time, Bobby, I'd like a word with you."

"No preaching," Bobby bargained. "It isn't Sunday."

Graham laughed pleasantly.

"It's about money. That talks any day."

Bobby edged a way out and followed Graham to an unoccupied room. There the big man turned on him.

"See here, Bobby! When are you going out to the Cedars?"

Bobby flushed.

"You're a dear friend, Hartley, and I've always loved you, but I'm in no mood for preaching tonight. Besides, I've got my own life to lead" - he glanced away - "my own reasons for leading it."

"I'm not going to preach," Graham answered seriously, "although it's obvious you're raising the devil with your life. I wanted to tell you that I've had a note from Katherine to-day. She says your grandfather's threats are taking too much form; that the new will's bound to come unless you do something. She cares too much for you, Bobby, to see you throw everything away. She's asked me to persuade you to go out."

"Why didn't she write to me?"

"Have you been very friendly with Katherine lately? And that's not fair. You're both without parents. You owe Katherine something on that account."

Bobby didn't answer, because it was clear that while Katherine's affection for him had weakened, her friendship for Graham had grown too fast. Looking at the other he didn't wonder.

"There's another thing," Graham was saying. "The gloomy old Cedars has got on Katherine's nerves, and she says there's been a change in the old man the last few days - wanders around as if he were afraid of something."

Bobby laughed outright.

"Him afraid of something! It's always been his system to make everybody and everything afraid of him. But you're right about Katherine. We have always depended on each other. I think I'll go out after dinner."

"Then come have a bite with me," Graham urged. "I'll see you off afterward. If you catch the eight-thirty you ought to be out there before half-past ten."

Bobby shook his head.

"An engagement for dinner, Hartley. I'm expecting Carlos Paredes to pick me up here any minute."

Graham's disapproval was belligerent.

"Why, in the name of heaven, Bobby, do you run around with that damned Panamanian? Steer him off to-night. I've argued with you before. It's unpleasant, I know, but the man carries every mark of crookedness."

"Easy with my friends, Hartley! You don't understand Carlos. He's good fun when you know him - awfully good fun."

"So," Graham said, "is this sort of thing. Too many cocktails, too much wine. Paredes has the same pleasant, dangerous quality."

A club servant entered.

"In the reception room, Mr. Blackburn."

Bobby took the card, tore it into little bits, and dropped them one by one into the waste-paper basket.

"Tell him I'll be right out." He turned to Graham.

"Sorry you don't like my playmates. I'll probably run out after dinner and let the old man terrorize me as a cure for his own fear. Pleasant prospect! So long."

Graham caught at his arm.

"I'm sorry. Can't we forget to-night that we disagree about

Paredes? Let me dine with you."

Bobby's laugh was uncomfortable.

"Come on, if you wish, and be my guardian angel. God knows I need one."

He walked across the hall and into the reception room. The light was not brilliant there. One or two men sat reading newspapers about a green-shaded lamp on the centre table, but Bobby didn't see Paredes at first. Then from the obscurity of a corner a form, tall and graceful, emerged with a slow monotony of movement suggestive of stealth. The man's dark, sombre eyes revealed nothing. His jet-black hair, parted in the middle, and his carefully trimmed Van Dyke beard gave him an air of distinction, an air, at the same time, a trifle too reserved. For a moment, as the green light stained his face unhealthily, Bobby could understand Graham's aversion. He brushed the idea aside.

"Glad you've come, Carlos."

The smile of greeting vanished abruptly from Paredes's face. He looked with steady eyes beyond Bobby's shoulder. Bobby turned. Graham stood on the threshold, his face a little too frank. But the two men shook hands.

"I'd an idea until I saw Bobby," Graham said, "that you'd gone back to Panama."

Paredes yawned.

"Each year I spend more time in New York. Business suggests it. Pleasure demands it."

His voice was deep and pleasant, but Bobby had often remarked that it, like Paredes's eyes, was too reserved. It seemed never to call on its obvious powers of expression. Its accent was noticeable only in a pleasant, polished sense.

"Hartley," Bobby explained, "is dining with us."

Paredes let no disapproval slip, but Graham hastened to explain.

"Bobby and I have an engagement immediately after dinner."

"An engagement after dinner! I didn't understand -"

"Let's think of dinner first," Bobby said. "We can talk about engagements afterward. Perhaps you'll have a cocktail here while we decide where we're going."

"The aperitif I should like very much," Paredes said. "About dinner there is nothing to decide. I have arranged everything. There's a table waiting in the Fountain Room at the C -- and there I have planned a little surprise for you."

He wouldn't explain further. While they drank their cocktails Bobby watched Graham's disapproval grow. The man glanced continually at his watch. In the restaurant, when Paredes left them to produce, as he called it, his surprise, Graham appraised with a frown the voluble people who moved intricately through the hall.

"I'm afraid Paredes has planned a thorough evening," he said, "for which he'll want you to pay. Don't be angry, Bobby. The situation is serious enough to excuse facts. You must go to the Cedars to-night. Do you understand? You must go, in spite of Paredes, in spite of everything."

"Peace until train time," Bobby demanded.

He caught his breath.

"There they are. Carlos *has* kept his word. See her, Hartley. She's glorious."

A young woman accompanied the Panamanian as he came

back through the hall. She appeared more foreign than her guide - the Spanish of Spain rather than of South America. Her clothing was as unusual and striking as her beauty, yet one felt there was more than either to attract all the glances in this room, to set people whispering as she passed. Clearly she knew her notoriety was no little thing. Pride filled her eyes.

Paredes had first introduced her to Bobby a month or more ago. He had seen her a number of times since in her dressing-room at the theatre where she was featured, or at crowded luncheons in her apartment. At such moments she had managed to be exceptionally nice to him. Bobby, however, had answered merely to the glamour of her fame, to the magnetic response her beauty always brought in places like this.

"Paredes," Graham muttered, "will have a powerful ally. You won't fail me, Bobby? You will go?"

Bobby scarcely heard. He hurried forward and welcomed the woman. She tapped his arm with her fan.

"Leetle Bobby!" she lisped. "I haven't seen very much of you lately. So when Carlos proposed - you see I don't dance until late. Who is that behind you? Mr. Graham, is it not? He would, maybe, not remember me. I danced at a dinner where you were one night, at Mr. Ward's. Even lawyers, I find, take enjoyment in my dancing."

"I remember," Graham said. "It is very pleasant we are to dine together." He continued tactlessly: "But, as I've explained to Mr. Paredes, we must hurry. Bobby and I have an early engagement."

Her head went up.

"An early engagement! I do not often dine in public."

"An unavoidable thing," Graham explained. "Bobby will tell you."

Bobby nodded.

"It's a nuisance, particularly when you're so condescending, Maria."

She shrugged her shoulders. With Bobby she entered the dining-room at the heels of Paredes and Graham.

Paredes had foreseen everything. There were flowers on the table. The dinner had been ordered. Immediately the waiter brought cocktails. Graham glanced at Bobby warningly. He wouldn't, as an example Bobby appreciated, touch his own. Maria held hers up to the light.

"Pretty yellow things! I never drink them."

She smiled dreamily at Bobby.

"But see! I shall place this to my lips in order that you may make pretty speeches, and maybe tell me it is the most divine aperitif you have ever drunk."

She passed the glass to him, and Bobby, avoiding Graham's eyes, wondering why she was so gracious, emptied it. And afterward frequently she reminded him of his wine by going through the same elaborate formula. Probably because of that, as much as anything else, constraint grasped the little company tighter. Graham couldn't hide his anxiety. Paredes mocked it with sneering phrases which he turned most carefully. Before the meal was half finished Graham glanced at his watch.

"We've just time for the eight-thirty," he whispered to Bobby, "if we pick up a taxi."

Maria had heard. She pouted.

"There is no engagement," she lisped, "as sacred as a dinner, no entanglement except marriage that cannot be easily broken. Perhaps I have displeased you, Mr. Graham. Perhaps you fancy

I excite unpleasant comment. It is unjust. I assure you my reputation is above reproach" - her dark eyes twinkled - "certainly in New York."

"It isn't that," Graham answered. "We must go. It's not to be evaded."

She turned tempestuously.

"Am I to be humiliated so? Carlos! Why did you bring me? Is all the world to see my companions leave in the midst of a dinner as if I were plague-touched? Is Bobby not capable of choosing his own company?"

"You are thoroughly justified, Maria," Paredes said in his expressionless tones. "Bobby, however, has said very little about this engagement. I did not know, Mr. Graham, that you were the arbiter of Bobby's actions. In a way I must resent your implication that he is no longer capable of caring for himself."

Graham accepted the challenge. He leaned across the table, speaking directly to Bobby, ignoring the others:

"You've not forgotten what I told you. Will you come while there's time? You must see. I can't remain here any longer."

Bobby, hating warfare in his present mood, sought to temporize:

"It's all right, Hartley. Don't worry. I'll catch a later train."

Maria relaxed.

"Ah! Bobby still chooses for himself."

"I'll have enough rumpus," Bobby muttered, "when I get to the Cedars. Don't grudge me a little peace here."

Graham arose. His voice was discouraged.

"I'm sorry. I'll hope, Bobby."

Without a word to the others he walked out of the room.

So far, when Bobby tried afterward to recall the details of the evening, everything was perfectly distinct in his memory. The remainder of the meal, made uncomfortable by Maria's sullenness and Paredes's sneers, his attempt to recapture the earlier gayety of the evening by continuing to drink the wine, his determination to go later to the Cedars in spite of Graham's doubt - of all these things no particular lacked. He remembered paying the check, as he usually did when he dined with Paredes. He recalled studying the time-table and finding that he had just missed another train.

Maria's spirits rose then. He was persuaded to accompany her and Paredes to the music hall. In her dressing-room, while she was on the stage, he played with the boxes of make-up, splashing the mirror with various colours while Paredes sat silently watching.

The alteration, he was sure, came a little later in the cafe at a table close to the dancing floor. Maria had insisted that Paredes and he should wait there while she changed.

"But," he had protested, "I have missed too many trains."

She had demanded his time-table, scanning the columns of close figures.

"There is one," she had said, "at twelve-fifteen - time for a little something in the cafe, and who knows? If you are agreeable I might forgive everything and dance with you once, Bobby, on the public floor."

So he sat for some time, expectant, with Paredes, watching the boisterous dancers, listening to the violent music, sipping absent-mindedly at his glass. He wondered why Paredes had grown so quiet.

"I mustn't miss that twelve-fifteen," he said, "You know, Carlos, you weren't quite fair to Hartley. He's a splendid fellow. Roomed with me at college, played on same team, and all that. Only wanted me to do the right thing. Must say it was the right thing. I won't miss that twelve-fifteen."

"Graham," Paredes sneered, "is a wonderful type - Apollo in the flesh and Billy Sunday in the conscience."

Then, as Bobby started to protest, Maria entered, more dazzling than at dinner; and the dancers swayed less boisterously, the chatter at the tables subsided, the orchestra seemed to hesitate as a sort of obeisance.

A man Bobby had never seen before followed her to the table. His middle-aged figure was loudly clothed. His face was coarse and clean shaven. He acknowledged the introductions sullenly.

"I've only a minute," Bobby said to Maria.

He continued, however, to raise his glass indifferently to his lips. All at once his glass shook. Maria's dark and sparkling face became blurred. He could no longer define the features of the stranger. He had never before experienced anything of the kind. He tried to account for it, but his mind became confused.

"Maria!" he burst out. "Why are you looking at me like that?"

Her contralto laugh rippled.

"Bobby looks so funny! Carlos! Leetle Bobby looks so queer! What is the matter with him?"

Bobby's anger was lost in the increased confusion of his senses, but through that mental turmoil tore the thought of Graham and his intention of going to the Cedars. With shaking fingers he dragged out his watch. He couldn't read the dial. He braced his hands against the table, thrust back his chair, and arose. The room tumbled about him. Before his eyes the dancers made long nebulous bands of colour in which nothing had form or coherence. Instinctively he felt he hadn't dined recklessly enough to account for these amazing symptoms. He was suddenly afraid.

"Carlos!" he whispered.

He heard Maria's voice dimly:

"Take him home."

A hand touched his arm. With a supreme effort of will he walked from the room, guided by the hand on his arm. And always his brain recorded fewer and fewer impressions for his memory to struggle with later.

At the cloak room some one helped him put on his coat. He was walking down steps. He was in some kind of a conveyance. He didn't know what it was. An automobile, a carriage, a train? He didn't know. He only understood that it went swiftly, swaying from side to side through a sable pit. Whenever his mind moved at all it came back to that sensation of a black pit in which he remained suspended, swinging from side to side, trying to struggle up against impossible odds. Once or twice words flashed like fire through the pit: "Tyrant! - Fool to go."

From a long immersion deeper in the pit he struggled frantically. He must get out. Somehow he must find wings. He realized that his eyes were closed. He tried to open them and failed. So the pit persisted and he surrendered himself, as one accepts death, to its hateful blackness.

Abruptly he experienced a momentary release. There was no more swaying, no more movement of any kind. He heard a strange, melancholy voice, whispering without words, always whispering with a futile perseverance as if it wished him to understand something it could not express.

"What is it trying to tell me?" he asked himself.

Then he understood. It was the voice of the wind, and it tried to tell him to open his eyes, and he found that he could. But in spite of his desire they closed again almost immediately. Yet, from that swift glimpse, a picture outlined itself later in his memory.

In the midst of wild, rolling clouds, the moon was a drowning face. Stunted trees bent before the wind like puny men who strained impotently to advance. Over there was one more like a real man - a figure, Bobby thought, with a black thing over its face - a mask.

"This is the forest near the Cedars," Bobby said to himself. "I've come to face the old devil after all."

He heard his own voice, harsh, remote, unnatural, speaking to the dim figure with a black mask that waited half hidden by the straining trees.

"Why am I here in the woods near the Cedars?"

And he thought the thing answered:

"Because you hate your grandfather."

Bobby laughed, thinking he understood. The figure in the black mask that accompanied him was his conscience. He could understand why it went masked.

The wind resumed its whispering. The figures, straining like puny men, fought harder. The drowning face disappeared, wet and helpless. Bobby felt himself sinking back, back into the sable pit.

"I don't want to go," he moaned.

A long time afterward he heard a whisper again, and he wondered if it was the wind or his conscience. He laughed through the blackness because the words seemed so absurd.

"Take off your shoes and carry them in your hand. Always do that. It is the only safe way."

He laughed again, thinking:

"What a careful conscience!"

He retained only one more impression. He was dully aware that some time had passed. He shivered. He thought the wind had grown angry with him, for it no longer whispered. It shrieked, and he could make nothing of its wrath. He struggled frantically to emerge from the pit. The quality of the blackness deepened. His fright grew. He felt himself slipping, slowly at first then faster, faster down into impossible depths, and there was nothing at all he could do to save himself.

*   *   *   *   *

"Go away! For God's sake, go away!"

Bobby thought he was speaking to the sombre figure in the mask. His voice aroused him to one more effort at escape, but he felt that there was no use. He was too deep.

Something hurt his eyes. He opened them and for a time was blinded by a narrow shaft, of sunlight resting on his face. With an effort he moved his head to one side and closed his eyes again, at first merely thankful that he had escaped from the black hell, trying to control his sensations of physical evil. Subtle curiosity forced its way into his sick brain and stung him wide awake. This time his eyes remained open, staring about him, dilating with a wilder fright than he had experienced in the dark mazes of his nightmare adventure.

He had never seen this place before. He lay on the floor of an empty room. The shaft of sunlight that had aroused him entered through a crack in one of the tightly drawn blinds. There were dust and grime on the wails, and cobwebs clustered in the corners.

In the silent, deserted room the beating of his heart became audible. He struggled to a sitting posture. He gasped for breath. He knew it was very cold in here, but perspiration moistened his face. He could recall no such suffering as this since, when a boy, he had slipped from the crisis of a destructive fever.

Had he been drugged? But he had been with friends. There was no motive.

What house was this? Was it, like this room, empty and deserted? How had he come here? For the first time he went through that dreadful process of trying to draw from the black pit useful memories.

He started, recalling the strange voice and its warning, for his shoes lay near by as though he might have dropped them carelessly when he had entered the room and stretched himself on the floor. Damp earth adhered to the soles. The leather above was scratched.

"Then," he thought, "that much is right. I was in the woods. What was I doing there? That dim figure! My imagination."

He suffered the agony of a man who realizes that he has wandered unawares in strange places, and retains no recollection of his actions, of his intentions. He went back to that last unclouded moment in the cafe with Maria, Paredes, and the stranger. Where had he gone after he had left them? He had looked at his watch. He had told himself he must catch the twelve-fifteen train. He must have gone from the restaurant, proceeding automatically, and caught the train. That would account for the sensation of motion in a swift vehicle, and perhaps there had been a taxicab to the station. Doubtless in the woods near the Cedars he had decided it was too late to go in, or that it was wiser not to. He had answered to the necessity of sleeping somewhere. But why had he come here? Where, indeed, was he?

At least he could answer that. He drew on his shoes - a pair of patent leather pumps. He fumbled for his handkerchief, thinking he would brush the earth from them. He searched each of his pockets. His handkerchief was gone. No matter. He got to his feet, lurching for a moment dizzily. He glanced with distaste at his rumpled evening clothing. To hide it as far as possible he buttoned his overcoat collar about his neck. On tip-toe he approached the door, and, with the emotions of a thief, opened it quietly. He sighed. The rest of the house was as empty as this room. The hall was thick with dust. The rear door by which he must have entered stood half open. The lock was broken and rusty.

He commenced to understand. There was a deserted farmhouse less than two miles from the Cedars. Since he had always known about it, it wasn't unusual he should have taken shelter there after deciding not to go in to his grandfather.

He stepped through the doorway to the unkempt yard about whose tumbled fences the woods advanced thickly. He recognized the place. For some time he stood ashamed, yet fair enough to seek the cause of his experience in some mental unhealth deeper than any reaction from last night's folly.

He glanced at his watch. It was after two o'clock. The mournful neighbourhood, the growing chill in the air, the sullen sky, urged him away. He walked down the road. Of course he couldn't go to the Cedars in this condition. He would return to his apartment in New York where he could bathe, change his clothes, recover from this feeling of physical ill, and remember, perhaps, something more.

It wasn't far to the little village on the railroad, and at this hour there were plenty of trains. He hoped no one he knew would see him at the station. He smiled wearily. What difference did that make? He might as well face old Blackburn, himself, as he was. By this time the thing was done. The new will had been made. He was penniless and an outcast. But his furtive manner clung. He didn't want Katherine to see him like this.

From the entrance of the village it was only a few steps to the station. Several carriages stood at the platform, testimony that a train was nearly due. He prayed that it would be for New York. He didn't want to wait around. He didn't want to risk Katherine's driving in on some errand.

His mind, intent only on escaping prying eyes, was drawn by a man who stepped from behind a carriage and started across the roadway in his direction, staring at him incredulously. His quick apprehension vanished. He couldn't recall that surprised face. There was no harm being seen, miserable as he was, dressed as he was, by this stranger. He looked at him closer. The man was plainly clothed. He had small, sharp eyes. His hairless face was intricately wrinkled. His lips were thin, making a straight line.

To avoid him Bobby stepped aside, thinking he must be going past, but the stranger stopped and placed a firm hand on Bobby's shoulder. He spoke in a quick, authoritative voice:

"Certainly you are Mr. Robert Blackburn?"

For Bobby, in his nervous, bewildered condition, there was an ominous note in this surprise, this assurance, this peremptory greeting.

"What's amazing about that?" he jerked out.

The stranger's lips parted in a straight smile.

"Amazing! That's the word I was thinking of. Hoped you might come in from New York. Seemed you were here all the time. That's a good one on me - a very good one."

The beating of Bobby's heart was more pronounced than it had been in the deserted house. He asked himself why he should shrink from this stranger who had an air of threatening him. The answer lay in that black pit of last night and this morning. Unquestionably he had been indiscreet. The man would tell him how.

"You mean," he asked with dry lips, "that you've been looking for me? Who are you? Please take your hand off."

The stranger's grasp tightened.

"Not so fast, Mr. Robert Blackburn. I daresay you haven't just now come from the Cedars?"

"No, no. I'm on my way to New York. There's a train soon, I think."

His voice trailed away. The stranger's straight smile widened. He commenced to laugh harshly and uncouthly.

"Sure there's a train, but you don't want to take it. And why haven't you been at the Cedars? Grandpa's death grieved you too much to go near his body?"

Bobby drew back. The shock robbed him for a moment of the power to reason.

"Dead! The old man! How -"

The stranger's smile faded.

"Here it is nearly three o'clock in the afternoon, and you're all dressed up for last night. That's lucky."

Bobby couldn't meet the narrow eyes.

"Who are you?"

The stranger with his free hand threw back his coat lapel.

"My name's Howells. I'm a county detective. I'm on the case, because your grandfather died very strangely. He was murdered, very cleverly murdered. Queerest case I've ever handled. What do you think?"

In his own ears Bobby's voice sounded as remote and unreal as it had through the blackness last night.

"Why do you talk to me like this?"

"Because I tell you I'm on the case, and I want you to turn about and go straight to the Cedars."

"This is - absurd. You mean you suspect - You're placing me under arrest?"

The detective's straight smile returned.

"How we jump at conclusions! I'm simply telling you not to bother me with questions. I'm telling you to go straight to the Cedars where you'll stay. Understand? You'll stay there until you're wanted - Until you're wanted."

The merciless repetition settled it for Bobby. He knew it would be dangerous to talk or argue. Moreover, he craved an opportunity to think, to probe farther into the black pit. He turned and walked away. When he reached the last houses he glanced back. The detective remained in the middle of the road, staring after him with that straight and satisfied smile.

Bobby walked on, his shaking hands tightly clenched, muttering to himself:

"I've got to remember. Good God! I've got to remember. It's the only way I can ever know he's not right, that I'm not a murderer."

CHAPTER II

THE CASE AGAINST BOBBY

Bobby hurried down the road in the direction of the Cedars. Always he tried desperately to recall what had occurred during those black hours last night and this morning before he had awakened in the empty house near his grandfather's home. All that remained were his sensation of travel in a swift vehicle, his impression of standing in the forest near the Cedars, his glimpse of the masked figure which he had called his conscience, the echo in his brain of a dream-like voice saying: "Take off your shoes and carry them in your hand. Always do that. It's the only safe way."

These facts, then, alone were clear to him: He had wandered, unconscious, in the neighbourhood. His grandfather had been strangely murdered. The detective who had met him in the village practically accused him of the murder. And he couldn't remember.

He turned back to his last clear recollections. When he had experienced his first symptoms of slipping consciousness he had been in the cafe in New York with Carlos Paredes, Maria, the dancer, and a strange man whom Maria had brought to the table. Through them he might, to an extent, trace his movements, unless they had put him in a cab, thinking he would catch the train, of which he had talked, for the Cedars.

Already the forest crowded the narrow, curving road. The

Blackburn place was in the midst of an arid thicket of stunted pines, oaks, and cedars. Old Blackburn had never done anything to improve the estate or its surroundings. Steadily during his lifetime it had grown more gloomy, less habitable.

With the silent forest thick about him Bobby realized that he was no longer alone. A crackling twig or a loose stone struck by a foot might have warned him. He went slower, glancing restlessly over his shoulder. He saw no one, but that idea of stealthy pursuit persisted. Undoubtedly it was the detective, Howells, who followed him, hoping, perhaps, that he would make some mad effort at escape.

"That," he muttered, "is probably the reason he didn't arrest me at the station."

Bobby, however, had no thought of escape. He was impatient to reach the Cedars where he might learn all that Howells hadn't told him about his grandfather's death.

A high wooden fence straggled through the forest. The driveway swung from the road through a broad gateway. The gate stood open. Bobby remembered that it had been old Blackburn's habit to keep it closed. He entered and hurried among the trees to the edge of the lawn in the centre of which the house stood.

Feeling as guilty as the detective thought him, he paused there and examined the house for some sign of life. At first it seemed as dead as the forest stripped by autumn - almost as gloomy and arid as the wilderness which straggled close about it. He had no eye for the symmetry of its wings which formed the court in the centre of which an abandoned fountain stood. He studied the windows, picturing Katherine alone, surrounded by the complications of this unexpected tragedy.

His feeling of an inimical watchfulness persisted. A clicking sound swung him back to the house. The front door had been opened, and in the black frame of the doorway, as he looked,

Katherine and Graham appeared, and he knew the resolution of his last doubt was at hand.

Katherine had thrown a cloak over her graceful figure. Her sunny hair strayed in the wind, but her face, while it had lost nothing of its beauty, projected even at this distance a sense of weariness, of anxiety, of utter fear.

Bobby was grateful for Graham's presence. It was like the man to assume his responsibilities, to sacrifice himself in his service. He straightened. He must meet these two. Through his own wretched appearance and position he must develop for Katherine more clearly than ever Graham's superiority. He stepped out, calling softly:

"Katherine!"

She started. She turned in his direction and came swiftly toward him. She spread her hands.

"Bobby! Bobby! Where have you been?"

There were tears in her eyes. They were like tears that have been too long coming. He took her hands. Her fingers were cold. They twitched in his.

"Look at me, Katherine," he said hoarsely. "I'm sorry."

Graham came up. He spoke with apparent difficulty.

"You've not been home. Then what happened last night? Quick! Tell us what you did - everything."

"I've seen the detective," he answered. "He's told you, too? Be careful. I think he's back there, watching and listening."

Katherine freed her hands. The tears had dried. She shook a little.

"Then you were at the station," she said. "You must have come from New York, but I tried so hard to get you there. For hours I telephoned and telegraphed. Then I got Hartley. Come away from the trees so we can talk without - without being overheard."

As they moved to the centre of the open space Graham indicated Bobby's evening clothes.

"Why are you dressed like that, Bobby? You *did* come from town? You can tell us everything you did last night after I left you, and early this morning?"

Bobby shook his head. His answer was reluctant.

"I didn't come from New York just now. I was evidently here last night, and I can't remember, Hartley. I remember scarcely anything."

Graham's face whitened.

"Tell us," he begged.

"You've got to remember!" Katherine cried.

Bobby as minutely as he could recited the few impressions that remained from last night.

When he had finished Graham thought for some time.

"Paredes and the dancer," he said at last, "practically forced me away from you last night. It's obvious, Bobby, you must have been drugged."

Bobby shook his head.

"I thought of that right away, but it won't do. If I had been drugged I wouldn't have moved around, and I did come out somehow, I managed to get to the empty house to sleep. It's more as if my mind had simply closed, as if it had gone on working its own ends without my knowing anything about it. And that's dreadful, because the detective has practically accused me of murdering my grandfather. How was it done? You see I know nothing. Tell me how - how he was killed. I can't believe I - I'm such a beast. Tell me. If I was in the house, some detail might start my memory."

So Katherine told her story while Bobby listened, shrinking from some disclosure that would convict him. As she went on, however, his sense of bewilderment increased, and when she had finished he burst out:

"But where is the proof of murder? Where is there even a suggestion? You say the doors were locked and he doesn't show a mark."

"That's what we can't understand," Graham said. "There's no evidence we know anything about that your grandfather's heart didn't simply give out, but the detective is absolutely certain, and - there's no use mincing matters, Bobby - he believes he has the proof to convict you. He won't tell me what. He simply smiles and refuses to talk."

"The motive?" Bobby asked.

Graham looked at him curiously. Katherine turned away.

"Of course," Bobby cried with a sharpened discomfort. "I'd forgotten. The money - the new will he had planned to make. The money's mine now, but if he had lived until this morning it never would have been. I see."

"It is a powerful motive," Graham said, "for any one who doesn't know you."

"But," Bobby answered, "Howells has got to prove first that my grandfather was murdered. The autopsy?"

"Coroner's out of the county," Graham replied, "and Howells won't have an assistant. Dr. Groom's waiting in the house. We're expecting the coroner almost any time."

Bobby spoke rapidly.

"If he calls it murder, Hartley, there's one thing we've got to find out: what my grandfather was afraid of. Tell me again, Katherine, everything he said about me. I can't believe he could have been afraid of me."

"He called you," Katherine answered, "a waster. He said: 'God knows what he'll do next.' He said he'd ordered you out last night and he hadn't had a word from you, but that he'd made up his mind anyway. He was going to have his lawyer this morning and change his will, leaving all his money to the Bedford Foundation, except a little annuity for me. He grew sentimental and said he had no faith left in his flesh and blood, and that it was sad to grow old with nobody caring for him except to covet his money. I asked him if he were afraid of you, and all he answered was: 'You and Bobby are thicker than thieves.' Oh, yes. When I saw him for the last time in the hall he said there was nothing for me to worry about except you. That's all. I remember perfectly. He said nothing more about you."

"I wonder," Bobby muttered, "if a jury wouldn't think it enough."

Katherine shook her head.

"There seemed so much more than that behind his fear," she said. "As I've told you, he gave me a feeling of superstition. I never once was afraid of a murderer - of a man in the house. I was afraid of something queer and active, but not human."

Bobby straightened.

"Would you," he asked, "call a man going about in an asphasia quite human? Somnambulists do unaccountable things - such as overcoming locked doors -"

"Don't, Bobby! Don't!" Katherine cried.

"Sh - h! Quiet!" Graham warned.

A foot scraped on gravel.

"Maybe the detective," Bobby suggested.

He stared at the bend, expecting to see the stiff, plain figure of the detective emerge from the forest. Instead with a dawning amazement he watched Carlos Paredes stroll into view. The Panamanian was calm and immaculate. His Van Dyke beard was neatly trimmed and combed. As he advanced he puffed in leisurely fashion at a cigarette.

Graham flushed.

"After last night he has the nerve -"

"Be decent to him," Bobby urged. "He might help me - might clear up last night."

"I wonder," Graham mused, "to what extent he could clear it up if he wished."

Paredes threw his cigarette away as he came closer. Solemnly he shook hands with Katherine and Bobby, expressing a profound sympathy. Even then Bobby remarked that those reserved features let slip no positive emotion. The man turned to Graham.

"Our little difference of last evening," he said suavely, "will, I hope, evaporate in this atmosphere of unexpected sorrow. If I was in the wrong I deeply regret it. My one wish now is to join you in being of use to Bobby and Miss Katherine in their bereavement. I saw the account in a paper at luncheon. I came as quickly as possible."

Graham answered this smooth effrontery with a blunt question.

"Do you know that Bobby is in very real trouble, that he may be implicated in Mr. Blackburn's death?"

Paredes flung up his hands, but Bobby, looking for emotion in the sallow face then, found none. Paredes's features, it occurred to him, were exactly like a mask.

Bobby checked himself. In his unhealthy way Paredes had been a good friend. The man's voice flowed smoothly, demanding particulars.

"But this," he said, when they had told him what they could, "changes the situation. I must stay here. I must watch that detective and learn what he has up his sleeve."

Graham turned away.

"I've tried. Maybe you'll succeed better than I."

"Then you'll excuse me," Paredes said quickly. "I should like your permission to telephone to my hotel in New York for some clothing. I want to see this through."

The three looked at each other. Katherine and Graham seemed about to speak. Bobby wouldn't let them.

"Carlos," he said, "you might help me. I'm almost afraid to ask. What happened in the cafe last night? The last thing I remember distinctly is sitting there with you and Maria and a stranger she had introduced. I didn't get his name. What did I do? Did any one leave the place with me?"

Paredes smiled a little, shaking his head.

"You behaved as if Mr. Graham's earlier fears had been accomplished. You insisted you were going to catch your train. I didn't think it wise, so I went to the cloak room with you, intending to see you home. Somehow, just the same you gave me the slip."

"You oughtn't to have let him get away," Graham said.

Paredes shrugged his shoulders.

"You weren't there. You don't know how sly Bobby was."

"I suppose it's useless to ask," Graham said. "You saw nothing put in his wine?"

Paredes laughed.

"Is it likely? Certainly not. I should have mentioned it. I should have stopped such a thing. What do you think I am, Mr. Graham?"

"Sorry," Graham said. "You must understand we can't let any lead slip. This stranger Maria brought up?"

"I didn't catch his name," Paredes answered.

"I'd never seen him before. I gathered he was a friend of hers - connected with the profession. Now I shall telephone with your permission, Miss Katherine; and don't you worry, Bobby. I will see you through; but we can't do much until the coroner comes, until the detective can be made to talk."

Katherine hesitated for a moment, then she surrendered.

"Please go with him, Hartley, and - and make him as comfortable as you can in this unhappy house."

Katherine detained Bobby with a nod. He saw the others go. He shrank, in his mental and physical discomfort, from this isolation with her. As soon as the door was closed she touched his hand. She burst out passionately:

"I don't believe it, Bobby. I'll never believe it no matter what happens."

"It's sweet of you, Katherine," he said huskily. "That helps when you don't know what to believe yourself."

"Don't talk that way. Such a crime would never have entered your head under any conditions. Only, Bobby, it ought never to have happened. You ought never to have been in this position. Why have you been friendly with people like - like that Spaniard? What can he want, forcing himself here? At any rate, you'll never lead that sort of life again?"

Her fingers sought his. He clasped them firmly.

"If I get past this," he said, "I'll always look you straight in the eye, Katherine. It was mad - silly. You don't quite understand -"

He broke off, glancing at the door through which Graham had disappeared.

"Then remember," she said softly, "I don't believe it."

She released his hand, sighing.

"That's all I can say, all I can do now. You're ill, Bobby. Go in. Rest for awhile. When you've had sleep you may remember something."

He shook his head. He walked slowly with her to the house.

As he climbed the stairs he heard Paredes telephoning. He couldn't understand the man's insistence on remaining where clearly he was an intruder.

He entered his bedroom which he had occupied only once or

twice during the last few months. The place seemed unfamiliar. As he bathed and dressed his sense of strangeness grew, and he understood why. The last time he had been here he had stood in no personal danger. There had been no black parenthesis in his life during the stretch of which he might have committed an unspeakable crime. For he couldn't believe as firmly as Katherine did. Since he couldn't remember, he might have done anything.

"Come!" he called in response to a stealthy rapping at the door.

Stealth, it occurred to him, had, since last night, become a stern condition of his life.

Graham entered and noiselessly closed the door.

"I had a chance to slip in," he explained. "Paredes is wandering about the place. I'd give a lot to know what he's after at the Cedars. Katherine is in her room, trying to rest after last night, I fancy."

"And," Bobby asked, "the detective - Howells?"

"If he's back from the station," Graham answered, "he's keeping low. I wonder if it was he or Paredes who followed you through the woods?"

"Why should Carlos have followed me?" Bobby asked. "I've been thinking it over, Hartley. It isn't a bad scheme having him here, since you think he hasn't told all he knows."

"I don't say that," Graham answered. "I don't know what to think about Paredes. I've come to talk about just that. I'm a lawyer, and I've had some criminal practice. Since this detective will be satisfied with you for a victim, I'm going to take your case, if you'll have me. I'll be your detective as well as your lawyer."

Bobby was a good deal touched.

"That's kind of you - more than I deserve, for I have resented you at times."

Graham, it was clear, didn't guess he referred to his friendship for Katherine, for he answered quickly:

"I must have seemed a nuisance, but I was only trying to get you back on the straight path where you've always belonged. I can't believe you did this thing, even unconsciously, until I'm shown proof without a single flaw. Until the autopsy the only thing we have to work on is that party last night. I've telephoned to New York and put a trustworthy man on the heels of Maria and the stranger. Meantime I think I'd better watch developments here."

"Please," Bobby agreed. "Stay with me, Hartley, until this man takes some definite action."

He picked at the fringe of the window curtain. "If the autopsy shows that my grandfather was murdered," he said, "either I killed him, or else some one has deliberately tried to throw suspicion on me, for with only a motive to go on this detective wouldn't be so sure. Why in the name of heaven should any one kill the old man, place all this money in my hands, and at the same time send me to the electric chair? Don't you see how absurd it is that Carlos, Maria, or any one else should have had a hand in it? There was nothing for them to gain from his death. I've thought and thought in such circles until I am almost convinced of the logic of my guilt."

He drew the curtain farther back and gazed across the court at the room where his grandfather lay dead. One of the two windows of the room was a little raised, but the blinds were closely drawn.

"I did hate him," he mused. "There's that. Ever since I can remember he did things to make me despise him. Have - have you seen him?"

Graham nodded.

"Howells took me in. He looked perfectly normal - not a mark."

"I don't want to see him," Bobby said.

He drew back from the window, pointing. The detective, Howells, had strolled into the court. His hands hung at his sides. They didn't swing as he walked. His lips were stretched in that thin, straight smile. He paused by the fountain, glancing for a moment anxiously downward. Then he came on and entered the house.

"He'll be restless," Graham said, "until the coroner comes, and proves or disproves his theory of murder. If he questions you, you'd better say nothing for the present. From his point of view what you remember of last night would be only damaging."

"I want him to leave me alone," Bobby said. "If he doesn't arrest me I won't have him bullying me."

Jenkins knocked and entered. The old butler was as white-faced as Bobby, more tremulous.

"The policeman, sir! He's asking for you."

"Tell him I don't wish to see him."

The detective, himself, stepped from the obscurity of the hall, smiling his queer smile.

"Ah! You are here, Mr. Blackburn! I'd like a word with you."

He turned to Graham and Jenkins.

"Alone, if you please."

Bobby mutely agreed, and Graham and the butler went out. The detective closed the door and leaned against it, studying Bobby with his narrow eyes.

"I don't suppose," he began, "that there's any use asking you about your movements last night?"

"None," Bobby answered jerkily, "unless you arrest me and take me before those who ask questions with authority."

The detective's smile widened.

"No matter. I didn't come to argue with you about that. I was curious to know if you'd tried to see your grandfather's body."

Bobby shook his head.

"I took it for granted the room was locked."

"Yes," the detective answered, "but some people, it seems, have skilful ways of overcoming locks."

He moved to one side, placing his hand on the door knob.

"I've come to open doors for you, to give you the opportunity an affectionate grandson must crave."

Bobby hesitated, fighting back his feeling of repulsion, his first instinct to refuse. The detective might take it as an evidence against him. On the other hand, if he went, the man would unquestionably try to tear from a meeting between the living and the dead some valuable confirmation of his theory.

"Well?" the detective said. "What's the matter? Thought the least I could do was to give you a chance. Wouldn't do it for everybody. Then everybody hasn't your affectionate nature."

Bobby advanced.

"For God's sake, stop mocking me. I'll go, since you wish."

The detective opened the door and stood aside to let Bobby pass.

"Daresay you know the room - the way to it?"

Bobby didn't answer. He went along the corridor and into the main hall where Katherine had met Silas Blackburn last night. He fought back his aversion and entered the corridor of the old wing. He heard the detective behind him. He was aware of the man's narrow eyes watching him with a malicious assurance.

Bobby, with a feeling of discomfort, sprung in part from the gloomy passageway, paused before the door his grandfather had had the unaccountable whim of entering last night. The detective took a key from his pocket and inserted it in the lock.

"Had some trouble repairing the lock this morning," he said. "That fellow, Jenkins, entered with a heavy hand - a good deal heavier than whoever was here before him."

He opened the door.

"Queerest case I've ever seen," he mumbled. "Step in, Mr. Blackburn."

Because of the drawn blinds the room was nearly as dark as the corridor. Bobby entered slowly, his nerves taut. Against the farther wall the bed was like an enormous shadow, without form.

"Stay where you are," the detective warned, "until I give you more light. You know, I wouldn't want you to touch anything, because the room is exactly as it was when he was murdered!"

Bobby experienced a swift impulse to strangle the brutal word in the detective's throat. But he stood still while the man went to the bureau, struck a match, and applied it to a candle. The wick burned reluctantly. It flickered in the wind that slipped past the curtain of the open window.

"Come here," the detective commanded roughly.

Bobby dragged himself forward until he stood at the foot of the four-poster bed. The detective lifted the candle and held it beneath the canopy.

"You look all you want now, Mr. Robert Blackburn," he said grimly.

Bobby conquered the desire to close his eyes, to refuse to obey. He stared at his grandfather, and a feeling of wonder grew upon him. For Silas Blackburn rested peacefully in the great bed. His eyes were closed. The thick gray brows were no longer gathered in the frown too familiar to Bobby. The face with its gray beard retained no fear, no record of a great shock.

Bobby glanced at the detective who bent over the bed watching him out of his narrow eyes.

"Why," he asked simply, "do you say he was murdered?"

"He was murdered," the detective answered. "Murdered in cold blood, and, look you here, young fellow, I know who did it. I'm going to strap that man in the electric chair. He's got just one chance - if he talks out, if he makes a clean breast of it."

Across the body he bent closer. He held the candle so that its light searched Bobby's face instead of the dead man's, and the uncertain flame was like an ambush for his eyes.

In response to those intolerable words Bobby's sick nerves stretched too tight. No masquerade remained before this huntsman who had his victim trapped, and calmly studied his agony. The horror of the accusation shot at him across the body of the man he couldn't be sure he hadn't murdered, robbed him of his last control. He cried out hysterically:

"Why don't you do something? For God's sake, why don't you arrest me?"

A chuckle came from the man in ambush behind the yellow flame.

"Listen to the boy! What's he talking about? Grief for his grandfather. That's what it is - grief."

"Stop!" Bobby shouted. "It's what you've been accusing me with ever since you stopped me at the station." He indicated the silent form of the old man. "You keep telling me I murdered him. Why don't you arrest me then? Why don't you lock me up? Why don't you put the case on a reasonable basis?"

He waited, trembling. The flame continued to flicker, but the hand holding the candlestick failed to move, and Bobby knew that the eyes didn't waver, either. He forced his glance from the searching flame. He managed to lower and steady his voice.

"You can't. That's the trouble. He wasn't murdered. The coroner will tell you so. Anybody who looks at him will tell you so. Since you haven't the nerve to arrest me. I'm going. I'm glad to have had this out with you. Understand. I'm my own master. I do what I please. I go where I please."

At last the candle moved to one side. The detective straightened and walked to Bobby. The multitude of small lines in his face twitched. His voice was too cold for the fury of his words.

"That's just what I want you to do, damn you - anything you please. I'm accusing nobody, but I'm getting somebody. I've got somebody right now for this old man's murder. My man's going to writhe and burn in the chair, confession or no confession. Now get out of this room since you're so anxious, and don't come near it again."

Bobby went. At the end of the corridor he heard the closing of the door, the scraping of the key. He was afraid the detective might follow him to his room to heckle him further. To avoid that he hurried to the lower floor. He wanted to be alone. He must have time to accustom himself to this degrading fate which loomed in the too-close future. Unless they could demolish the detective's theory he, Bobby Blackburn, would go to the death house.

A fire blazed in the big hall fireplace. Paredes stood with his back to it, smoking and warming his hands. A man sat in the shadow of a deep leather chair, his rough, unpolished boots stretched toward the flaming logs. As he came down the stairs Bobby heard the heavy, rumbling voice of the man in the chair:

"Certainly it's a queer case, but not the way Howells means. I daresay the old fool died what the world will call a natural death. If you smoke so much you will, too, before long."

Bobby tried to slip past, but Paredes saw him.

"Feeling better, Bobby?"

The boots were drawn in. From the depths of the chair arose a figure nearly gigantic in the firelight. The man's face, at first glance, appeared to be covered with hair. Black and curling, it straggled over his forehead. It circled his mouth, and fell in an unkempt beard down his waistcoat. The huge man must have been as old as Silas Blackburn, but he showed no touch of gray. His only concession to age was the sunken and bloodshot appearance of his eyes.

Bobby and Katherine had always been afraid of this great, grim country practitioner who had attended their childish illnesses.

That sense of an overpowering and incomprehensible personality had lingered. Even through his graver fear Bobby felt a sharp discomfort as he surrendered his hand to the other's absorbing grasp.

"I'm afraid you came too late this time, Doctor Groom."

The doctor looked him up and down.

"Not for you, I guess," he grumbled. "Don't you know you're sick, boy?"

Bobby shook his head.

"I'm very tired. That's all. I'm on my way to the library to try to rest."

He freed his hand. The big man nodded approvingly.

"I'll send you a dose," he promised, "and don't you worry about your grandfather's having been murdered by any man. I've seen the body. Stuff and nonsense! Detective's an ass. Waiting for coroner, although I know he's one, too."

"I pray," Bobby answered listlessly, "that you're right."

"If there's any little thing I can do," Paredes offered formally.

"No, no. Thanks," Bobby answered.

He went on to the library. He glanced with an unpleasant shrinking from the door of the enclosed staircase leading to the private hall just outside the room in which his grandfather lay dead. There was no fire here, but he wrapped himself in a rug and lay on the broad, high-backed lounge which was drawn close to the fireplace, facing it. His complete weariness conquered his premonitions, his feeling of helplessness. The entrance of Jenkins barely aroused him.

"Where are you, Mr. Robert?"

"Here," Bobby answered sleepily.

The butler walked to the lounge and looked over the back.

"To be sure, sir. I didn't see you here."

He held out a glass.

"Doctor Groom said you were to drink this. It would make you sleep, sir."

Bobby closed his eyes again.

"Put it on the table where I can reach it when I want it."

"Yes, sir. Mr. Robert! The policeman? Did he say anything, if I might make so bold as to ask?"

"Go away," Bobby groaned. "Leave me in peace."

And peace for a little time came to him. It was the sound of voices in the room that aroused him. He lay for a time, scarcely knowing where he was, but little by little the sickening truth came back, and he realized that it was Graham and the detective, Howells, who talked close to the window, and Graham had already fulfilled his promise.

Bobby didn't want to eavesdrop, but it was patent he would embarrass Graham by disclosing himself now, and it was likely Graham would be glad of a witness to anything the detective might say.

It was still light. A ray from the low sun entered the window and rested on the door of the enclosed staircase.

Graham's anxious demand was the first thing Bobby heard distinctly - the thing that warned him to remain secreted.

"I think now with the coroner on his way it's time you defined your suspicions a trifle more clearly. I am a lawyer. In a sense I represent young Mr. Blackburn. Please tell me why you are so sure his grandfather was murdered."

"All right," the detective's level voice came back. "Half an hour ago I would have said no again, but now I've got the evidence I wanted. I appreciate, Mr. Graham, that you're a friend of that young rascal, and what I have to say isn't pleasant for a friend to hear. But first you want to know why I'm so sure the case is murder, in spite of the doctor who made his diagnosis without really looking."

"Go on," Graham said softly.

Bobby waited - his nerves as tense as they had grown in the presence of the dead man.

"Two days ago," the detective went on quietly, "old Mr. Blackburn came to the court house in Smithtown and asked for the best detective the district attorney could put his hand on. I don't want to blow my own trumpet, but I've got away with one or two pretty fair jobs. I've had good offers from private firms in New York. So they turned him over to me. It was easy to see the old man was scared, just as his niece says he was last night. The funny part was he wouldn't say definitely what he was afraid of. I thought he might be shielding somebody until he was a little surer of his ground. He told me he was afraid of being murdered, and he wanted a good man he could call on to come out here to the Cedars if things got too hot for him. I can hear his voice now as distinctly as if he was standing where you are.

"'My heart's all right,' he said. 'It won't stop awhile yet unless it's made to. So if I'm found cold some fine morning you can be sure I was put out of the way.'

"I tried to pump him, naturally, but he wouldn't say another word except that he'd send for me if there was time. He didn't want any fuss made, and he gave me a handsome present to keep my mouth shut and not to bother him with any more questions. I figured - you can't blame me, Mr. Graham - that the old boy was a little cracked. So I took his money and let it go at that. I didn't think much more about it until they told me early this morning he lay dead here under peculiar circumstances."

"Odd!" Graham commented. "It does make it more like murder, Howells. But he doesn't look like a murdered man."

"When you know as much about crime as I do, Mr. Graham, you'll realize that murders which are a long time planning are likely to take on one of two appearances - suicide or natural death."

"All right," Graham said. "For the purpose of argument let us agree it's murder. Even so, why do you suspect young Blackburn?"

"Without a scrap of evidence it's plain as the nose on your face," the detective answered. "If old Blackburn had lived until this morning our young man would have been a pauper. As it is, he's a millionaire, but I don't think he'll enjoy his money. The two had been at sword's points for a long time. Robert hated the old man - never made any bones about it. You couldn't ask for a more damaging motive."

"You can't convict a man on motive," Graham said shortly. "You spoke of evidence."

"More," the detective replied, "than any jury in the land would ask."

Bobby held his breath, shrinking from this information, which, however, he realized it was better he should know.

"When I got here," the detective said, "I decided on the theory of murder to make a careful search as soon as day broke. I didn't have to wait for day, though, to find one crying piece of evidence. For a long time I was alone in the room with the body. Queer feeling about that room, Mr. Graham. Don't know how to describe it except to say it's uncomfortable. Too old, maybe. Maybe it was just being there alone with the dead man before the dawn, although I thought I was hardened to that sort of thing. Anyway, I didn't like it. To keep my spirits up, as well as to save time, I commenced searching the place with a candle. Nothing about the bed. Nothing in the closets or the bureau."

He grinned sheepishly.

"You know I kind of was afraid to open the closet doors. Then I got on my knees and looked under the bed. The light was bad and I didn't see anything at first. After a minute, close against the wall, I noticed something white. I reached in and pulled it out. It was a handkerchief, and it had a monogram, Mr. Graham - R. B. in purple and green."

He paused. Graham exclaimed sharply. Bobby felt the net tighten. If that evidence was conclusive to the others, how much more so was it for him! He recalled how, after awaking in the empty house, he had searched unsuccessfully in all his pockets for his handkerchief, intending to brush the dirt from his shoes.

"I went to his room," the detective hurried on, "and found a lot of his clothes and his stationery and his toilet articles marked with the same cipher. I knew my man had made a big mistake - the sort of mistake every criminal makes no matter how clever he is - and I had him. But that isn't, by any means, all. Don't look so distressed, Mr. Graham. There isn't the slightest chance for him. You see I repaired the lock, and, as soon as it was day, closed the room and went outside to look for signs. Since nightfall no one had come legitimately through the court except Doctor Groom and myself. Our footprints were all right - making a straight line along the path to the front door. In the soft earth by the fountain I found another and a smaller print, made by a very neat shoe, sir, and I said to myself: 'There is almost certainly the footprint of the murderer.'

"There were plenty of others coming across the grass. He'd evidently avoided the path. And there was one directly under the open window where the body lies. It's still there. Perhaps you can see it. No matter. That's the last one I found. The prints ceased there. There wasn't a one going back, and I was fair up a stump. Then I saw a little undefined sign of pressure on the grass, and I got an idea. 'Suppose,' I says, 'my man took his shoes off and went around in his stockinged feet!' I couldn't understand, though, why he hadn't thought of that before. I went back to Robert Blackburn's room and got one of his shoes, and ran into a snag again. The sole of the shoe was a trifle larger than the footprints. Every one of his shoes I tried was the same way. I argued that the handkerchief was enough, but I wanted this other evidence. I simply had to clear up these queer footprints.

"I figured, since the murder had been made to look so much like a natural death, that he'd come out here some time to-day, expecting to carry it off. I wanted to go to the station, anyway, to find out if he'd been seen coming through last night or early this morning. While I was talking to the station agent I had my one piece of luck. I couldn't believe my eyes. Mr. Robert walks up from the woods. He'd been hiding around the neighbourhood all the time. Probably had missed his handkerchief and decided he'd better not take any chances. Yet it must have seemed a pretty sure thing that the station wouldn't be watched, and it's those nervy things, doing the obvious, that skilful criminals get away with all the time. I needed only one look at him, and I had the answer to the mystery of the footprints. I gave him plenty of time to come here and change his clothes, then I manoeuvered him out of his room and went there and found the pumps he'd worn last night and to-day. You see, they'd be a little smaller than his ordinary shoes. Not only did they fit the footprints exactly, but they were stained with soil exactly like that in the court. There you are, sir. I've made a plaster cast of one of the prints. I've got it here in my pocket where I intend to keep it until I clear the whole case up and turn in my report."

Graham's tone was shocked and discouraged.

"What more do you want? Why haven't you arrested him?"

In this room the detective's satisfied chuckle was an offence.

"No good detective would ask that, Mr. Graham. I want my report clean. The coroner will tell us how the old man was killed. I want to tell how young Blackburn got into that room. One of the windows was raised a trifle, but that's no use. I've figured on the outside of the wing until I'm dizzy. There's no way up for a normal man. An orangoutang would make hard work of it. His latch key would have let him into the house, and it would have been simple enough for him to find out that the old man had changed his room. I've got to find out how he got past those doors, locked on the inside."

He chuckled again.

"Almost like a sleep-walker's work."

Bobby shivered. Was that where the evidence pointed? Already the net was too finely woven. The detective continued earnestly:

"I'm figuring on some scheme to make him show me the way. I've a sort of plan for to-night, but it's only a chance."

"What?" Graham asked.

"Oh, no, sir," Howells laughed. "You'll learn about that when the time comes."

"I don't understand you," Graham said. "You're sure of your man but you keep no close watch on him. Do you know where he is now?"

"Haven't the slightest idea, Mr. Graham."

"What's to prevent his running away?"

"I'm offering him every opportunity. He wouldn't get far, and I've a feeling that if he confessed by running he'd break down and give up the whole thing. You've no idea how it frets me, Mr. Graham. I've got my man practically in the chair, but from a professional point of view it isn't a pretty piece of work until I find out how he got in and out of that room. The thing seems impossible, and yet here we are, knowing that he did it. Well, maybe I'll find out to-night. Hello!"

The door opened. Bobby from his hiding place could see Paredes on the threshold, yawning and holding a cigarette in his fingers.

"Here you are," he said drowsily. "I've just been in the court. It made me seek company. That court's too damp, Mr. Detective."

His laugh was lackadaisical.

"When the sun leaves it, the court seems full of, unfriendly things - what the ignorant would call, ghosts. I'm Spanish and I know."

The detective grunted.

"Funny!" Paredes went on. "Observation doesn't seem to interest you. I'd rather fancied it might."

He yawned again and put his cigarette to his lips. Puffing placidly, he turned and left.

"What do you suppose he means by that?" the detective said to Graham.

Without waiting for an answer he followed Paredes from the room. Graham went after him. Bobby threw back the rug and arose. For a moment he was as curious as the others as to Paredes's intention. He slipped across the dining room. The hall was deserted. The front door stood open. From the court came Paredes's voice, even, languid, wholly without expression:

"Mean to tell me you don't react to the proximity of unaccountable forces here, Mr. Howells?"

The detective's laugh was disagreeable.

"You trying to make a fool of me? That isn't healthy."

As Bobby hurried across the hall and up the stairs he heard Paredes answer:

"You should speak to Doctor Groom. He says this place is too crowded by the unpleasant past -"

Bobby climbed out of hearing. He entered his bedroom and locked the door. He resented Paredes's words and attitude which he defined as studied to draw humour out of a tragic and desperate situation. He thought of them in no other way. His tired mind dismissed them. He threw himself on the bed, muttering:

"If I run away I'm done for. If I stay I'm done for."

He took a fierce twisted joy in one phase of the situation.

"If I was there last night," he thought, "Howells will never find out how I got into the room, because, no matter what trap he sets, I can't tell him."

His leaden weariness closed his eyes. For a few minutes he slept again.

Once more it was a voice that awakened him - this time a woman's, raised in a scream. He sprang up, flung open the door, and stumbled into the corridor. Katherine stood there, holding her dressing gown about her with trembling hands. The face she turned to Bobby was white and panic-stricken. She beckoned, and he followed her to the main hall. The others came tearing up the stairs - Graham, Paredes, the detective, and the black and gigantic doctor.

In answer to their quick questions she whispered breathlessly:

"I heard. It was just like last night. It came across the court and stole in at my window."

She shook. She stretched out her hands in a terrified appeal.

"Somebody - something moved in that room where he - he's dead."

"Nonsense," the detective said. "Both doors are locked, and I have the keys in my pocket."

Paredes fumbled with a cigarette.

"You're forgetting what I said about my sensitive apprehension of strange things -"

The detective interrupted him loudly, confidently:

"I tell you the room is empty except for the murdered man - unless someone's broken down a door."

Katherine cried out:

"No. I heard that same stirring. Something moved in there."

The detective turned brusquely and entered the old corridor.

"We'll see."

The others followed. Katherine was close to Bobby. He touched her hand.

"He's right, Katherine. No one's there. No one could have been there. You mustn't give way like this. I'm depending on you - on your faith."

She pressed his hand, but her assurance didn't diminish.

The key scraped in the lock. They crowded through the doorway after the detective. He struck a match and lighted the candle. He held it over the bed. He sprang back with a sharp cry, unlike his level quality, his confident conceit. He pointed. They all approximated his helpless gesture, his blank amazement. For on the bed had occurred an abominable change.

The body of Silas Blackburn no longer lay peacefully on its back. It had been turned on its side, and remained in a stark and awkward attitude. For the first time the back of the head was disclosed.

Their glances focussed there - on the tiny round hole at the base of the brain, on the pillow where the head had rested and which they saw now was stained with an ugly and irregular splotch of blood.

Bobby saw the candle quiver at last in the detective's hand. The man strode to the door leading to the private hall and examined the lock.

"Both doors," he said, "were locked. There was no way in -"

He turned to the others, spreading his hands in justification. The candle, which he seemed to have forgotten, cast gross, moving shadows over his face and over the face of the dead man.

"At least you'll all grant me now that he was murdered."

They continued to stare at the body of Silas Blackburn. Cold for many hours, it was as if he had made this atrocious revealing movement to assure them that he had, indeed, been murdered; to expose to their startled eyes the sly and deadly method.

CHAPTER III

HOWELLS DELIVERS HIMSELF TO THE ABANDONED ROOM

For a long time no one spoke. The body of Silas Blackburn had been alone in a locked room, yet before their eyes it lay, turned on its side, as if to inform them of the fashion of this murder. The tiny hole at the base of the brain, the blood-stain on the pillow, which the head had concealed, offered their mute and ghastly testimony.

Doctor Groom was the first to relax. He raised his great, hairy hand to the bed-post and grasped it. His rumbling voice lacked its usual authority. It vibrated with a childish wonder:

"I'm reminded that it isn't the first time there's been blood from a man's head on that pillow."

Katherine nodded.

"What do you mean?" the detective snarled. "There's only one answer to this. There must have been a mechanical post-mortem reaction."

For a moment Doctor Groom's laugh filled the old room. It ceased abruptly. He shook his head.

"Don't be a fool, Mr. Policeman. At the most conservative estimate this man has been dead more than thirteen hours.

Even a few instants after death the human body is incapable of any such reaction."

"What then?" the detective asked. "Some one of us, or one of the servants, must have overcome the locks again and deliberately disturbed the body. That must be so, but I don't get the motive."

"It isn't so," Doctor Groom answered bluntly.

Already the detective had to a large extent controlled his bewilderment.

"I'd like your theory then," he said dryly. "You and Mr. Paredes have both been gossiping about the supernatural. When you first came you hinted dark things. You said he'd probably died what the world would call a natural death."

"I meant," the doctor answered, "only that Mr. Blackburn's heart might have failed under the impulse of a sudden fright in this room. I also said, you remember, that the room was nasty and unhealthy. Plenty of people have remarked it before me."

Graham touched the detective's arm.

"A little while ago you admitted yourself that the room was uncomfortable."

Doctor Groom smiled. The detective faced him with a fierce belligerency.

"You'll agree he was murdered."

"Certainly, if you wish to call it that. But I ask for the sharp instrument that caused death. I want to know how, while Blackburn lay on his back, it was inserted through the bed, the springs, the mattress, and the pillow."

"What are you driving at?"

Doctor Groom pointed to the dead man.

"I merely repeat that it isn't the first time that pillow's been stained from unusual wounds in the head. Being, as you call it, a trifle superstitious, I merely ask if the coincidence is significant."

Katherine cried out. Bobby, in spite of his knowledge that sooner or later he would be arrested for his grandfather's murder, stepped forward, nodding.

"I know what you mean, doctor."

"Anybody," the doctor said, "who's ever heard of this house knows what I mean. We needn't talk of that."

The detective, however, was insistent. Paredes in his unemotional way expressed an equal curiosity. Bobby and Katherine had been frightened as children by the stories clustering about the old wing. They nodded from time to time while the doctor held them in the desolate room with the dead man, speaking of the other deaths it had sheltered.

Silas Blackburn's great grandfather, he told the detective, had been carried to that bed from a Revolutionary skirmish with a bullet at the base of his brain. For many hours he had raved deliriously, fighting unsuccessfully against the final silence.

"It has been a legend in the family, as these young people will tell you, that Blackburns die hard, and there are those who believe that people who die hard leave something behind them - something that clings to the physical surroundings of their suffering. If it was only that one case! But it goes on and on. Silas Blackburn's father, for instance, killed himself here. He had lost his money in silly speculations. He stood where you stand, detective, and blew his brains out. He fell over and lay where his son lies, his head on that pillow. Silas Blackburn was a money grubber. He started with nothing but this property, and he made a fortune, but even he had enough imagination to lock this room up after one more death of that kind. It was this girl's father. You were too young, Katherine, to remember it, but I took care of him. I saw it. He was carried here after he had been struck at the back of the head in a polo match. He died, too, fighting hard. God! How the man suffered. He loosened his bandages toward the end. When I got here the pillow was redder than it is to-day. It strikes me as curious that the first time the room has been slept in since then it should harbour a death behind locked doors - from a wound in the head."

Paredes's fingers were restless, as if he missed his customary cigarette. The detective strolled to the window.

"Very interesting," he said. "Extremely interesting for old women and young children. You may classify yourself, doctor."

"Thanks," the doctor rumbled. "I'll wait until you've told me how these doors were entered, how that wound was made, how this body turned on its side in an empty room."

The detective glanced at Bobby. His voice lacked confidence.

"I'll do my best. I'll even try to tell you why the murderer came back this afternoon to disturb his victim."

Bobby went, curiously convinced that the doctor had had the better of the argument.

For a moment Katherine, Graham, Paredes, and he were alone in the main hall.

"God knows what it was," Graham said, "but it may mean something to you, Bobby. Tell us carefully, Katherine, about the sounds that came to you across the court."

"It was just what I heard last night when he died," she answered. "It was like something falling softly, then a long-drawn sigh. I tried to pay no attention. I fought it. I didn't call at first. But I couldn't keep quiet. I knew we had to go to that room. It never occurred to me that the detective or the coroner might be there moving around."

"You were alone up here?" Graham said.

"I think so."

"No," Bobby said. "I was in my room."

"What were you doing?" Graham asked.

"I was asleep. Katherine's call woke me up."

"Asleep!" Paredes echoed. "And she didn't call at once -"

He broke off. Bobby grasped his arm.

"What are you trying to do?"

"I'm sorry," Paredes said. "Now, really, you mustn't think of that. I shouldn't have spoken. I'm more inclined to agree with the doctor's theory, impossible as it seems."

"Yesterday," Katherine said, "I would have thought it impossible. After last night and just now I'm not so sure. I - I wish the doctor were right. It would clear you, Bobby."

He smiled.

"Do you think any jury would listen to such a theory?"

Katherine put her finger to her lips. Howells and the doctor came from the corridor of the old wing. At the head of the stairs the detective turned.

"You will find it very warm and comfortable by the fire in the lower hall, Mr. Blackburn."

He waited until Katherine had slipped to her room until Graham, Paredes, the doctor, and Bobby were on the stairs. Then he walked slowly into the new corridor.

Bobby knew what he was after. The detective had made no effort to disguise his intention. He wanted Bobby out of the way while he searched his room again, this time for a sharp, slender instrument capable of penetrating between the bones at the base of a man's brain.

Paredes lighted a cigarette and warmed his back at the fire. The doctor settled himself in his chair. He paid no attention to the others. He wouldn't answer Paredes's slow remarks.

"Interesting, doctor! I am a little psychic. Always in this house I have responded to strange, unfriendly influences. Always, as now, the approach of night depresses me."

Bobby couldn't sit still. He nodded at Graham, arose, got his coat and hat, and stepped into the court. The dusk was already thick there. Dampness and melancholy seemed to exude from the walls of the old house. He paused and gazed at one of the foot-prints in the soft earth by the fountain. Shreds of plaster adhered to the edges, testimony that the detective had made his cast from this print. He tried to realize that that mute, familiar impression had the power to send him to his execution. Graham, who had come silently from the house, startled him.

"What are you looking at?"

"No use, Hartley. I was on the library lounge. I heard every word Howells said."

"Perhaps it's just as well," Graham said. "You know what you face. But I hate to see you suffer. We've got to find a way around that evidence."

Bobby pointed to the windows of the room of death.

"There's no way around except the doctor's theory."

He laughed shortly.

"Much as I've feared that room, I'm afraid the psychic explanation won't hold water. Paredes put his finger on it. I would have had time to get back to my room before Katherine called -"

"Stop, Bobby!"

"Hartley! I'm afraid to go to sleep. It's dreadful not to know whether you are active in your sleep, whether you are evil and ingenious to the point of the miraculous in your sleep. I'm so tired, Hartley."

"Why should you have gone to that room this afternoon?" Graham asked. "You must get this idea out of your head. You must have sleep, and, perhaps, when you're thoroughly rested, you will remember."

"I'm not so sure," Bobby said, "that I want to remember."

He pointed to the footprint.

"There's no question. I was here last night."

"Unless," Graham said, "your handkerchief and your shoes were stolen."

"Nonsense!" Bobby cried. "The only motive would be to commit a murder in order to kill me by sending me to the chair. And who would know his way around that dark house like me? Who would have found out so easily that my grandfather had changed his room?"

"It's logical," Graham admitted slowly, "but we can't give in. By the way, has Paredes ever borrowed any large sums?"

Bobby hesitated. After all, Paredes and he had been good friends.

"A little here and there," he answered reluctantly.

"Has he ever paid you back?"

"I don't recall," Bobby answered, flushing. "You know I've never been exactly calculating about money. Whenever he wanted it I was always glad to help Carlos out. Why do you ask?"

"If any one," Graham answered, "looked on you as a certain source of money, there would be a motive in conserving that source, in increasing it. Probably lots of people knew Mr. Blackburn was out of patience with you; would make a new will to-day."

"Do you think," Bobby asked, "that Carlos is clever enough to have got through those doors? And what about this afternoon - that ghastly disturbing of the body?"

He smiled wanly.

"It looks like me or the ghosts of my ancestors."

"If Paredes," Graham insisted, "tries to borrow any money from you now, tell me about it. Another thing, Bobby. We can't afford to keep your experiences of last night a secret any longer."

He stepped to the door and asked Doctor Groom to come out.

"He won't be likely to pass your confidences on to Howells," he said. "Those men are natural antagonists."

After a moment the doctor appeared, a slouch hat drawn low over his shaggy forehead.

"What you want?" he grumbled. "This court's a first-class place to catch cold. Dampest hole in the neighbourhood. Often wondered why."

"I want to ask you," Graham began, "something about the effects of such drugs as could be given in wine. Tell him, will you, Bobby, what happened last night?"

Bobby vanquished the discomfort with which the gruff, opinionated physician had always filled him. He recited the story of last night's dinner, of his experience in the cafe, of his few blurred impressions of the swaying vehicle and the woods.

"Hartley thinks something may have been put in my wine."

"What for?" the doctor asked. "What had these people to gain by drugging you? Suppose for some far-fetched reason they wanted to have Silas Blackburn put out of the way. They couldn't make you do it by drugging you. At any rate, they couldn't have had a hand in this afternoon. Mind, I'm not saying you had a thing to do with it yourself, but I don't believe you were drugged. Any drug likely to be used in wine would probably have sent you into a deep sleep. And your symptoms on waking up are scarcely sharp enough. Sorry, boy. Sounds more like aphasia. The path you've been treading sometimes leads to that black country, and it's there that hates sharpen unknown. I remember a case where a tramp returned and killed a farmer who had refused him food. Retained no recollection of the crime - hours dropped out of his life. They executed him while he still tried to remember."

"I read something about the case," Bobby muttered.

"Been better if you hadn't," the doctor grumbled. "Suggestions work in a man's brain without his knowing it."

He thought for a moment, his heavy, black brows coming closer together. He glanced at the windows of the old room. His sunken, infused eyes nearly closed.

"I know how you feel, and that's a little punishment maybe you deserve. I'll say this for your comfort. You probably followed the plan that had been impressed on your brain by Mr. Graham. You came here, no doubt, and stood around. With an automatic appreciation of your condition you may have taken that old precaution of convivial men returning home, and removed your shoes. Then your automatic judgment may have warned you that you weren't fit to go in at all, and you probably wandered off to the empty house."

"Then," Bobby asked, "you don't think I did it?"

"God knows who did it. God knows what did it. The longer I live the surer I become that we scientists can't probe everything. Whenever I go near Silas Blackburn's body I receive a very powerful impression that his death in that room from such a wound goes deeper than ordinary murder, deeper than a case of recurrent aphasia."

His eyes widened. He turned with Graham and Bobby at the sound of an automobile coming through the woods.

"Probably the coroner at last," he said.

The automobile, a small runabout, drew up at the entrance to the court. A little wizened man, with yellowish skin stretched across high cheek bones, stepped out and walked up the path.

"Well!" he said shrilly. "What you doing, Doctor Groom?"

"Waiting to witness another reason why coroners should be abolished," the doctor rumbled. "This is the dead man's grandson, Coroner; and Mr. Graham, a friend of the family's."

Bobby accepted the coroner's hand with distaste.

"Howells," the coroner said in his squeaky voice, "seems to think it's a queer case. Inconvenient, I call it. Wish people wouldn't die queerly whenever I go on a little holiday. I had got five ducks, gentlemen, when they came to me with that damned telegram. Bad business mine, 'cause people will die when you least expect them to. Let's go see what Howells has got on his mind. Bright sleuth, Howells! Ought to be in New York."

He started up the path, side by side with Doctor Groom.

"Are you coming?" Graham asked Bobby. Bobby shook his head. "I don't want to. I'd rather stay outside. You'd better be there, Hartley."

Graham followed the others while Bobby wandered from the court and started down a path that entered the woods from the rear of the house.

Immediately the forest closed greedily about him. Here and there, where the trees were particularly stunted, branches cut against a pallid, greenish glow in the west - the last light.

Bobby wanted, if he could, to find that portion of the woods where he had stood last night, fancying the trees straining in the wind like puny men, visualizing a dim figure in a black mask which he had called his conscience.

The forest was all of a pattern - ugly, unfriendly, melancholy. He went on, however, hoping to glimpse that particular picture he remembered. He left the path, walking at haphazard among the undergrowth. Ahead he saw a placid, flat, and faintly luminous stretch. He pushed through the bushes and paused on the shore of a lake, small and stagnant. Dead, stripped trunks of trees protruded from the water. At the end a bird arose with a sudden flapping of wings; it cried angrily as it soared above the trees and disappeared to the south.

The morbid loneliness of the place touched Bobby's spirit with chill hands. As a child he had never cared to play about the stagnant lake, nor, he recalled, had the boys of the village fished or bathed there. Certainly he hadn't glimpsed it last night. He was about to walk away when a movement on the farther bank held him, made him gaze with eager eyes across the sleepy water.

He thought there was something black in the black shadows of the trees - a thing that stirred through the heavy dusk without sound. He received, moreover, an impression of anger and haste as distinct as the bird had projected. But he could see nothing clearly in this bad light. He couldn't be sure that there was any one over there.

He started around the end of the lake, and for a moment he thought that the shape of a woman, clothed in black, detached itself from the shadow. The image dissolved. He wondered if it had been more substantial than fancy.

"Who is that?" he called.

The woods muffled his voice. There was no answer. Nor was there, he noticed, any crackling of twigs or rustling of dead leaves. If there had been a woman there she had fled noiselessly, yet, as he went on around the lake, his own progress was distinctly audible through the decay of autumn.

It was too dark on the other side to detect any traces of a recent human presence in the thicket. He couldn't quiet, however, the feeling that he had had a glimpse of a woman clothed in black who had studied him secretly across the stagnant stretch of the lake.

On the other hand, there was no logic in a woman's presence here at such an hour, no logic in a stranger's running away from him. While he pondered the night invaded the forest completely, making it impossible for him to search farther. It had grown so dark, indeed, that he found his way out with difficulty. The branches caught at his clothing. The underbrush tangled itself about his feet. It was as if the thicket were trying to hold him away from the house.

As he entered the court he noticed a discoloured glow diffusing itself through the curtains of the room of death.

He opened the front door. Paredes and Graham alone sat by the fire.

"Then they're not through yet," Bobby said.

Graham arose. He commenced to pace the length of the hall.

"They've had Katherine in that room. One would think she'd been through enough. Now they've sent for the servants."

Paredes laughed lightly.

"After this," he said, "I'm afraid, Bobby, you'll need the powers of the police to keep servants in your house."

Muttering, frightened voices came from the dining-room. Jenkins entered, and, shaking his head, went up the stairs. The two women who followed him, were in tears. They paused, as if seeking an excuse to linger on the lower floor, to postpone as long as possible their entrance of the room of death.

Ella, a pretty girl, whose dark hair and eyes suggested a normal vivacity, spoke to Bobby.

"It's outrageous, Mr. Robert. He found out all we knew this morning. What's he after now? You might think we'd murdered Mr. Blackburn."

Jane was older. An ugly scar crossed her cheek. It was red and like an open wound as she demanded that Bobby put a stop to these inquisitions.

"I can do nothing," he said. "Go on up and answer or they can make trouble for you."

Muttering again to each other, they followed Jenkins, and in the lower hall the three men waited.

Jenkins came down first. His face was white. It twitched.

"The body!" he mouthed. "It's moved! I saw it before."

He stretched out his hands to Bobby.

"That's why they wanted us, to find out where we were this afternoon, and everything we've done, as if we might have gone there, and disturbed -"

Angry voices in the upper hall interrupted him. The two women ran down, as white as Jenkins. At an impatient nod from Bobby the three servants went on to the kitchen. Howells, the coroner, and Doctor Groom descended.

"What ails you, Doctor?" the coroner was squeaking. "I agree it's an unpleasant room. Lots of old rooms are. I follow you when you say no post-mortem contraction would have caused such an alteration in the position of the body. There's no question about the rest of it. The man was clearly murdered with a sharp tool of some sort, and the murderer was in the room again this afternoon, and disturbed the corpse. Howells says he knows who. It's up to him to find out how. He says he has plenty of evidence and that the guilty person's in this house, so I'm not fretting myself. I'm cross with you, Howells, for breaking up my holiday. One of my assistants would have done as well."

Howells apparently paid no attention to the coroner. His narrow eyes followed the doctor with a growing curiosity. His level smile seemed to have drawn his lips into a line, inflexible, a little cruel. The doctor grunted:

"Instead of abolishing coroners we ought to double their salaries."

The coroner made a long squeak as an indication of mirth.

"You think unfriendly spooks did it. I've always believed you were an old fogy. Hanged if that doesn't sound modern."

The doctor ran his fingers through his thick, untidy hair.

"I merely ask for the implement that caused death. I only ask to know how it was inserted through the bed while Blackburn lay on his back. And if you've time you might tell me how the murderer entered the room last night and to-day."

The coroner repeated his squeak. He glanced at the little group by the fire.

"Out in the kitchen, upstairs, or right here under our noses is almost certainly the person who could tell us. Interesting case, Howells!"

Howells, who still watched the doctor, answered dryly:

"Unusually interesting."

The coroner struggled into his coat.

"Permits are all available," he squeaked. "Have your undertakers out when you like."

Graham answered him brusquely.

"Everything's arranged. I've only to telephone."

The coroner nodded at Doctor Groom. His voice pointed its humour with a thinner tone.

"If I were you, Howells, I'd take this hairy old theorist up as a suspicious character."

The doctor made a movement in his direction while Howells continued to stare. The doctor checked himself. He went to the closet and got his hat and coat.

"Want me to drop you, old sawbones?" the coroner asked.

Savagely the doctor shook his head.

"My buggy's in the stable."

The coroner's squeak was thinner, more irritating than ever.

"Then don't let the spooks get you, driving through the woods. Old folks say there are a-plenty there."

Bobby arose. He couldn't face the prospect of the man's squeaking again.

"We find nothing to laugh at in this situation," he said. "You're quite through?"

The coroner's eyes blazed.

"I'm through, if that's the way you feel. Goodnight." He added with a sharp maliciousness: "I leave my sympathy for whoever Howells has his eagle eye on."

Howells, when the doctor and the coroner had gone, excused himself with a humility that mocked the others:

"With your permission I shall write in the library until dinner."

He bowed and left.

"He wants to work on his report," Graham suggested.

"An exceptional man!" Paredes murmured.

"Has he questioned you?" Graham asked.

"I'd scarcely call it that," Paredes replied. "We've both questioned, and we've both been clams. I fancy he doesn't think much of me since I believe in ghosts, yet the doctor seems to interest him."

"Where were you?" Graham asked, "when Miss Perrine's scream called us?"

Paredes stifled a yawn.

"Dozing here by the fire. I am very tired after last night."

"You don't look particularly tired."

"Custom, I'm ashamed to say, constructs a certain armour. To-morrow, with a fresh mind, I hope to be able to dissect all I have seen and heard, all that has happened here to-day."

"The thing that counts is what happened to me last night, Carlos," Bobby said. "It's the only way you can help me."

As Paredes strolled to the foot of the stairs Bobby waited for a defensive reply, for a sign, perhaps, that the Panamanian was offended and proposed to depart. Paredes, however, went upstairs, yawning. He called back:

"I must make myself a trifle more presentable for dinner."

Graham faced Bobby with the old question:

"What can he want hanging around here unless it's money?" And after a moment: "He's clever - hard to sound. I have to leave you, Bobby. I must telephone - the ugly formalities."

"It's good of you to take them off my mind," Bobby answered.

He remained in his chair, gazing drowsily at the fire, trying, always trying to remember, yet finding no new light among the shadows of his memory.

Just before dinner Katherine joined him. She wore a sombre

gown that made her face seem too white, that heightened the groping curiosity of her eyes.

Without speaking she sat down beside him and stared, too, at the smouldering fire. From her presence, from her tactful silence he drew comfort - to an extent, rest.

"You make me ashamed," he whispered once. "I've been a beast, leaving you here alone these weeks. You don't understand quite, why that was." She wouldn't let him go on. She shook her head. They remained silently by the fire until Graham and Paredes joined them.

When dinner was announced the detective came from the library, and, uninvited, sat at the table with them. His report evidently still filled his mind, for he spoke only when it was unavoidable and then in monosyllables. Paredes alone ate with a show of enjoyment, alone attempted to talk. Eventually even he fell silent before the lack of response.

Afterward he arranged a small card table by the fire in the hall. He found cards, and, with a package of cigarettes and a box of matches convenient to his hand, commenced to play solitaire. The detective, Bobby gathered, had brought his report up to date, for he lounged near by, watching the Panamanian's slender fingers as they handled the cards deftly. Bobby, Graham, and Katherine were glad to withdraw beyond the range of those narrow, searching eyes. They entered the library and closed the door.

Graham, expectant of a report from his man in New York as to the movements of Maria and the identity of the stranger, was restless.

"If we could only get one fact," he said, "one reasonable clue that didn't involve Bobby! I've never felt so at sea. I wonder if, in spite of Howells's evidence, we're not all a little afraid since this afternoon, of something such as Katherine felt last night - something we can't define. Howells alone is satisfied. We must believe in the hand of another man. Doctor Groom talks about indefinable hands."

"Uncle Silas was so afraid last night!" Katherine whispered.

"That," Bobby cried, "is the fact we must have."

He paused.

"What's that?" he asked sharply.

They sat for some time, listening to the sound of wheels on the gravel, to the banging of the front door, and, later, to the pacing of men in the room of death overhead. They tried again to thread the mazes of this problem whose only conceivable exit led to Bobby's guilt. The movements upstairs persisted. At last they became measured and dragging, like the footsteps of men who carried some heavy burden.

They looked at each other then. Katherine hid her eyes.

"It's like a tomb here," Bobby said.

He arranged kindling in the fireplace and touched a match to it. It hadn't occurred to him to ring for Jenkins. None of them wished to be disturbed. Eventually it was the detective who intruded. He strolled in, glanced at them curiously for a moment, then walked to the door of the enclosed staircase. He grasped the knob.

"To-night," he announced, "I am trying a small experiment on the chance of clearing up the last details of the mystery. Since it depends on the courage of whoever murdered Mr. Blackburn I've small hope of its success."

He indicated the ceiling. "You've heard, I daresay, what's been going on up there. Mr. Blackburn's body has been removed to his own room. The room where he was killed is empty. I mean to go up and enter and lock the doors as he did last night. I shall leave the window up as it was last night. I shall blow out the candle as he did."

He lowered his voice. He looked directly at Bobby. His words carried a definite challenge.

"I shall lie on the bed and await the murderer under the precise conditions Mr. Blackburn did."

"What do you expect to gain by that?" Graham asked.

"Probably nothing," Howells answered, "because, as I have said, success depends upon the courage of a man who kills in the dark while his victim sleeps. I simply give him the chance to attack me as he did Mr. Blackburn. Of course he realizes it would be a good deal to his advantage to have me out of the way. I ask him to come, therefore, as stealthily as he did last night. I beg him to match his skill with mine. I want him to play his miracle with the window or one of the locks. But I'll wager he hasn't the nerve, although I don't see why he should hesitate. He's a doomed man. I shall make my arrest in the morning. I shall publish all my evidence."

Bobby wouldn't meet the narrow, menacing eyes, for he knew that Howells challenged him to a duel of slyness with the whole truth at stake. The detective's manner increased the hatred which had blazed in Bobby's mind when he had stood in the bedroom over his grandfather's body. For a moment he wished with all his heart that he might accept the challenge. He did the best he could.

"I gather," he said, "that you haven't unearthed the motive for disturbing the body. And have you found the sharp instrument that caused death?"

The detective answered tolerantly:

"I have found a number of sharp instruments. None of them, however, seems quite slender or round enough. I'll get all that out of my man when I lock him up. I'll get it to-night if he dares come."

"Why," Graham said, "do you announce your plans so accurately to us?"

The detective's level smile widened.

"You shouldn't ask that, Mr. Graham. I've caused the servants to know my plans. Mr. Paredes knows them. I wish every one in the house to know them. That is in order that the murderer, who is in the house, may come if he wishes."

Katherine arose abruptly.

"When you come down to it," she said, "you are accusing one of us. It's brutal, unfair - absurd."

"I am a detective, Miss," Howells answered. "I have my own methods."

Bobby stared at the slight protuberance in the breast pocket of the detective's coat. The cast of his footprint must be secreted there, and almost certainly the handkerchief which had been found beneath the bed. He shrank from his own thoughts.

If he had consciously committed this murder he could understand a desire to get that evidence.

Katherine had gone closer to the detective.

"In any case," she urged him, "I wish you wouldn't try to spend the night in that room. It isn't pleasant. After what the doctor has said, it - well, it isn't safe."

Howells burst out laughing.

"Never fear, Miss. I'm content to give Doctor Groom's spirits as much chance to take a fall out of me as anybody. I'll be going up now." He bowed. "Good-night to you all, and pleasant dreams."

He opened the door and slipped into the darkness of the private staircase. They heard him, after he had closed the door, climbing upward. Katherine shivered.

"He has plenty of courage, Hartley! If nothing happens to him to-night he'll finish Bobby in the morning. That mustn't happen. He mustn't go to jail. You understand. Things would never be the same for him again."

Graham spread his hands.

"What am I to do? I might go to New York and get after these people myself."

"Don't leave the Cedars," Bobby begged, "until he does arrest me. There'll be plenty of time for the New York end then. I've no faith in it. Watch Carlos if you want, but most important of all, find out - somehow you've got to find out - what my grandfather was afraid of."

Graham nodded.

"And if it does come to an arrest, Bobby, you're not to say a word to anybody without my advice. You ought to get to bed now. You must have rest, and Katherine, too. Don't listen to-night, Katherine, for messages from across the court."

"I'll try," she said, "but, Hartley, I wish that man wasn't there. I wish no one was in that room."

She took Bobby's hand.

"Good-night, Bobby, and don't give up hope. We'll do something. Somehow we'll pull you through."

Bobby waited, hoping that Graham would offer to share his

room with him. For, as he had said earlier, the prospect of going to sleep, of losing control of his thoughts and actions, appalled him. Yet such an offer, he realized, must impress Graham as delicate, as an indication that he really doubted Bobby's innocence, as a sort of spying. He wasn't surprised, therefore, when Graham only said:

"I'll be in the next room, Bobby. If you're restless or need me you've only to knock on the wall."

Bobby didn't leave the library with them. The warmth with which Katherine had just filled him faded as he watched her go out side by side with Graham. Her hand was on Graham's arm. There was, he fancied, in her eyes an emotion deeper than gratitude or friendship. He sighed as the door closed behind them. He was himself largely to blame for that situation. His very revolt against its imminence had hastened its shaping.

He walked anxiously to the table. He had remembered the medicine Doctor Groom had prepared for him that afternoon to make him sleep. He hadn't taken it then. If it remained where he had left it, which was likely enough in the disordered state of the household, he would drink it now. Reinforced by his complete weariness, it ought to send him into a sleep profound enough to drown any possible abnormal impulses of unconsciousness.

The glass was there. He drained it, and stood for a time looking at the pinkish sediment in the bottom. That was all right for to-night, but afterward - he couldn't shrink perpetually from sleep. He shrugged his shoulders, remembering it would make little difference what he did in his sleep when they had him behind prison bars. Perhaps this would be his last night of freedom.

He found Paredes still in the hall. The Panamanian, with languid gestures, continued to play his solitaire. His box of cigarettes was much reduced.

"I thought you were tired, Carlos."

Paredes glanced up. His eyes were neither weary nor alert. As usual his expression disclosed nothing of his thoughts, yet he must have read in Bobby's tone a reproach at this indifference.

"The game intrigues me," he murmured, "and you know," he added dreamily. "I sometimes think better while I amuse myself."

Bobby nodded good-night and went on up to his room. Even while he undressed the effects of the doctor's narcotic were perceptible. His eyes had grown heavy, his brain a trifle numb.

Almost apathetically he assured himself that he couldn't accomplish these mad actions in his sleep.

"Yet last night -" he murmured. "That finishes me in the eyes of the law. The doctor will testify to aphasia. According to him I am two men - two men!"

He yawned, recalling snatches of books he had read and one or two scientific reports of such cases. He climbed into bed and blew out his candle. His drowsiness thickened. In his dulled mind one recollection remained - the picture of Howells coldly challenging him with his level smile to make a secret entrance of the old bedroom in a murderous effort to escape the penalty of the earlier crime. And Howells had been right. His death would give Bobby a chance. The destruction of the evidence, the bringing into the case of a broader-minded man, a man without a carefully constructed theory - all that would help Bobby, might save him. Howells, moreover, had indicated that he had so far withheld his evidence. But that was probably a bait.

In his drowsy way Bobby hated more powerfully than before this detective who, with a serene malevolence, made him writhe in his net. Thought ceased. He drifted into a trance-like sleep. He swung in the black pit again, fighting out against crushing odds. The darkness thundered as though informing him that graver forces than any he had ever imagined had definitely grasped him. Then he understood. He was in a black cell, and the thundering was the steady advance of men along an iron floor to take him -

"Bobby! Bobby!"

He flung out his hands. He sat upright, opening his eyes. The blackness assumed the familiar, yielding quality of the night. The thunder, the footfalls, became a hurried knocking at his door.

"Bobby! You're there -" It was Katherine. Her tone made the night as frightening as the blackness of the pit.

"What's the matter?"

"You're there. I didn't know. Get up. Hartley's putting some clothes on. Hurry! The house is so dark - so strange."

"Tell me what's happened."

She didn't answer at first. He struck a match, lighted his candle, threw on a dressing gown, and stepped to the door. Katherine shrank against the wall, hiding her eyes from the light of his candle. He thought it odd she should wear the dress in which she had appeared at dinner. But it seemed indifferently fastened, and her hair was in disorder. Graham stepped from his room.

"What is it?" Bobby demanded.

"You wouldn't wake up, Bobby. You were so hard to wake." The idea seemed to fill her mind. She repeated it several times.

"It's nothing," Graham said. "Go back to your room, Katherine. She's fanciful -"

She lowered her hands. Her eyes were full of terror. "No. We have to go to that room as I went last night, as we went to-day."

Graham tried to quiet her. "We'll go to satisfy you."

Her voice hardened. "I know. I was asleep. It woke me up, stealing in across the court again."

Bobby grasped her arm. "You came out and aroused up at once?"

She shook her head. "I - I couldn't find my dressing gown. This dress was by the bed. I put it on, but I couldn't seem to fasten it."

Bobby stepped back, remembering his last thought before drifting into the trance-like sleep. She seemed to know what was in his mind.

"But when I knocked you were sleeping so soundly."

"Too soundly, perhaps."

"Come. We're growing imaginative," Graham said. "Howells would take care of himself. He'll probably give us the deuce for disturbing him, but to satisfy you, Katherine, we'll wake him up."

"If you can," she whispered.

They entered the main hall. Light came through the stair well from the lower floor. Graham walked to the rail and glanced down. Bobby followed him. On the table by the fireplace the cards were arranged in neat piles. A strong draft blew cigarette smoke up to them.

"Paredes," Graham said, amazed, "is still downstairs. The front door's open. He's probably in the court."

"It must be very late," Bobby said.

Katherine shivered.

"Half-past two. I looked at my watch. The same time as last night."

With a gesture of resolution she led the way into the corridor. Bobby shrank from the damp and musty atmosphere of the narrow passage.

"Why do you come, Katherine?" he asked.

"I have to know, as I had to know last night."

Graham raised his hand and knocked at the door which again was locked on the inside. The echoes chattered back at them. Graham knocked again. With a passionate revolt Katherine raised her hands, too, and pounded at the panels. Suddenly she gave up. She let her hands fall listlessly.

"It's no use."

"Howells! Howells!" Graham called. "Why don't you answer?"

"When he boasted to-night," Katherine whispered, "the murderer heard him."

"Suppose he's gone down to the library?" Graham said.

Bobby gave Katherine the candle.

"No. He'd have stayed. We've got to break in here. We've got to find out."

Graham placed his powerful shoulder against the door. The lock strained. Bobby added his weight. With a splintering of wood the door flew open, precipitating them across the threshold. Through the darkness Graham sprang for the opposite door.

"It's locked," he called, "and the key's on this side."

Bobby took the candle from Katherine and forced himself to approach the bed. The flame flickered a little in the breeze which stole past the curtain of the open window. It shook across the body of Howells, fully clothed with his head on the stained pillow. His face, intricately lined, was as peaceful as Silas Blackburn's had been. Its level smile persisted.

Bobby caught his breath.

"Howells -"

He set the candle on the bureau.

"It's no use. We must look at the back of his head."

"The back of his head!" Katherine echoed.

"It's illegal," Graham said.

"Look!" Bobby cried. "We've got to look!"

Graham tiptoed forward. He stretched out his hand. With a motion of abhorrence he drew it back. Bobby watched him hypnotically, thinking:

"I wanted this. I hated him. I thought of it just before I went to sleep."

Graham reached out again. This time he touched Howells's head. It rolled over on the pillow.

"Good God!" he said.

They stared at the red hole, near the base of the brain, at a fresh crimson splotch, straying beyond the edges of the darker one they had seen that afternoon.

Graham turned away, his hand still outstretched, as if it had touched some poisonous thing and might retain a contamination.

"He was prepared against it," he whispered, "expected it, yet it got him."

He glanced rapidly around the room whose shadows seemed crowding about the candle to stifle it.

"Unless we're all mad," he cried, "the murderer must be hidden in this room now. Don't you see? He's got to be, or Groom's right, and we're fighting the dead. Go out, Katherine. Stand by that broken door, Bobby. I'm going to look."

CHAPTER IV

A STRANGE LIGHT APPEARS AT
THE DESERTED HOUSE

Graham's intention, logical as it was, impressed Bobby as quite futile. Silas Blackburn had died in this ancient, melancholy room behind locked doors. This afternoon, with a repetition of the sounds that had probably accompanied his death, they had been drawn to find that, behind locked doors again, the position of the body had changed incredibly, as if to expose to them the tiny fatal wound at the base of the brain. Now for the third time those stealthy movements had aroused Katherine, and they had found, once more behind locked doors, the determined and malicious detective, murdered precisely as old Blackburn had been.

Of course Graham was logical. By every rational argument the murderer must still be in the room. Yet Bobby foresaw that, as always, no one would be found, that nothing would be unearthed to explain the succession of tragic mysteries. While Graham commenced his search, indeed, he continued to stare at the little round hole in Howells's head, at the fresh, irregular stain on the pillow, and he became absorbed in his own predicament. Again and again he asked himself if he could be responsible for these murders which had been committed with an inhuman ingenuity. He knew only that he had wandered, unconscious, in the vicinity of the Cedars last night; that he had been asleep when his grandfather's body had altered its position; that he had gone to sleep a little while ago too profoundly, brooding over Howells's challenge to the murderer to invade the room of death and kill him if he could. Howells had been confident that he could handle a man and so solve the riddle of how the room had been entered. Certainly Howells's challenge had been accepted, and Bobby knew that he had fallen into that deep sleep hating the detective, telling himself that the man's death might save him from arrest, from conviction, from an intolerable walk to a little room with a single chair.

"Recurrent aphasia." The doctor's expression came back to him. In such a state a man could overcome locked doors, could accomplish apparent miracles and retain no recollection. And Bobby had hated and feared Howells more than he had his grandfather.

Dully he saw Katherine go out at Graham's direction. As one in a dream he moved toward the door they had had to break down on entering.

"Stand close to it," Graham said. "We'll cover everything."

"You'll find no one," Bobby answered with a perfect assurance.

He saw Graham take the candle and explore the large closets. He watched him examine the spaces behind the window curtains. He could smile a little as Graham stooped, peering beneath the bed, as he moved each piece of furniture large enough to secrete a man.

"You see, Hartley, it's no use."

Graham's lack of success, however, stimulated his anger.

"Then," he said, "there must be some hiding place in the walls. Such devices are common in houses as old as this."

Bobby indicated the silent form of the detective.

"He believed I killed my grandfather. The only reason he didn't arrest me was his failure to find out how the room had been entered and left. Don't you suppose he looked for a hiding place or a secret entrance the first thing? It's obvious."

But Graham's savage determination increased. He sounded each panel. None gave the slightest revealing response. He got a tape from Katherine and measured the dimensions of the room, the private hall, and the corridor. At last he turned to Bobby, his anger dead, his face white and tired.

"Everything checks," he admitted. "There's no secret room, no way in or out. Logically Groom's right. We're fighting the dead who resent the intrusion of your grandfather and Howells."

He laughed mirthlessly.

"After all, we can't surrender to that. There must be another answer."

"From the first Howells was satisfied with me," Bobby said.

Graham flung up his hands.

"Then tell me how you got in without disturbing those locks. I grant you, Bobby, you had sufficient motive for both murders, but I don't believe you have two personalities, one decent and lovable, the other cruel and cunning to the point of magic. I don't believe if a man had two such personalities the actions of one would be totally closed to the memory of the other."

Bobby smiled wanly.

"It isn't pleasant to confess it, Hartley, but I have read of such cases."

"Fiction!"

"Scientific fact."

"I wish to the devil I had shared your room with you to-night," Graham muttered. "I might have furnished you an alibi for this affair at least."

"Either that," Bobby answered frankly, "or you might have followed me and learned the whole secret. Honestly, isn't that what you were thinking of, Hartley? And I did go to sleep, telling myself it would help me if something of the sort happened to Howells. Now I'm not so sure that it will. I - I suppose you've got to notify the police."

Graham held up his hand.

"What's that? In the corridor!"

There were quiet footsteps in the corridor. Bobby turned quickly. Paredes strolled slowly through the passage, a cigarette held in his slender, listless fingers. Bobby stared at him, remembering his surprise a few minutes ago that the Panamanian should have sat up so late, should have been, probably, in the court when they had followed Katherine to the discovery of this new crime.

Paredes paused in the doorway. He took in the tragic picture framed by the sinister room without displaying the slightest interest. He continued to hold his cigarette until it expired. Then he crossed the threshold. Graham and Bobby watched the expressionless face. Gracefully Paredes raised his finger and pointed to the bed. When he spoke his voice was low and pleasant:

"Appalling! I feared something of the kind when I heard you come to this room."

He glanced at the broken door.

"The same unbelievable circumstance," he drawled. "I see you had to break in."

The colour flashed back to Graham's face.

"You have taken plenty of time to solve your misgivings."

"It hasn't been so long. I fancied everything was all right, and I was immersed in my solitaire. Then I heard a stirring upstairs. As I've told you, the house frightens me. It is not natural or healthy. So I came up to investigate this stirring, and there was Miss Katherine in the hall. She told me."

Graham faced him with undisguised enmity.

"Immersed in your solitaire! We were attracted by a light in the lower hall at such an hour. We looked down. You were not there. The front door was open."

Paredes glanced at his cold cigarette. He yawned.

"When Howells died precisely as Mr. Blackburn did," Graham hurried on, "you alone were awake about the house. Weren't you at that moment in the court?"

Paredes laughed tolerantly.

"It is clear, in spite of my apologies, that we are not friends, Graham; but, may I ask, are you accusing me of this strange - accident?"

"I should like to know what you were doing in the court."

"Perhaps," Paredes answered, "I was attracted there by the sounds that aroused Miss Katherine."

Graham shook his head.

"From her description I doubt if those sounds would have been audible in the hall."

"No matter," Paredes said. "I merely suggest that it's a case for Groom. His hint of a spiritual enmity may be saner than you think."

Katherine appeared in the doorway. She had evidently over-heard Paredes's comment, for she nodded. The determination in her eyes suggested that she had struggled with the situation during these last moments and had reached a definite conclusions That quality was in her voice.

"At least, Hartley," she said, "you must send for Doctor Groom before you notify the police."

Graham waved his hand.

"Why?" he asked. "The man is dead."

With a movement, hidden from Paredes, she indicated Bobby.

"Last time there was a good deal of delay before the doctor came. If we get him right away he may be able to do something for this poor fellow. At least his advice would be useful."

Bobby realized that she was fighting for time for him. Any delay would be useful that would give them a chance to plan before the police with unimaginative efficiency should invade the house and limit their opportunities. Graham showed that he caught her point.

"Maybe it's better," he said. "Then, Bobby, telephone Groom to be ready for you, and take my runabout. It's in the stable. You'll get him here much faster than he could come in his carriage."

"While I'm gone," Bobby asked, "what will you do?"

"Watch this room," Graham jerked out. "See that no one enters or leaves it, or touches the body. I'll hope for some clue."

"You've plenty of courage," Paredes drawled. "I shouldn't care to watch alone in this room."

He followed Katherine into the corridor. Bobby looked at Graham.

"You'll take no chances, Hartley?"

Graham's smile wasn't pleasant.

"According to you and the dead detective there's no risk while you're out of the house. Still, I shall be nervous, but don't worry."

Bobby joined the others before they had reached the hall.

"Of course Hartley found nothing," Katherine said to him.

"Nothing," Paredes answered, "except a very bad temper."

Katherine's distaste for the man was no longer veiled.

"You don't like Mr. Graham," she said, "but he is our friend, and he is in this house to help us."

Paredes bowed.

"I regret that the amusement Mr. Graham causes me sometimes finds expression. He is so earnest, so materialistic in his relation to the world. That is why he will see nothing psychic in the situation."

Paredes's easy contempt was like a tonic for Katherine. Her fear seemed to drop from her. She turned purposefully to Bobby, ignoring the Panamanian.

"I shall watch with Hartley," she said.

He was ashamed that jealousy should creep into such a

moment, but her resolve recalled his amorous discontent. The prospect of Graham and her, watching alone, drawn to each other by their fright and uncertainty, by their surroundings, by the hour, became unbearable. It placed him, to an extent, on Paredes's side. It urged him, when Paredes had gone on downstairs, to spring almost eagerly to his defence.

"As Hartley says," Katherine began, "he makes you think of a snake. He must see we dislike and resent him."

"You and Hartley, perhaps," Bobby said. "Carlos says he is here to help me. I've no reason to disbelieve him."

A little colour came into Katherine's face. She half stretched out her hand as if in an appeal. But the colour faded and her hand dropped.

"We are wasting time," she said. "You had better go."

"I am sorry we disagree about Carlos," he commenced.

She turned deliberately away from him.

"You must hurry," she said. "Hurry!"

He saw her enter the corridor to join Graham. The obscurity of the narrow place seemed to hold for him a new menace.

He walked downstairs slowly. While he telephoned, instructing a servant to tell the doctor to be dressed and ready in twenty minutes, he saw Paredes go to the closet and get his hat and coat.

"I shall keep you company," the Panamanian announced.

Bobby was glad enough to have him. He didn't want to be alone. He was aware by this time that no amount of thought would persuade useful memories to emerge from the black pit. They walked to the stable, half gone to ruin like the rest of the estate. Bobby started Graham's car. The servants' quarters, he saw, were dark. Then Jenkins and the two women hadn't been aroused, were still ignorant of the new crime. As they drove smoothly past the gloomy house they glimpsed through the court the dimly lit windows of the old room that persistently guarded its grim secret. Bobby pictured the living as well as the dead there, and his mind revolted, and he shivered. He opened the throttle wider. The car sprang forward. The divergent glare from the headlights forced back the reluctant thicket. Paredes drawled unexpectedly:

"There is nothing as lonely anywhere in the world."

He stooped behind the windshield and lighted a cigarette.

"At least. Bobby," he said between puffs, "the Cedars has taken from you the fear of Howells."

And after a time, staring at the glow of his cigarette, he went on softly:

"Have you noticed anything significant about the discovery of each mystery at the Cedars?"

"Many things," Bobby muttered.

"Think," Paredes urged him.

Bobby answered angrily:

"You've suggested that to me once to-day, Carlos. You mean that each time I have been asleep or unconscious."

"I mean something quite different," Paredes said.

He hesitated. When he continued, his drawl was more pronounced.

"Then you haven't remarked that each time it has been Miss

Katherine who has made the discovery, who has aroused the rest of the house?"

The car swerved sharply. Bobby's first impulse had been to take his hands from the wheel, to force Paredes to retract his sly insinuation.

"That's the rottenest thing I've ever known you to do, Carlos. Take it back."

Paredes shrugged his shoulders.

"There is nothing to take back. I accuse no one. I merely call attention to a chain of exceptional coincidences."

"You make me wonder," Bobby said, "if Hartley isn't justified in his dislike of you. You'll kill such a ridiculous suspicion."

"Or?" Paredes drawled. "Very well. It seems my fate recently to offend those I like best. I merely thought that any theory leading away from you would be welcome."

"Any theory," Bobby answered, "involving Katherine is unthinkable."

Paredes smiled.

"I didn't understand exactly how you felt. I rather took it for granted that Graham - Never mind. I take it back."

"Then drop it," Bobby answered sullenly, sorry that there was nothing else he could say.

They continued in silence through the deserted forest whose aggressive loneliness made words seem trivial. Bobby was asking himself again where he had stood last night when he had glimpsed for a moment the straining trees and the figure in a mask which he had called his conscience. If he could only prove that figure substantial! Then Graham would have some ground for his suspicion of Paredes and the dancer Maria. He glanced at Paredes. Could there have been a conspiracy against him in the New York cafe? Did Paredes, in fact, have some devious purpose in remaining at the Cedars?

The automobile took a sharp curve in the road. Bobby started, gazing ahead with an interest nearly hypnotic. The headlights had caught in their glare the deserted farmhouse in which he had awakened just before Howells had told him of his grandfather's death and practically placed him under arrest. In the white light the frame of the house from which the paint had flaked, appeared ghastly, unreal, like a structure seen in a nightmare from which one recoils with morbid horror. The light left the building. As the car tore past, Bobby could barely make out the black mass in the midst of the thicket.

Paredes had observed it, too.

"I daresay," he remarked casually, "the Cedars will become as deserted as that. It is just that it should, for the entire neighbourhood impresses one as unfriendly to life, as striving through death to drive life out."

"Have you ever seen that house before?" Bobby asked quickly.

"I have never seen it before. I do not care ever to see it again."

It was a relief when the forest thinned and fields stretched, flat and pleasant, like barriers against the stunted growth. Bobby stopped the car in front of one of a group of houses at a crossroads. He climbed the steps and rang. Doctor Groom opened the door himself. His gigantic, hairy figure was silhouetted against the light from within.

"What's the matter now?" he demanded in his gruff voice. "Fortunately I hadn't gone to bed. I was reading some books on psychic manifestations. Who's sick? Or -"

Bobby's face must have told him a good deal, for he broke off.

"Get your things on," Bobby said, "and I will tell you as we drive back, for you must come. Howells has been killed precisely as my grandfather was."

For a moment Doctor Groom's bulky frame remained motionless in the doorway. Instead of the surprise and horror Bobby had foreseen, the old man expressed only a mute wonder. He got his hat and coat and entered the runabout, Paredes made room for him, sitting on the floor, his feet on the running board.

Bobby had told all he knew before they had reached the forest. The doctor grunted then:

"The wound at the back of the head was the same as in your grandfather's case?"

"Exactly."

"Then what good am I? Why am I routed out?"

"A formality," Bobby answered. "Katherine thought if we got you quickly you might do something. Anyway, she wanted your advice."

The woods closed about them. Again the lights seemed to push back a palpable barrier.

"I can't work miracles," the doctor was murmuring. "I can't bring men back to life. Such a wound leaves no ground for hope. You'd better have sent for the police at once. Hello!"

He strained forward, peering around the windshield.

"Funny!" Paredes called.

Bobby's eyes were on the road.

"What do you see?"

"The house, Bobby!" Paredes cried.

"No one, to my certain knowledge," the doctor said, "has lived in that house for ten years. You say it was empty and falling to pieces when you woke up there this morning."

Bobby knew what they meant then, and he reduced the speed of the car and looked ahead to the right. A pallid glow sifted through the trees from the direction of the deserted house.

Bobby guided the car to the side of the road, stopped it, and shut off the engine. At first no one moved. The three men stared as if in the presence of an unaccountable phenomenon. Even when Bobby had extinguished the headlights the glow failed to brighten. Its pallid quality persisted. It seemed to radiate from a point close to the ground.

"It comes from the front of the house," Bobby murmured.

He stepped from the automobile.

"What are you going to do?" Paredes wanted to know.

"Find out who is in that house."

For Bobby had experienced a quick hope. If there was a man or a woman secreted in the building the truth as to his own remarkable presence there last night might not be so far to seek after all. There was, moreover, something lawless about this light escaping from the place at such an hour. A little while ago, when Paredes and he had driven past, the house had been black. They had remarked its lonely, abandoned appearance. It had led Paredes to speak of the neighbourhood as the domain of death. Yet the strange, pallid quality of the light itself made him pause by the broken fence. It did come from the lower part of the front of the house, yet, so faint was it, it failed to outline the aperture through which it escaped. The doctor and Paredes joined him.

"When I was here," he said, "all the shutters were closed. This glow is too white, too diffused. We must see."

As he started forward Paredes grasped his arm.

"There are too many of us. We would make a noise. Suppose I creep up and investigate."

"There is one way in - at the back," Bobby told the doctor. "Let us go there. We'll have whoever's inside trapped. Meantime, Carlos, if he wishes, will steal up to the front; he'll find out where the light comes from. He'll look in if he can."

"That's the best plan," Paredes agreed.

But they had scarcely turned the corner of the house, beyond reach of the glow, when Paredes rejoined them. His feet were no longer careful in the underbrush. He came up running. For the first time in their acquaintance Bobby detected a lessening of the man's suave, unemotional habit.

"The light!" the Panamanian gasped. "It's gone! Before I could get close it faded out."

Bobby called to the doctor and ran toward the door at the rear. It was unhinged and half open as it had been when he had awakened to his painful and inexplicable predicament. He went through, fumbling in his pocket for matches. The damp chill of the hall nauseated him as it had done before, seemed to place about his throat an intangible band that made breathing difficult. Before he could get his match safe out the doctor had struck a wax vesta. Its strong flame played across the dingy, streaked walls.

"There's a flashlight, Carlos," Bobby said, "in the door flap of the automobile."

Paredes started across the yard with a haste, it seemed to Bobby, almost eager.

Striking matches as they went, the doctor and Bobby hurried to the front of the house. The rooms appeared undisturbed in their decay. The shutters were closed. The front door was barred. The broken walls from which the plaster hung in shreds leered at them.

Suddenly Bobby turned, grasping the doctor's arm.

"Did you hear anything?"

The doctor shook his head.

"Or feel anything?"

"No."

"I thought," Bobby said excitedly, "that there was some one in the hall. I - I simply got that impression, for I saw nothing myself. My back was turned."

Paredes strolled silently in.

"It may have been Mr. Paredes," the doctor said.

But Bobby wasn't convinced.

"Did you see or hear anything coming through the hall, Carlos?"

"No," Paredes said.

He had brought the light. With its help they explored the tiny cellar and the upper floor. There was no sign of a recent occupancy. Everything was as Bobby had found it on awakening. A vagrant wind sighed about the place. They looked at each other with startled eyes. They filed out with an incongruous stealth.

"Then there are ghosts here, too!" Paredes whispered.

"Who knows?" Doctor Groom mused. "It is as puzzling as anything that has happened at the Cedars unless the light we saw was some phosphorescent effect of decaying wood or vegetation."

"Then why should it go out all at once?" Bobby asked. "Is there any connection between this light and what has happened at the Cedars?"

"The house at least," Paredes put in, "is connected with what has happened at the Cedars through your experience here."

At Doctor Groom's suggestion they sat in the automobile for some time, watching the house for a repetition of the pallid light. After several minutes, when it failed to come, Bobby set his gears.

"Graham and Katherine will be worried."

They drove quickly away from the black, uncommunicative mass of the abandoned building. The woods were lonelier than before. They impressed Bobby as guarding something.

He drove straight to the stable. As they walked into the court they saw the uncertain candlelight diffused from the room of death. In the hall Bobby responded to a quick alarm. The Cedars was too quiet. What had happened since he and Paredes had left?

"Katherine! Hartley!" he called.

He heard running steps upstairs. Katherine leaned over the banister. Her quiet voice reassured him. "Is the doctor with you?"

He nodded. Paredes yawned and lighted a cigarette. He settled himself in an easy chair. Bobby and Doctor Groom hurried up. Katherine led them down the old corridor. Two chairs had been placed in the broken doorway.

Graham sat there. He arose and greeted the doctor.

"Nothing has happened since I left?" Bobby asked.

Graham shook his head.

"Katherine and I have watched every minute."

Doctor Groom walked to the bed and for a long time looked down at Howells. Once he put out his hand, quickly withdrawing it.

"It's simply a repetition," he said at last, and his voice was softer than its custom. "It may be a warning, for all we know, that no one may sleep in this room without attracting death. Yet why should that be? I miss this poor fellow's materialistic viewpoint. There's nothing I can do for him, nothing I can say, except that death must have been instantaneous. The police must seek again for a man to place in the electric chair."

Graham touched his arm with an odd reluctance.

"Sitting here for so long I've been thinking. I have always been materialistic, too. Tell me seriously, doctor, do you believe there is any psychic force capable of killing two men in this incisive fashion?"

"No one," the doctor answered, "can say what psychic force is capable of doing. Some scientists have started to explore, but it is still uncharted country. From certain places - I daresay you've noticed it - one gets an impression of peace and content; from others a depression, a sense of suffering. I think we have all experienced psychic force to that extent. Remember that this room has a history of intense and rebellious suffering. Some of it I have seen with my own eyes. Your father's fight for life, Katherine, was horrible for those of us who knew he had no chance. As I watched beside him I used to wonder if such violent agony could ever drift wholly into silence, and when we had to tell him finally that the fight was lost, it was beyond bearing."

"If these men had been found dead without marks of violence," Graham said, "I might consider such a possibility, irrational as it seems."

"Irrational," Doctor Groom answered, "must not be confused with impossible. The marks of a physical violence, far from proving that the attack was physical, strengthens the case of the supernatural. Certainly you have heard and read of pictures being dashed from walls by invisible hands, of objects moved about empty rooms, of cases where human beings have been attacked by inanimate things - heavy things - hurtling through the air. Some scientists recognize such irrational possibilities. Policemen don't."

"Very well," Graham said stubbornly. "I'll follow you that far, but you must show me in this room the sharp object with which these men were attacked, no matter what the force behind it."

The doctor spread his hands. His infused eyes nearly closed.

"That I can't do. At any rate, Robert, this isn't wholly tragic to you. I don't see how any one could accuse you of aphasia to-night."

"You've not forgotten," Bobby said slowly, "that you spoke of a recurrent aphasia."

"That's the trouble," Graham put in under his breath. "He has no more alibi now than he had when his grandfather was murdered."

Bobby told of his heavy sleep, of the delay in Katherine's arousing him.

The doctor's gruff voice was disapproving.

"You shouldn't have drunk that medicine. It had stood too long. It would only have approximated its intended effect."

"You mean," Bobby asked, "that I wasn't sleeping as soundly as I thought?"

"Probably not, but you're by no means a satisfactory victim. Men do unaccountable things in a somnambulistic state, but asleep they haven't wings any more than they have awake. You've got to show us how you entered this room without disturbing the locks. Now, Mr. Graham, we must comply with the law. Call in the police."

"There's nothing else to do," Bobby agreed.

So they went along the dingy corridor and downstairs. From the depths of the easy chair in which Paredes lounged smoke curled with a lazy indifference. The Panamanian didn't move.

While Graham and the doctor walked to the back of the hall to telephone, Katherine, an anxious figure, a secretive one, beckoned Bobby to the library. He went with her, wondering what she could want.

It was quite dark in the library. As Bobby fumbled with the lamp and prepared to strike a match he was aware of the girl's provocatively near presence. He resisted a warm impulse to reach out and touch her hand. He desired to tell her all that was in his heart of the division that had increased between them the last few months. Yet to follow that impulse would, he realized, place a portion of his burden on her shoulders; would also, in a sense, be disloyal to Graham, for he no longer questioned that the two had reached a definite sentimental understanding. So he sighed and struck the match. Even before the lamp was lighted Katherine was speaking with a feverish haste:

"Before the police come - you've a chance, Bobby - the last chance. You must do before the police arrive whatever is to be done."

He replaced the shade and glanced at her, astonished by her intensity, by the forceful gesture with which she grasped his arm. For the first time since Silas Blackburn's murder all of her vitality had come back to her.

"What do you mean?"

She pointed to the door of the private staircase.

"Just what Howells told you before he went up there to his death."

Bobby understood. He reacted excitedly to her attitude of conspirator.

"He said," she went on, "that the criminal had nothing to lose. That it would be to his advantage to have him out of the way, to destroy that evidence."

"I thought of it," Bobby answered, "just before I went to sleep."

"Don't you see?" she said. "If you had killed him you would have taken the cast and the handkerchief and destroyed them? Hartley has told me everything, and I could see his coat for myself. The cast and the handkerchief are still in Howells's pocket."

"Why should I have killed him if not to destroy those?" Bobby took her up with a quick hope.

"You didn't," she cried. "Nothing would ever make me believe that you killed him, but you will be charged with it unless the evidence - disappears. You'll have no defence."

Bobby drew back a little.

"You want me to go there - and - and take from his pocket those things?"

She nodded.

"You remember he suggested that he hadn't sent his report. That may be there, too."

Bobby shook his head. "He must have said that as a bait."

"At the worst," she urged, "a report without evidence could only turn suspicion against you. It wouldn't convict you as those other things may. You must get them. You must destroy them."

Graham slipped quietly in and closed the door.

"The district attorney is coming himself with another detective," he said. "I can guess what Katherine has been talking about. She's right. I'm a lawyer, an I know the penalty of tampering with evidence. But I don't believe you're a murderer, and I tell you as long as that evidence exists they can convict you. They can send you to the chair. They may arrest you and try you anyway on his report, but I don't believe they can convict you on it alone. You're justified in protecting yourself, Bobby, in the only way you can. No one will see you go in the room. We'll arrange it so that no one can testify against you."

Bobby felt himself at a cross roads. During the commission of those crimes he had been unconscious. If he had, in fact, had anything to do with them, his personality, his real self, had known nothing, had done no wrong. His body had merely reacted to hideous promptings whose source lurked at the bottom of the black pit. To tamper with evidence would be a conscious crime. All the more, because of his doubt of himself, he shrank from that. Katherine saw his hesitation.

"It's a matter of your life or death."

But although Katherine decided him it wasn't with that. She came closer. She looked straight at him, and her eyes were full of an affection that stirred him profoundly:

"For my sake, Bobby -"

He studied the dead ashes of the fire which a little while ago had played on Howells, vital and antagonistic, by the door of the private staircase. The man had challenged him to do just the thing from which he shrank. But Howells was no longer vital or antagonistic, and it occurred to him that a little of his shrinking arose from the thought of approaching and robbing the still thing upstairs, all that was left of the man who had not been afraid of the mystery of the locked room.

"For my sake," Katherine repeated.

Bobby squared his shoulders. He fought back his momentary cowardice. The affection in Katherine's eyes was stronger than that.

"All right," he said. "Howells never gave me a chance while he was alive. He'll have to now he's dead."

Katherine relaxed. Graham's face was quite white, but he gave his instructions in a cold, even tone:

"We'll go to the hall now. Katherine will go on upstairs. She mustn't see you enter the room, but she will watch in the corridor while you are there to be sure you aren't disturbed. You and I will chat for awhile with the others, Bobby, then you will go up. You understand? Paredes mustn't even guess what you are doing. I'll keep him and Groom downstairs. If he spied, if he knew what you were at, he'd have a weapon in his hands I'd hate to think about. He may be all right, but we can't risk any more than we have to. We must go on tiptoe."

He opened the door. Katherine gave Bobby's hand a quick, encouraging pressure.

"Take the stuff to my room," Graham whispered. "The first chance, we'll destroy it so that no trace will be left."

They went to the hall. Without speaking, Katherine climbed the stairs. Graham drew a chair between Paredes and the doctor. Bobby lounged against the mantel, trying to find in the Panamanian's face some clue as to his real feelings. But Paredes's eyes were closed. His hand drooped across the chair arm. His slender, pointed fingers held, as if from mere habit, a lifeless cigarette.

"Asleep," Graham whispered.

Without opening his eyes Paredes spoke: "No; I feel curiously awake." He yawned.

Doctor Groom glanced at his watch. "The powers of prosecution," he grumbled, "ought to be here within the next fifteen or twenty minutes."

Bobby glanced at Graham. Then it wasn't safe to delay too long. More and more as he waited he shrank from the invasion of the room of death. The prospect of reaching out and touching the still, cold thing on the bed revolted him. Was there anything in that room capable of forbidding his intention? Was there, in short, a surer, more malicious force for evil than his unconscious self, at work in the house? He was about to make some formal comment to the others, to embark on his distasteful adventure, when Paredes, as if he had read Bobby's mind, opened his eyes, languidly left his chair, and walked to the foot of the stairs.

"Where you going?" Graham asked sharply.

Paredes waved his hand indifferently and walked on up. There was something of stealth in his failure to reply, in his cat-like tread on the stairs. Graham and Bobby stared after him, unable to meet this new situation audibly because of Groom. Yet five minutes had gone. There was no time to be lost.

Paredes mustn't rob Bobby of his chance. With a sort of desperation he started for the stairs. Graham held out his hand as if to restrain him, then nodded. Bobby had his foot on the first step when Katherine's cry reached them, shaping the moment to their use. For there was no fright in her cry. It was, rather, angry. And Bobby and Graham ran up while Doctor Groom remained in his chair, an expression of blank amazement on his face.

A candle burned on the table in the upper hall. Katherine and Paredes stood near the entrance of the old corridor. Paredes, as usual, was quite unruffled. Katherine's attitude was defensive. She seemed to hold the corridor against him. The anger of her cry was active in her eyes. Paredes laughed lightly.

"Sorry to have given the household one more shock. Fortunately no harm done."

"What is it, Katherine?" Graham demanded.

"I don't know," she answered. "He startled me. He entered the corridor."

Paredes nodded.

"Quite right. She was there. I was on my way to my room. If your house had electricity, Bobby, this incident would have been avoided. I saw something dark in the corridor."

"You may not know," Graham said, "that ever since we found Howells, one of us has tried, more or less, to keep the entrance of that room under observation."

"Yet you were all downstairs a little while ago," Paredes yawned. "It's too bad. I might have taken my turn then. At any rate, since I was excluded from your confidence, I overcame my natural fear, and, for Bobby's sake, slipped in, and, I am afraid, startled Miss Katherine."

"Yes," she said.

His explanation was reasonable. There was nothing more to be said, but Bobby's doubt of his friend, sown by Graham and stimulated by the incidents of the last hour, was materially strengthened. He felt a sharp fear of Paredes. Such reserve, such concealment of emotion, was scarcely human.

"If," Graham was saying, "you really want to help Bobby, there is something you can do. Will you come downstairs with me for a moment? I'd like to suggest one or two things before the police arrive."

Without hesitation Paredes followed Graham down the stairs.

Katherine turned immediately to Bobby, her eyes eager, full of the tense determination that had dictated her plan in the library.

"Now, Bobby!" she whispered. "And there's no time to waste. They may be here any minute. I won't see you go, but I'll be back at once to guard you against Paredes if he slips up again."

She walked across the hall and disappeared in the newer corridor. Without witness he faced the old corridor, and with the attempt directly ahead his repugnance achieved a new power. The black entrance with its scarcely dared memories reminded him that what he was about to do was directed against more than human law, was an outrage against the dead man. He had to remind himself of the steely purpose with which Howells had marked him as the murderer; and the man's power persisted after death. In such a contest he was justified.

He took the candle from the table. Through the stair-well the murmur of Graham's voice, occasionally interrupted by Groom's heavy tones or the languid accents of Paredes, drifted encouragingly. Trying to crush his premonitions, Bobby entered the corridor. Instead of illuminating the narrow passage the candle seemed half smothered by its blackness. For the first time in his memory Bobby faced the entrance of the sinister room alone. He pushed open the broken door. He paused on the threshold. It impressed him as not unnatural that he should experience such misgivings. They sprang not alone from the fact that within twenty-four hours two men had died unaccountably within these faded walls. Nor did the evidence pointing to his own unconscious guilt wholly account for them. At the bottom of everything was the fact that from his earliest childhood he had looked upon the room as consecrated to death; had consequently feared it; had, he recalled, always hurried past the disused corridor leading in its direction.

Through its wide spaces the light of the candle scarcely penetrated. No more than an indefinite radiance thrust back the obscurity and outlined the bed. He could barely see the stark, black form outstretched there.

The dim, vast room, as he advanced, imposed upon him a sense of isolation. Katherine in the upper hall, the others downstairs, whose voices no longer reached him, seemed all at once far away. He stood in a place lonelier and more remote than the piece of woods where he had momentarily opened his eyes last night; and, instead of the straining trees and the figure in the black mask which he had called his conscience, he had for motion and companionship only the swaying of the curtains in the breeze from the open window and the dark, prostrate thing whose face as he went closer was like a white mask - a mask with a fixed and malevolent sneer.

The wind caught the flame of the candle, making it flicker. Tenuous shadows commenced to dance across the walls. He paused with a tightening throat, for the form on the bed seemed moving, too, with sly and scarcely perceptible gestures. Then he understood. It was the effect of the shaking candle, and he forced himself to go on, but a sense of a multiple companionship accompanied him - a sense of a shapeless, soundless companionship that projected an idea of a steady regard. There swept through his mind a procession of figures in quaint dress and with faces not unlike his own, remembered from portraits and family legends, men and women to whom this room had been familiar, within whose limits they had suffered, cried out a too-powerful agony, and died. It seemed to him that he waited for voices to guide him, to urge him on as Katherine had urged him, or to drive him back, because he was an intruder in a company whose habit was strange and terrifying.

He forced his glance from the shadows which seemed more active along the walls. He raised his candle and stared at the dead man. The cast was undoubtedly there. The coat, stretched tightly across the breast, outlined it. He stood at the side of the bed. He had only to bend and place his hand in the pocket which the cast filled awkwardly. The wind alone, he saw, wasn't responsible for the shaking of the candle. His hand shook as the shadows shook, as the thing on the bed shook. The sense of loneliness grew upon him until it became complete, appalling. For the first time he understood that loneliness can possess a ponderable quality. It was, he felt, potent and active in the room - a thing he couldn't understand, or challenge, or overcome.

His hand tightened. He thought of Katherine guarding the corridor; of Paredes and Doctor Groom, held downstairs by Graham; of the county authorities hurrying to seize this evidence that would convict him; and he realized that his duty and his excuse were clear. He understood that just now he had been captured by a force undefinable in terms of the world he knew. For a moment he eluded the stealthy fleshless hands of its impalpable skirmishers. He reached impulsively out to the dead man. He was about to place his fingers in the pocket, which, after all was said and done, held his life.

In the light of the candle the face seemed alive and more menacing than it had ever done in life. About the straight smile was a wider, more triumphant quality.

The candle flickered sharply. It expired. The conquering blackness took his breath.

He told himself it was the draft from the window which was strong, but the companionship of the night was closer and more numerous. The darkness wreathed itself into mocking and tortuous bodies whose faces were hidden.

In an agony of revolt against these incorporeal, these fanciful horrors, he reached in the pocket.

He sprang back with a choked, inaudible cry, for the dead thing beneath his hand was stirring. The dead, cold thing with a languid and impossible rebuke, moved beneath his touch. And the pocket he had felt was empty. The coat, a moment ago bulging and awkward, was flat. There sprang to his mind the mad thought that the detective, malevolent in life, had long after death snatched from his hand the evidence, carefully gathered, on which everything for him depended.

CHAPTER V

THE CRYING THROUGH THE WOODS

Bobby's inability to cry out alone prevented his alarming the others and announcing to Paredes and Doctor Groom his unlawful presence in the room. During the moment that the shock held him, silent, motionless, bent in the darkness above the bed, he understood there could have been no ambiguity about his ghastly and loathsome experience. The dead detective had altered his position as Silas Blackburn had done, and this time someone had been in the room and suffered the appalling change. Bobby's fingers still responded to the charnel feeling of cold, inactive flesh suddenly become alive and potent beneath his touch. And a reason for the apparent miracle offered itself. Between the extinction of his candle and the commencement of that movement! - only a second or so - the evidence had disappeared from the detective's pocket.

Bobby relaxed. He stumbled across the room and into the corridor. He went with hands outstretched through the blackness, for no candle burned in the upper hall, but he knew that Katherine was on guard there. When he left the passage he saw her, an unnatural figure herself, in the yellowish, unhealthy twilight which sifted through the stair well from the lamp in the hall below.

She must have sensed something out of the way immediately, for she hurried to meet him and her whisper held no assurance.

"You got the cast and the handkerchief, Bobby?"

And when he didn't answer at once she asked with a sharp rush of fear:

"What's the matter? What's happened?"

He shuddered. At last he managed to speak.

"Katherine! I have felt death cease to be death."

Later he was to recall that phrase with a sicker horror than he experienced now.

"You saw something!" she said. "But your candle is out. There is no light in the room."

He took her hand. He pressed it.

"You're real!" he said with a nervous laugh. "Something I can understand. Everything is unreal. This light -"

He strode to the table, found a match, and lighted his candle. Katherine, as she saw his face, drew back.

"Bobby!"

"My candle went out," he said dully, "and he moved through the darkness. I tell you he moved beneath my hand."

She drew farther away, staring at him.

"You were frightened -"

"No. If we go there with a light now," he said with the same dull conviction, "we will find him as we found my grandfather this afternoon."

The monotonous voices of the three men in the lower hall

weaved a background for their whispers. The normal, familiar sound was like a tonic. Bobby straightened. Katherine threw off the spell of his
announcement.

"But the evidence! You got -"

She stared at his empty hands. He fancied that he saw contempt in her eyes.

"In spite of everything you must go back. You must get that."

"Even if I had the courage," he said wearily, "it would be no use, for the evidence is gone."

"But I saw it. At least I saw his pocket -"

"It was there," he answered, "when my light went out. I did put my hand in his pocket. In that second it had gone."

"There was no one there," she said, "no one but you, because I watched."

He leaned heavily against the wall.

"Good God, Katherine! It's too big. Whatever it is, we can't fight it."

She looked for some time down the corridor at the black entrance of the sinister room. At last she turned and walked to the banister. She called:

"Hartley! Will you come up?"

Bobby wondered at the steadiness of her voice. The murmuring below ceased. Graham ran up the stairs. Her summons had been warning enough. Their attitudes, as Graham reached the upper hall, were eloquent of Bobby's failure.

"You didn't get the cast and the handkerchief?" he said.

Bobby told briefly what had happened.

"What is one to do?" he ended. "Even the dead are against me."

"It's beyond belief," Graham said roughly.

He snatched up the candle and entered the corridor. Uncertainly Katherine and Bobby followed him. He went straight to the bed and thrust the candle beneath the canopy. The others could see from the door the change that had taken place. The body of Howells was turned awkwardly on its side. The coat pocket was, as Bobby had described it, flat and empty.

Katherine turned and went back to the hall. Graham's hand shook as Bobby's had shaken.

"No tricks, Bobby?"

Bobby couldn't resent the suspicion which appeared to offer the only explanation of what had happened. The candle flickered in the draft.

"Look out!" Bobby warned.

The misshapen shadows danced with a multiple vivacity across the walls. Graham shaded the candle flame, and the shadows became like morbid decorations, gargantuan and motionless.

"It's madness," Graham said. "There's no explanation of this that we can understand."

Howells's straight smile mocked them. As if in answer to Graham a voice sighed through the room. Its quality was one with the shadows, unsubstantial and shapeless. Bobby grasped one of the bed posts and braced himself, listening. The candle in Graham's hand commenced to flicker again, and Bobby knew that it hadn't been his fancy, for Graham listened, too.

It shook again through the heavy, oppressive night, merely accentuated by the candle - a faint ululation barely detaching itself from silence, straying after a time into the silence again. At first it was like the grief of a woman heard at a great distance. But the sound, while it gained no strength, forced on them more and more an abhorrent sense of intimacy. This crying from an infinite distance filled the room, seemed finally to have its source in the room itself. After it had sobbed thinly into nothing, its pulsations continued to sigh in Bobby's ears. They seemed timed to the renewed and eccentric dancing of the amorphous shadows.

Graham straightened and placed the candle on the bureau. He seemed more startled than he had been at the unbelievable secretiveness of a dead man.

"You heard it?" Bobby breathed.

Graham nodded.

"What was it? Where did you think it came from?" Bobby demanded. "It was like someone mourning for this - this poor devil."

Graham couldn't disguise his effort to elude the sombre spell of the room, to drive from his brain the illusion of that unearthly moaning.

"It must have come from outside the house," he answered "There's no use giving way to fancies where there's a possible explanation. It must have come from outside - from some woman in great agony of mind."

Bobby recalled his perception of a woman moving with a curious absence of sound about the edges of the stagnant lake. He spoke of it to Graham.

"I couldn't be sure it was a woman, but there's no house within two miles. What would a woman be doing wandering around the Cedars?"

"At any rate, there are three women in the house," Graham said, "Katherine and the two servants, Ella and Jane. The maids are badly frightened. It may have come from the servants' quarters. It must have been one of them."

But Bobby saw that Graham didn't believe either of the maids had released that poignant suffering.

"It didn't sound like a living voice," he said simply.

"Then how are we to take it?" Graham persisted angrily. "I shall question Katherine and the two maids."

He took up the candle with a stubborn effort to recapture his old forcefulness, but as they left the room the shadows thronged thickly after them in ominous pursuit; and it wasn't necessary to question Katherine. She stood in the corridor, her lips parted, her face white and shocked.

"What was it?" she said. "That nearly silent grief?"

She put her hands to her ears, lowering them helplessly after a moment.

"Where did you think it came from?" Graham asked.

"From a long ways off," she answered. "Then I - I thought it must be in the room with you, and I wondered if you saw -"

Graham shook his head.

"We saw nothing. It was probably Ella or Jane. They've been badly frightened. Perhaps a nightmare, or they've heard us moving around the front part of the house. I am going to see."

Katherine and Bobby followed him downstairs. Doctor Groom and Paredes stood in front of the fireplace, questioningly looking upward. Paredes didn't speak at first, but Doctor Groom burst out in his grumbling, bass voice:

"What's been going on up there?"

"Did you hear just now a queer crying?" Graham asked.

"No."

"You, Paredes?"

"I've heard nothing," Paredes answered, "except Doctor Groom's disquieting theories. It's an uncanny hour for such talk. What kind of a cry - may I ask?"

"Like a woman moaning," Bobby said, "and, Doctor, Howells has changed his position."

"What are you talking about?" the doctor cried.

"He has turned on his side as Mr. Blackburn did," Graham told him.

Paredes glanced at Bobby.

"And how was this new mystery discovered?"

Bobby caught the implication. Then the Panamanian clung to his slyly expressed doubt of Katherine which might, after all, have had its impulse in an instinct of self-preservation. Bobby knew that Graham and Katherine would guard the fashion in which the startling discovery had been made. Before he could speak for himself, indeed, Graham was answering Paredes:

"This crying seemed after a time to come from the room. We entered."

"But Miss Katherine called you up," Paredes said. "I supposed she had heard again movements in the room."

Bobby managed a smile.

"You see, Carlos, nothing is consistent in this case."

Paredes bowed gravely.

"It is very curious a woman should cry about the house."

"The servants may make it seem natural enough," Graham said. "Will you come, Bobby?"

As they crossed the dining room they heard a stirring in the kitchen. Graham threw open the door. Jenkins stood at the foot of the servants' stairs. The old butler had lighted a candle and placed it on the mantel. The disorder of his clothing suggested the haste with which he had left his bed and come downstairs. His wrinkled, sunken face had aged perceptibly. He advanced with an expression of obvious relief.

"I was just coming to find you, Mr. Robert."

"What's up?" Bobby asked. "A little while ago I thought you were all asleep back here."

"One of the women awakened him," Graham said. "It's just as I thought."

"Was that it?" the old butler asked with a quick relief. But immediately he shook his head. "It couldn't have been that, Mr. Graham, for I stopped at Ella's and Jane's doors, and there was no sound. They seemed to be asleep. And it wasn't like that."

"You mean," Bobby said, "that you heard a woman crying?"

Jenkins nodded. "It woke me up."

"If you didn't think it was one of the maids," Graham asked, "what did you make of it?"

"I thought it came from outside. I thought it was a woman prowling around the house. Then I said to myself, why should a woman prowl around the Cedars? And it was too unearthly, sir, and I remembered the way Mr. Silas was murdered, and the awful thing that happened to his body this afternoon, and I - you won't think me foolish, sirs? - I doubted if it was a human voice I had heard."

"No," Graham said dryly, "we won't think you foolish."

"So I thought I'd better wake you up and tell you."

Graham turned to Bobby.

"Katherine and you and I," he said, "fancied the crying was in the room with us. Jenkins is sure it came from outside the house. That is significant."

"Wherever it came from," Bobby said softly, "it was like some one mourning for Howells."

Jenkins started.

"The policeman!"

Bobby remembered that Jenkins hadn't been aroused by the discovery of Howells's murder.

"You'd know in a few minutes anyway," he said. "Howells has been killed as my grandfather was."

Jenkins moved back, a look of unbelief and awe in his wrinkled face.

"He boasted he was going to sleep in that room," he whispered.

Bobby studied Jenkins, not knowing what to make of the old man, for into the awe of the wrinkled face had stolen a positive relief, an emotion that bordered on the triumphant.

"It's terrible," Jenkins whispered.

Graham grasped his shoulder.

"What's the matter with you, Jenkins? One would say you were glad."

"No. Oh, no, sir. It is terrible. I was only wondering about the policeman's report."

"What do you know about his report?" Bobby cried.

"Only that - that he gave it to me to mail just before he went up to the old room."

"You mailed it?" Graham snapped.

Jenkins hesitated. When he answered his voice was self-accusing.

"I'm an old coward, Mr. Robert. The policeman told me the letter was very important, and if anything happened to it I would get in trouble. He couldn't afford to leave the house himself, he said. But, as I say, I'm a coward, and I didn't want to walk through the woods to the box by the gate. I figured it all out. It wouldn't be taken up until early in the morning, and if I waited until daylight it would only be delayed one collection. So I made up my mind I'd sleep on it, because I knew he had it in for you, Mr. Robert. I supposed I'd mail it in the morning, but I decided I'd think it over anyway and not harrow myself walking through the woods."

"You've done a good job," Graham said excitedly. "Where is the report now?"

"In my room. Shall I fetch it, sir?"

Graham nodded, and Jenkins shuffled up the stairs.

"What luck!" Graham said. "Howells must have telephoned his suspicions to the district attorney. He must have mentioned the evidence, but what does that amount to since it's disappeared along with the duplicate of the report, if Howells made one?"

"I can fight with a clear conscience," Bobby cried. "I wasn't asleep when Howells's body altered its position. Do you realize what that means to me? For once I was wide awake when the old room was at its tricks."

"If Howells were alive," Graham answered shortly, "he would look on the fact that you were awake and alone with the body as the worst possible evidence against you."

Bobby's elation died.

"There is always something to tangle me in the eyes of the law with these mysteries. But I know, and I'll fight. Can you find any trace of a conspiracy against me in this last ghastly adventure?"

"It complicates everything," Graham admitted.

"It's beyond sounding," Bobby said, "for my grandfather's death last night and the disturbance of his body this afternoon seemed calculated to condemn me absolutely, yet Howells's murder and the movement of his body, with the disappearance of the cast and the handkerchief, seem designed to save me. Are there two influences at work in this house - one for me, one against me?"

"Let's think of the human elements," Graham answered with a frown. "I have no faith in Paredes. My man has failed to report on Maria. That's queer. You fancy a woman in black slipping through the woods, and we hear a woman cry. I want to account for those things before I give in to Groom's spirits. I confess at times they seem the only logical explanation. Here's Jenkins."

"If trouble comes of his withholding the report I'll take the blame," Bobby said.

Graham snatched the long envelope from Jenkins' hand. It was addressed in a firm hand to the district attorney at the county seat.

"There's no question," Graham said. "That's it. We mustn't open it. We'd better not destroy it. Put it where it won't be easily found, Jenkins. If you are questioned you have no recollection of Howells having given it to you. Mr. Blackburn promises he will see you get in no trouble."

The old man smiled.

"Trouble!" he scoffed. "Mr. Blackburn needn't fret himself about me. He's the last of this family - that is Miss Katherine and he. I'm old and about done for. I don't mind trouble. Not a bit, sir."

Bobby pressed his hand. His voice was a little husky: "I didn't think you'd go that far in my service, Jenkins."

The old butler smiled slyly: "I'd go a lot further than that, sir."

"We'd better get back," Graham said. "The blood hounds ought to be here, and they'll sniff at the case harder than ever because it's done for Howells."

They watched Jenkins go upstairs with the report.

"We're taking long chances," Graham said, "desperately long chances, but you're in a desperately dangerous position. It's the only way. You'll be accused of stealing the evidence; but remember, when they question you, they can prove nothing unless the cast and the handkerchief turn up. If they've been taken by an enemy in some magical fashion to be produced at the proper moment, there's no hope. Meantime play the game, and Katherine and I will help you all we can. The doctor, too, is friendly. There's no doubt of him. Come, now. Let's face the music."

Bobby followed Graham to the hall, trying to strengthen his nerves for the ordeal. Even now he was more appalled by the apparently supernatural background of the case than he was by the material details which pointed to his guilt. More than the report and the cast and the handkerchief, the remembrance of that impossible moment in the blackness of the old room filled his mind, and the unearthly and remote crying still throbbed in his ears.

Katherine, Graham, and the doctor waited by the fireplace. They had heard nothing from the authorities.

"But they must be here soon," Doctor Groom said.

"Did you learn anything back there, Hartley?" Katherine asked.

"It wasn't the servants," he said. "Jenkins heard the crying. He's certain it came from outside the house."

Paredes looked up.

"Extraordinary!" he said.

"I wish I had heard it," Doctor Groom grumbled.

Paredes laughed.

"Thank the good Lord I didn't. Perpetually, Bobby, your house reminds me that I've nerves sensitive to the unknown world. I will go further than the doctor. I will say that this house *is* crowded with the supernatural. It shelters things that we cannot understand, that we will never understand. When I was a child in Panama I had a nurse who, unfortunately, developed too strongly my native superstition. How she frightened me with her bedtime stories! They were all of men murdered or dead of fevers, crossing the trail, or building the railroad, or digging insufficient ditches for De Lesseps. Some of her best went farther back than that. They were thick with the ghosts of old Spaniards and the crimson hands of Morgan's buccaneers. Really that tiny strip across the isthmus is crowded with souls snatched too quickly from torn and tortured bodies. If you are sensitive you feel they are still there."

"What has all this to do with the Cedars?" Doctor Groom grumbled.

"It explains my ability to sense strange elements in this old house. There are in Panama - if you don't mind, doctor - improvised graveyards, tangled by the jungle, that give you a feeling of an active, unseen population precisely as this house does."

He arose and strolled with a cat-like lack of sound about the hall. When he spoke again his voice was scarcely audible. It was the voice of a man who thinks aloud, and the doctor failed to interrupt him again.

"I have felt less spiritually alarmed in those places of grinning skulls, which always seem trying to recite agonies beyond expression, than I feel in this house. For here the woods are more desolate than the jungle, and the walls of houses as old as this make a prison for suffering."

A vague discomfort stole through Bobby's surprise. He had never heard Paredes speak so seriously. In spite of the man's unruffled manner there was nothing of mockery about his words. What, then, was their intention?

Paredes said no more, but for several minutes he paced up and down the hall, glancing often with languid eyes toward the stairs. He had the appearance of one who expects and waits.

Katherine, Graham, and the doctor, Bobby could see, had been made as uneasy as himself by the change in the Panamanian. The doctor cleared his throat. His voice broke the silence tentatively:

"If this house makes you so unhappy, young man, why do you stay?"

Paredes paused in his walk. His thin lips twitched. He indicated Bobby.

"For the sake of my very good friend. What are a man's personal fears and desires if he can help his friends?"

Graham's distaste was evident. Paredes recognized it with a smile. Bobby watched him curiously, realizing more and more that Graham was right to this extent: they must somehow learn the real purpose of the Panamanian's continued presence here.

Paredes resumed his walk. He still had that air of expectancy. He seemed to listen. This feeling of imminence reached Bobby; increased his restlessness. He thought he heard an automobile horn outside. He sprang up, went to the door, opened it, and stood gazing through the damp and narrow court. Yet, he confessed, he listened for a repetition of that unearthly crying through the thicket rather than for the approach of those who would try to condemn him for two murders. Paredes was right. The place was unhealthy. Its dark walls seemed to draw closer. They had a desolate and unfriendly secretiveness. They might hide anything.

The whirring of a motor reached him. Headlights flung gigantic, distorted shadows of trees across the walls of the old wing. Bobby faced the others.

"They're coming," he said, and his voice was sufficiently

apprehensive now.

Graham joined him at the door. "Yes," he said. "There will be another inquisition. You all know that Howells for some absurd reason suspected Bobby. Bobby, it goes without saying, knows no more about the crimes than any of us. I dare say you'll keep that in mind if they try to confuse you. After all, there's very little any of us can tell them."

"Except," Paredes said with a yawn, "what went on upstairs when the woman cried and Howells's body moved. Of course I know nothing about that."

Graham glanced at him sharply.

"I don't know what you mean, but you have told us all that you are Bobby's friend."

"Quite so. And I am not a spy."

He moved his head in his grave and dignified bow.

The automobile stopped at the entrance to the court. Three men stepped out and hurried up the path. As they entered the hall Bobby recognized the sallow, wizened features of the coroner. One of the others was short and thick set. His round and florid face, one felt, should have expressed friendliness and good-humour rather than the intolerant anger that marked it now. The third was a lank, bald-headed man, whose sharp face released more determination than intelligence.

"I am Robinson, the district attorney," the stout one announced, "and this is Jack Rawlins, the best detective I've got now that Howells is gone. Jack was a close friend of Howells, so he'll make a good job of it, but I thought it was time I came myself to see what the devil's going on in this house."

The lank man nodded.

"You're right, Mr. Robinson. There'll be no more nonsense about the case. If Howells had made an arrest he might be alive this minute."

Bobby's heart sank. These men would act from a primary instinct of revenge. They wanted the man who had killed Silas Blackburn principally because it was certain he had also killed their friend. Rawlins's words, moreover, suggested that Howells must have telephoned a pretty clear outline of the case. Robinson stared at them insolently.

"This is Doctor Groom, I know. Which is young Mr. Blackburn?"

Bobby stepped forward. The sharp eyes, surrounded by puffy flesh, studied him aggressively. Bobby forced himself to meet that unfriendly gaze. Would Robinson accuse him now, before he had gone into the case for himself? At least he could prove nothing. After a moment the man turned away.

"Who is this?" he asked, indicating Graham.

"A very good friend - my lawyer, Mr. Graham," Bobby answered.

Robinson walked over to Paredes.

"Another lawyer?" he sneered.

"Another friend," Paredes answered easily.

Robinson glanced at Katherine.

"Of course you are Miss Perrine. Good. Coroner, these are all that were in the front part of the house when you were here before?"

"The same lot," the coroner squeaked.

"There are three servants, a man and two women," Robinson went on. "Account for them, Rawlins, and see what they have to say. Come upstairs when you're through. All right, Coroner."

But he paused at the foot of the steps.

"For the present no one will leave the house without my permission. If you care to come upstairs with me, Mr. Blackburn, you might be useful."

Bobby shrank from the thought of returning to the old room even with this determined company. He didn't hesitate, however, for Robinson's purpose was clear. He wanted Bobby where he could watch him. Graham prepared to accompany them.

"If you need me," the doctor said. "I looked at the body -"

"Oh, yes," Robinson sneered. "I'd like to know exactly what time you found the body."

Graham flushed, but Katherine answered easily:

"About half-past two - the hour at which Mr. Blackburn was killed."

"And I," Robinson sneered, "was aroused at three-thirty. An hour during which the police were left out of the case!"

"We thought it wise to get a physician first of all," Graham said.

"You knew Howells never had a chance. You knew he had been murdered the moment you looked at him," Robinson burst out.

"We acted for the best," Graham answered.

His manner impressed silence on Katherine and Bobby.

"We'll see about that later," Robinson said with a clear threat. "If it doesn't inconvenience you too much we'll go up now."

In the upper hall he snatched the candle from the table.

"Which way?"

Katherine nodded to the old corridor and slipped to her room. Robinson stepped forward with the coroner at his heels. Bobby, Graham, and the doctor followed. Inside the narrow, choking passage Bobby saw the district attorney hesitate.

"What's the matter?" the doctor rumbled.

The district attorney went on without answering. He glanced at the broken lock.

"So you had to smash your way in?"

He walked to the bed and looked down at Howells.

"Poor devil!" he murmured. "Howells wasn't the man to get caught unawares. It's beyond me how any one could have come close enough to make that wound without putting him on his guard."

"It's beyond us, as it was beyond him," Graham answered, "how any one got into the room at all."

In response to Robinson's questions he told in detail about the discovery of both murders. Robinson pondered for some time.

"Then you and Mr. Blackburn were asleep," he said. "Miss Perrine aroused you. This foreigner Paredes was awake and dressed and in the lower hall."

"I think he was in the court as we went by the stair-well,"

Graham corrected him.

"I shall want to talk to your foreigner," Robinson said. He shivered. "This room is like a charnel house. Why did Howells want to sleep here?"

"I don't think he intended to sleep," Graham said. "From the start Howells was bound to solve the mystery of the entrance of the room. He came here, hoping that the criminal would make just such an attempt as he did. He was confident he could take care of himself, get his man, and clear up the last details of the case."

Robinson looked straight at Bobby.

"Then Howells knew the criminal was in the house."

"Howells, I daresay," Graham said, "telephoned you something of his suspicions." Robinson nodded.

"He was on the wrong line," Graham argued, "or he wouldn't have been so easily overcome. You can see for yourself. Locked doors, a wound that suggests the assailant was close to him, yet he must have been awake and watchful; and if there had been a physical attack before the sharp instrument was driven into his brain he would have cried out, yet Miss Perrine was aroused by nothing of the sort, and the coroner, I daresay, will find no marks of a struggle about the body."

The coroner who had been busy at the bed glanced up.

"No mark at all. If Howells wasn't asleep, his murderer must have been invisible as well as noiseless."

Doctor Groom smiled. The coroner glared at him.

"I suggest, Mr. District Attorney," he squeaked, "that the ordinary layman wouldn't know that this type of wound would cause immediate death."

"Nor would any man," the doctor answered angrily, "be able to make such a wound with his victim lying on his back."

"On his back!" Robinson echoed. "But he isn't on his back."

The doctor told of the amazing alteration in the positions of both victims. Bobby regretted with all his heart that he had made the attempt to get the evidence. Already complete frankness was impossible for him. Already a feeling of guilt sprang from the necessity of withholding the first-hand testimony which he alone could give.

"And a woman cried!" Robinson said, bewildered. "All this sounds like a ghost story."

"You've more sense than I thought," Doctor Groom said dryly. "I never could get Howells to see it that way."

"What are you driving at?" Robinson snapped.

"These crimes," the doctor answered, "have all the elements of a ghostly impulse."

Robinson's laugh was a little uncomfortable.

"The Cedars is a nice place for spooks, but it won't do. I'll be frank. Howells telephoned me. He had found plenty of evidence of human interference. It's evident in both cases that the murderer came back and disturbed the bodies for some special purpose. I don't know what it was the first time, but it's simple to understand the last. The murderer came for evidence Howells had on his person."

Bobby couldn't meet the sharp, puffy eyes. He alone was capable of testifying that the evidence had been removed as if to secrete it from his unlawful hand. Yet if he spoke he would prove the district attorney's point. He would condemn himself.

"Curious," Graham said slowly, "that the murderer didn't take the evidence when he killed his man."

"I don't know about that," Robinson said, "but I know Howells had evidence on his person. You through, Coroner? Then we'll have a look, although it's little use."

He walked to the bed and searched Howells's pockets.

"Just as I thought. Nothing. He told me he was preparing a report. If he didn't mail it, that was stolen with the rest of the stuff. Rawlins's right. He waited too long to make his arrest."

Again Bobby wondered if the man would bring matters to a head now. He could appreciate, however, that Robinson, with nothing to go on but Howells's telephoned suspicions, might spoil his chances of a solution by acting too hastily. Rawlins strolled in.

"The two women were asleep," he said. "The old man knows nothing beyond the fact that he heard a woman crying outside a little while ago."

"I don't think we need bother about the back part of the house for the present," Robinson said. "Howells's evidence has been stolen. It's your job to find it unless it's been destroyed. Your other job is to discover the instrument that caused death in both cases. Then maybe our worthy doctor will desert his ghosts. Mr. Blackburn, if you will come with me there's a slight possibility of checking up some of the evidence of which Howells spoke. Our fine fellow may have made a slip in the court."

Bobby understood and was afraid - more afraid than he had been at any time since he had overheard Howells catalogue his case to Graham in the library. Why, even in so much confusion, had Graham and he failed to think of those tell-tale marks in the court? They had been intact when he had stood there just before dark. It was unlikely any one had walked across the grass since. He saw Graham's elaborate precautions demolished, the case against him stronger than it had been before Howells's murder. Graham's face revealed the same helpless comprehension. They followed Robinson downstairs. Graham made a gesture of surrender. Bobby glanced at Paredes who alone had remained below. The Panamanian smoked and lounged in the easy chair. His eyes seemed restless.

"I shall wish to ask you some questions in a few minutes, Mr. Paredes," the district attorney said.

"At your service, I'm sure," Paredes drawled.

He watched them until they had entered the court and closed the door. The chill dampness of the court infected Bobby as it had always done. It was a proper setting for his accusation and arrest. For Robinson, he knew, wouldn't wait as Howells had done to solve the mystery of the locked doors.

Robinson, while the others grouped themselves about him, took a flashlight from his pocket and pressed the control. The brilliant cylinder of light illuminated the grass, making it seem unnaturally green. Bobby braced himself for the inevitable denouement. Then, while Robinson exclaimed angrily, his eyes widened, his heart beat rapidly with a vast and wondering relief. For the marks he remembered so clearly had been obliterated with painstaking thoroughness, and at first the slate seemed perfectly clean. He was sure his unknown friend had avoided leaving any trace of his own. Each step in the grass had been carefully scraped out. In the confusion of the path there was nothing to be learned.

The genuine surprise of Bobby's exclamation turned Robinson to him with a look of doubt.

"You acknowledge these footmarks were here, Mr. Blackburn?"

"Certainly," Bobby answered. "I saw them myself just before dark. I knew

Howells ridiculously connected them with the murderer."

"You made a good job of it when you trampled, them out," Robinson hazarded.

But it was clear Bobby's amazement had not been lost on him.

"Or," he went on, "this foreigner who advertises himself as your friend! He was in the court tonight. We know that."

Suddenly he stooped, and Bobby got on his knees beside him. The cylinder of light held in its centre one mark, clear and distinct in the trampled grass, and with a warm gratitude, a swift apprehension, Bobby thought of Katherine. For the mark in the grass had been made by the heel of a woman's shoe.

"Not the foreigner then," Robinson mused, "not yourself, Blackburn, but a woman, a devoted woman. That's something to get after."

"And if she lies, the impression of the heel will give her away," the coroner suggested.

Robinson grinned.

"You'd make a rotten detective, Coroner. Women's heels are cut to a pattern. There are thousands of shoes whose heels would fit this impression. We need the sole for identification, and that she hasn't left us. But she's done one favour. She's advertised herself as a woman, and there are just three women in the house. One of those committed this serious offence, and the inference is obvious."

Before Bobby could protest, the doctor broke in with his throaty rumble: "One of those, or the woman who cried about the house."

Bobby started. The memory of that eerie grief was still uncomfortable in his brain. Could there have been actually a woman at the stagnant lake that afternoon and close to the house to-night - some mysterious friend who assumed grave risks in his service? He recognized Robinson's logic. Unless there were something in that far-fetched theory, Katherine faced a situation nearly as serious as his own. Robinson straightened. At the same moment the scraping of a window reached them. Bobby glanced at the newer wing. Katherine leaned from her window. The coincidence disturbed him. In Robinson's mind, he knew, her anxiety would assume a colour of guilt. Her voice, moreover, was too uncertain, too full of misgivings:

"What is going on down there? There have been no - no more tragedies?"

"Would you mind joining us for a moment?" Robinson asked.

She drew back. The curtain fell over her lighted window. The darkness of the court was disturbed again only by the limited radiance of the flashlight. She came hurriedly from the front door.

"I saw you gathered here. I heard you talking. I wondered."

"You knew there were footprints in this court," Robinson said harshly, "that Howells connected them with the murderer of your uncle."

"Yes," she answered simply.

"Why then," he asked, "did you attempt to obliterate them?"

She laughed.

"What do you mean? I didn't. I haven't been out of the house since just after luncheon."

"Can you prove that?"

"It needs no proof. I tell you so."

The flashlight exposed the ugly confidence of Robinson's smile.

"I am sorry to suggest the need of corroboration."

"You doubt my word?" she flashed.

"A woman," he answered, "has obliterated valuable testimony, I shall make it my business to punish her."

She laughed again. Without another word she turned and reentered the house. Robinson's oath was audible to the others.

"We can't put up with that sort of thing, sir," Rawlins said.

"I ought to place this entire household under arrest," Robinson muttered.

"As a lawyer," Graham said easily, "I should think with your lack of evidence it might be asking for trouble. There is Paredes who acknowledges he was in the court."

"All right. I'll see what he's got to say."

He started for the house. Bobby lingered for a moment with Graham.

"Do you know anything about this, Hartley?"

"Nothing," Graham whispered.

"Then you don't think Katherine -"

"If she'd done it she'd have taken good care not to be so curious. I doubt if it was Katherine."

They followed the others into the hall. Bobby, scarcely

appreciating why at first, realized there had been a change there. Then he understood:

Robinson faced an empty chair. The hall was pungent with cigarette smoke, but Paredes had gone.

Robinson pointed to the stairs.

"Get him down," he said to Rawlins.

"He wouldn't have gone to bed," Graham suggested. "Suppose he's in the old room where Howells lies?"

But Rawlins found him nowhere upstairs. With an increasing excitement Robinson joined the search. They went through the entire house. Paredes was no longer there. He had, to all appearances, put a period to his unwelcome visit. He had definitely disappeared from the Cedars.

His most likely exit was through the kitchen door which was unlocked, but Jenkins who had returned to his room had heard no one. With their electric lamps Robinson and Rawlins ferreted about the rear entrance for traces. The path there was as trampled and useless as the one in front. Rawlins, who had gone some distance from the house, straightened with a satisfied exclamation. The others joined him.

"Here's where he left the path right enough," he said. "And our foreigner wasn't making any more noise than he had to."

He flashed his lamp on a fresh footprint in the soft soil at the side of the path. The mark of the toe was deep and firm. The impression of the heel was very light. Paredes, it was clear, had walked from the house on tiptoe.

"Follow on," Robinson commanded. "I told this fellow I wanted to question him. I've scared him off."

Keeping his light on the ground, Rawlins led the way across

the clearing. The trail was simple enough to follow. Each of the Panamanian's footprints was distinct. Each had that peculiarity that suggested the stealth of his progress.

As they continued Bobby responded to an excited premonition. He sensed the destination of the chase. He could picture Paredes now in the loneliest portion of the woods, for the trail unquestionably pointed to the path he had taken that afternoon toward the stagnant lake.

"Hartley!" he said. "Paredes left the house to go to the stagnant lake where I fancied I saw a woman in black. Do you see? And he didn't hear the crying of a woman a little while ago, and when we told him he became restless. He wandered about the hall talking of ghosts."

"A rendezvous!" Graham answered. "He may have been waiting for just that. The crying may have been a signal. Perhaps you'll believe now, Bobby, that the man has had an underhanded purpose in staying here."

"I've made too many hasty judgments in my life, Hartley. I'll go slow on this. I'll wait until we see what we find at the lake."

Rawlins snapped off his light. The little party paused at the black entrance of the path into the thicket.

"He's buried himself in the woods," Rawlins said.

They crowded instinctively closer in the sudden darkness. A brisk wind had sprung up. It rattled among the trees, and set the dead leaves in gentle, rustling motion. It suggested to Bobby the picture which had been forced into his brain the night of his grandfather's death. The moon now possessed less light, but it reminded him again of a drowning face, and through the darkness he could fancy the trees straining in the wind like puny men. Abruptly the thought of penetrating the forest became frightening. The silent loneliness of the stagnant lake seemed as unfriendly and threatening as the melancholy of the old room.

"There are too many of us," Robinson was saying. "You'd better go on alone, Rawlins, and don't take any chances. I've got to have this man. You understand? I think he knows things worth while."

The rising wind laughed at his whisper. The detective flashed his lamp once, shut it off again, and stepped into the close embrace of the thicket.

Suddenly Bobby grasped Graham's arm. The little group became tense, breathless. For across the wind with a diffused quality, a lack of direction, vibrated to them again the faint and mournful grief of a woman.

CHAPTER VI

THE ONE WHO CREPT IN THE PRIVATE STAIRCASE

The odd, mournful crying lost itself in the restless lament of the wind. The thicket from which it had seemed to issue assumed in the pallid moonlight a new unfriendliness. Instinctively the six men moved closer together. The coroner's thin tones expressed his alarm:

"What the devil was that? I don't really believe there could be a woman around here."

"A queer one!" the detective grunted.

The district attorney questioned Bobby and Graham.

"That's the voice you heard from the house?"

Graham nodded.

"Perhaps not so far away."

Doctor Groom, hitherto more captured than any of them by the imminence of a spiritual responsibility for the mystery of the Cedars, was the first now to reach for a rational explanation of this new phase.

"We mustn't let our fancies run away with us. The coroner's right for once. No excuse for a woman hiding in that thicket.

A bird, maybe, or some animal -"

"Sounded more like a human being," Robinson objected.

The detective reasoned in a steady unmoved voice: "Only a mad woman would wander through the woods, crying like that without a special purpose. This man Paredes has left the house and come through here. I'd guess it was a signal."

"Graham and I had thought of that," Bobby said.

"Howells was a sharp one," Robinson mused, "but he must have gone wrong on this fellow. He 'phoned me the man knew nothing. Spoke of him as a foreigner who lolled around smoking cigarettes and trying to make a fool of him with a lot of talk about ghosts."

"Howells," Graham said, "misjudged the case from the start. He wasn't to blame, but his mistake cost him his life."

Robinson didn't answer. Bobby saw that the man had discarded his intolerant temper. From that change he drew a new hope. He accepted it as the beginning of fulfilment of his prophecy last night that an accident to Howells and the entrance of a new man into the case would give him a fighting chance. It was clearly Paredes at the moment who filled the district attorney's mind.

"Go after him," he said shortly to Rawlins. "If you can get away with it bring him back and whoever you find with him."

Rawlins hesitated.

"I'm no coward, but I know what's happened to Howells. This isn't an ordinary case. I don't want to walk into an ambush. It would be safer not to run him down alone."

"All right," Robinson agreed, "I don't care to leave the Cedars for the present. Perhaps Mr. Graham -"

But Graham wasn't enthusiastic. It never occurred to Bobby that he was afraid. Graham, he guessed, desired to remain near Katherine.

"I'll go, if you like," Doctor Groom rumbled.

It was probable that Graham's instinct to stay had sprung from service rather than sentiment. The man, it was reasonable, sought to protect Katherine from the Cedars itself and from Robinson's too direct methods of examination. As an antidote for his unwelcome jealousy Bobby offered himself to Rawlins.

"Would you mind if I came, too? I've known Paredes a long time."

Robinson sneered.

"What do you think of that, Rawlins?"

But the detective stepped close and whispered in the district attorney's ear.

"All right," Robinson said. "Go with 'em, if you want, Mr. Blackburn."

And Bobby knew that he would go, not to help, but to be watched.

The others strayed toward the house. The three men faced the entrance of the path alone.

"No more loud talk now," the detective warned. "If he went on tiptoe so can we."

Even with this company Bobby shrank from the dark and restless forest. With a smooth skill the detective followed the unfamiliar path. From time to time he stooped close to the ground, shaded his lamp with his hand, and pressed the control. Always the light verified the presence of Paredes ahead of them. Bobby knew they were near the stagnant lake. The underbrush was thicker. They went with more care to limit the sound of their passage among the trees. And each moment the physical surroundings of the pursuit increased Bobby's doubt of Paredes. No ordinary impulse would bring a man to such a place in this black hour before the dawn - particularly Paredes, who spoke constantly of his superstitious nature, who advertised a thorough-paced fear of the Cedars. The Panamanian's decision to remain, his lack of emotion before the tragic succession of events at the house, his attempt to enter the corridor just before Bobby had gone himself to the old room for the evidence, his desire to direct suspicion against Katherine, finally this excursion in response to the eerie crying, all suggested a definite, perhaps a dangerous, purpose in the brain of the serene and inscrutable man.

They slipped to the open space about the lake. The moon barely distinguished for them the flat, melancholy stretch of water. They listened breathlessly. There was no sound beyond the normal stirrings of the forest. Bobby had a feeling, similar to the afternoon's, that he was watched. He tried unsuccessfully to penetrate the darkness across the lake where he had fancied the woman skulking. The detective's keen senses were satisfied.

"Dollars to doughnuts they're not here. They've probably gone on. I'll have to take a chance and show the light again."

Fresh footprints were revealed in the narrow circle of illumination. Testifying to Paredes's continued stealth, they made a straight line to the water's edge. Rawlins exclaimed:

"He stepped into the lake. How deep is it?"

The black surface of the water seemed to Bobby like an opaque glass, hiding sinister things. Suppose Paredes, instead of coming to a rendezvous, had been led?

"It's deep enough in the centre," he answered.

"Shallow around the edges?"

"Quite."

"Then he knew we were after him," Groom said.

Rawlins nodded and ran his light along the shore. A few yards to the right a ledge of smooth rock stretched from the water to a grove of pine trees. The detective arose and turned off his light.

"He's blocked us," he said. "He knew he wouldn't leave his marks on the rocks or the pine needles. No way to guess his direction now."

Doctor Groom cleared his throat. With a hesitant manner he recited the discovery of the queer light in the deserted house, its unaccountable disappearances their failure to find its source.

"I was thinking," he explained, "that Paredes alone saw the light give out. It was his suggestion that he go to the front of the house to investigate. This path might be used as a short cut to the deserted house. The rendezvous may have been there."

Rawlins was interested again.

"How far is it?"

"Not much more than a mile," Groom answered.

"Then we'll go," the detective decided. "Show the way."

Groom in the lead, they struck off through the woods. Bobby, who walked last, noticed the faint messengers of dawn behind the trees in the east. He was glad. The night cloaked too much in this neighbourhood. By daylight the empty house would guard its secret less easily. Suddenly he paused and stood quite still. He wanted to call to the others, to point out what he had seen. There was no question. By chance he had accomplished the task that had seemed so hopeless yesterday. He had found the spot where his consciousness had come back momentarily to record a wet moon, trees straining in the wind like puny men, and a figure in a mask which he had called his conscience. He gazed, his hope retreating before an unforeseen disappointment, for with the paling moon and the bent trees survived that very figure on the discovery of whose nature he had built so vital a hope; and in this bad light it conveyed to him an appearance nearly human. Through the underbrush the trunk of a tree shattered by some violent storm mocked him with its illusion. The dead leaves at the top were like cloth across a face. Therefore, he argued, there had been no conspiracy against him. Paredes was clean as far as that was concerned. He had wandered about the Cedars alone. He had opened his eyes at a point between the court and the deserted house.

Rawlins turned back suspiciously, asking why he loitered. He continued almost indifferently. He still wanted to know Paredes's goal, but his disappointment and its meaning obsessed him.

When they crept up the growing light exposed the scars of the deserted house. Everything was as Bobby remembered it. At the front there was no decayed wood or vegetation to strengthen the doctor's half-hearted theory of a phosphorescent emanation.

The tangle of footsteps near the rear door was confusing and it was some time before the three men straightened and glanced at each other, knowing that the doctor's wisdom was proved. For Paredes had been there recently; for that matter, might still be in the house. Moreover, he hadn't hidden his tracks, as he could have done, in the thick grass. Instead he had come in a straight line from the woods across a piece of sandy ground which contained the record of his direction and his continued stealth. But inside they found nothing except burnt-out matches strewn across the floor, testimony of their earlier search. The fugitive had evidently left more carefully than he had come. The chill emptiness of the deserted house had drawn and released him ahead of the chase.

"I guess he knew what the light meant," the detective said, "as well as he did that queer calling. It complicates matters that I can't find a woman's footprints around here. She may have kept to the grass and this marked-up path, for, since I don't believe in banshees, I'll swear there's been a woman around, either a crazy woman, wandering at large, who might be connected with the murders, or else a sane one who signalled the foreigner. Let's get back and see what the district attorney makes of it."

"It might be wiser not to dismiss the banshees, as you call them, too hurriedly," Doctor Groom rumbled.

As they returned along the road in the growing light Bobby lost the feeling he had had of being spied upon. The memory of such an adventure was bound to breed something like confidence among its actors. Rawlins, Bobby hoped, would be less unfriendly. The detective, in fact, talked as much to him as to the doctor. He assured them that Robinson would get the Panamanian unless he proved miraculously clever.

"He's shown us that he knows something," he went on. "I don't say how much, because I can't get a motive to make it worth his while to commit such crimes."

The man smiled blandly at Bobby.

"While in your case there's a motive at least - the money."

He chuckled.

"That's the easiest motive to understand in the world. It's stronger than love."

Bobby wondered. Love had been the impulse for the last few months' folly that had led him into his present situation.

Graham, over his stern principles of right, had already stepped outside the law in backing Katherine's efforts to save Bobby. So he wondered how much Graham would risk, how far he was capable of going himself, at the inspiration of such a motive.

The sun was up when they reached the Cedars. Katherine had gone to her room. The coroner had left. Robinson and Graham had built a fresh fire in the hall. They sat there, talking.

"Where you been?" Robinson demanded. "We'd about decided the spooks had done for you."

The detective outlined their failure. The district attorney listened with a frown. At the end he arose and, without saying anything, walked to the telephone. When he returned he appeared better satisfied.

"Mr. Paredes," he said, "will have to be a slick article to make a clean getaway. And I'm bringing another man to keep reporters out. They'll know from Howells's murder that Mr. Blackburn didn't die a natural death. If reporters get in don't talk to them. I don't want that damned foreigner reading in the papers what's going on here. I'd give my job to have him in that chair for five minutes now."

Graham cleared his throat.

"I scarcely know how to suggest this, since it is sufficiently clear, because of Howells's suspicions, that you have Mr. Blackburn under close observation. But he has a fair idea of Paredes's habits, his haunts, and his friends in New York. He might be able to learn things the police couldn't. I've one or two matters to take me to town. I would make myself personally responsible for his return -"

The district attorney interrupted.

"I see what you mean. Wait a minute."

He clasped his hands and rolled his fat thumbs one around the other. The little eyes, surrounded by puffy flesh, became enigmatic. All at once he glanced up with a genial smile.

"Why not? I haven't said anything about holding Mr. Blackburn as more than a witness."

His tone chilled Bobby as thoroughly as a direct accusation would have done.

"And," Robinson went on, "the sooner you go the better. The sooner you get back the better."

Graham was visibly puzzled by this prompt acquiescence. He started for the stairs, but the district attorney waved him aside.

"Coats and hats are downstairs. No need wasting time."

Graham turned to Doctor Groom.

"You'll tell Miss Perrine, Doctor?"

The doctor showed that he understood the warning Graham wished to convey.

The district attorney made a point of walking to the stable to see them off. Graham gestured angrily as they drove away.

"It's plain as the nose on your face. I was too anxious to test their attitude toward you, Bobby. He jumped at the chance to run us out of the house. He'll have several hours during which to turn the place upside down, to give Katherine the third degree. And we can't go back. We'll have to see it through."

"Why should he give me a chance to slip away?" Bobby asked.

But before long he realized that Robinson was taking no

chances. At the junction of the road from Smithtown a car picked them up and clung to their heels all the way to the city.

"Rawlins must have telephoned," Graham said, "while we went to the stable. They're still playing Howells's game. They'll give you plenty of rope."

He drove straight to Bobby's apartment. The elevator man verified their suspicions. Robinson had telephoned the New York police for a search. A familiar type of metropolitan detective met them in the hall outside Bobby's door.

"I'm through, gentlemen," he greeted them impudently.

Graham faced him in a burst of temper.

"The city may have to pay for this outrage."

The man grinned.

"I should get gray hairs about that."

He went on downstairs. They entered the apartment to find confusion in each room. Bureau drawers had been turned upside down. The desk had been examined with a reckless thoroughness. Graham was frankly worried.

"I wonder if he found anything. If he did you won't get out of town."

"What could he find?" Bobby asked.

"If the court was planted," Graham answered, "why shouldn't these rooms have been?"

"After last night I don't believe the court was planted," Bobby said.

In the lower hall the elevator man handed Bobby the mail that had come since the night of his grandfather's murder. In the car again he glanced over the envelopes. He tore one open with a surprised haste.

"This is Maria's handwriting," he told Graham.

He read the hastily scrawled note aloud with a tone that failed toward the end.

"DEAR BOBBY;

"You must not, as you say, think me a bad sport. You were very wicked last night. Maybe you were so because of too many of those naughty little cocktails. Why should you threaten poor Maria? And you boasted you were going out to the Cedars to kill your grandfather because you didn't like him any more. So I told Carlos to take you home. I was afraid of a scene in public. Come around. Have tea with me. Tell me you forgive me. Tell me what was the matter with you."

"She must have written that yesterday morning," Bobby muttered. "Good Lord, Hartley! Then it was in my mind!"

"Unless that letter's a plant, too," Graham said. "Yet how could she know there'd be a search? Why shouldn't she have addressed it to the Cedars where there was a fair chance of its being opened and read by the police? Why hasn't my man made any report on her? We've a number of questions to ask Maria."

But word came down from the dancer's apartment that Maria wasn't at home.

"When did she go out?" Graham asked the hall man.

"Not since I came on duty at six o'clock."

Graham slipped a bill in the man's hand.

"We've an important message for her. We'd better leave it with the maid."

When they were alone in the upper hall he explained his purpose to Bobby.

"We must know whether she's actually here. If she isn't, if she hasn't been back for the last twenty-four hours - don't you see? It was yesterday afternoon you thought you saw a woman at the lake, and last night a woman cried about the Cedars -"

"That's going pretty far, Hartley."

"It's a chance. A physical one."

A pretty maid opened the door. Her face was troubled. She studied them with frank disappointment.

"I thought -" she began.

"That your mistress was coming back?" Graham flashed.

There was no concealment in the girl's manner. It was certain that Maria was not in the apartment.

"You remember me?" Bobby asked.

"Yes. You have been here. You are a friend of mademoiselle's. You can, perhaps, tell me where she is."

Bobby shook his head. The girl spread her hands. She burst out excitedly:

"What is one to do? I have telephoned the theatre. There was no one there who knew anything at all, except that mademoiselle had not appeared at the performance last night."

Graham glanced at Bobby.

"When," he asked, "did you see her last?"

"It was before luncheon yesterday."

"Did she leave no instructions? Didn't she say when she would be back?"

The girl nodded.

"That's what worries me, for she said she would be back after the performance last night."

"She left no instructions?" Graham repeated.

"Only that if any one called or telephoned I was to make no appointments. What am I to do? Perhaps I shouldn't be talking to you. She would never forgive me for an indiscretion."

"For the present I advise you to do nothing," Graham said. "You can safely leave all that to her managers. I am going to see them now. I will tell them what you have said."

The girl's eyes moistened.

"Thank you, sir. I have been at my wits' end."

Apparently she withheld nothing. She played no part to confuse the dancer's friends.

On the way to the managers' office, with the trailing car behind them, Graham reasoned excitedly:

"For the first time we seem to be actually on the track. Here's a tangible clue that may lead to the heart of the case. Maria pulled the wool over the maid's eyes, too. She didn't want her to know her plans, but her instructions show that she had no intention of returning last night. She probably made a bee line for the Cedars. It was probably she that you saw at the lake, probably she who cried last night. If only she hadn't written that note! I can't get the meaning of it. It's up to her managers now. If they haven't heard from her it's a safe guess she's playing a deep game, connected with the crying, and the light at the deserted house, and the disappearance of Paredes before dawn. You mustrealize the connection between that and your condition the other evening after you had left them."

Bobby nodded. He began to hope that at the managers' office they would receive no explanation of Maria's absence destructive to Graham's theory. Early as it was they found a bald-headed man in his shirt sleeves pacing with an air of panic a blantantly furnished office.

"Well!" he burst out as they entered. "My secretary tells me you've come about this temperamental Carmen of mine. Tell me where she is. Quick!"

Graham smiled at Bobby. The manager ran his fingers across his bald and shining forehead.

"It's no laughing matter."

"Then she has definitely disappeared?" Graham said.

"Disappeared! Why did I come down at this ungodly hour except on the chance of getting some word? She didn't even telephone last night. I had to show myself in front of the curtain and give them a spiel about a sudden indisposition. And believe me, gentlemen, audiences ain't what they used to be. Did these ginks sit back and take the show for what it was worth? Not by a darn sight. Flocked to the box office and howled for their money back. If she doesn't appear to-night I might as well close the house. I'll be ruined."

"Unless," Graham suggested, "you get your press agent to make capital out of her absence. The papers would publish her picture and thousands of people would look her up for you."

The manager ceased his perplexed massage of his forehead. He shook hands genially.

"I'd thought of that with some frills. 'Has beautiful dancer met foul play? Millions in jewels on her person when last seen.' Old stuff, but they rise to it."

"That will help," Graham said to Bobby when they were in the car again. "The reporters will find Maria quicker than any detective I can put my hand on. My man evidently fell down because she had gone before I got him on the case." At his office they learned that was the fact. The private detective had been able to get no slightest clue as to Maria's whereabouts. Moreover, Bobby's description of the stranger who had entered the cafe with her merely suggested a type familiar to the Tenderloin. For purposes of identification it was worthless. Always followed by the car from Smithtown, they went to the hotel where Paredes had lived, to a number of his haunts. Bobby talked with men who knew him, but he learned nothing. Paredes's friends had had no word since the man's departure for the Cedars the day before. So they turned their backs on the city, elated by the significance of Maria's absence, yet worried by the search and the watchful car which never lost sight of them. When they were in the country Graham sighed his relief. "You haven't been stopped. Therefore, nothing was found at your apartment, but if that wasn't planted why should Maria have sent an incriminating note there?" "Unless," Bobby answered, "she told the truth. Unless she was sincere when she mailed it. Unless she learned something important between the time she wrote it and her disappearance from her home."

"Frankly, Bobby," Graham said, "the note and the circumstances under which it came to you are as damaging as the footprints and the handkerchief, but it doesn't tell us how any human being could have entered that room to commit the murders and disturb the bodies. At least we've got one physical fact, and I'm going to work on that."

"If it is Maria prowling around the Cedars," Bobby said, "she's amazingly slippery, and with Paredes gone what are you going to do with your physical fact? And how does it explain the friendly influence that wiped out my footprints? Is it a friendly or an evil influence that snatched away the evidence and that keeps it secreted?"

"We'll see," Graham said. "I'm going after a flesh-and-blood criminal who isn't you. I'm going to try to find out what your grandfather was afraid of the night of his murder."

After a time he glanced up.

"You've known Paredes for a long time, Bobby, but I don't think you've ever told me how you met him."

"A couple of years ago I should think," Bobby answered. "Somebody brought him to the club. I've forgotten who. Carlos was working for a big Panama importing firm. He was trying to interest this chap in the New York end. I saw him off and on after that and got to like him for his quiet manner and a queer, dry wit he had in those days. Two or three months ago he - he seemed to fit into my humour, and we became pretty chummy as you know. Even after last night I hate to believe he's my enemy."

"He's your enemy," Graham answered, "and last night's the weak joint in his armour. I wonder if Robinson didn't scare him away by threatening to question him. Paredes isn't connected with that company now, is he? I gather he has no regular position."

"No. He's picked up one or two temporary things with the fruit companies. More than his running away, the thing that worries me about Carlos is his ridiculous suspicion of Katherine."

He told Graham in detail of that conversation. Graham frowned. He opened the throttle wider. Their anxiety increased to know what had happened at the Cedars since their departure. The outposts of the forest imposed silence, closed eagerly about them, seemed to welcome them to its dead loneliness. There was a man on guard at the gate. They hurried past. The house showed no sign of life, but when they entered the court Bobby saw Katherine at her window, doubtless attracted by the sounds of their arrival. Her face brightened, but she raised her arms in a gesture suggestive of despair.

"Does she mean the evidence has been found?" Bobby asked.

Graham made no attempt to conceal his real interest, the impulse at the back of all his efforts in Bobby's behalf.

"More likely Robinson has worried the life out of her since we've been gone. I oughtn't to have left her. I set the trap myself."

When they were in the house their halting curiosity was lost in a vast surprise. The hall was empty but they heard voices in the library. They hurried across the dining room, pausing in the doorway, staring with unbelieving eyes at the accustomed picture they had least expected to see.

Paredes lounged on the divan, smoking with easy indifference. His clothing and his shoes were spotless. He had shaved, and his beard had been freshly trimmed. Rawlins and the district attorney stood in front of the fireplace, studying him with perplexed eyes. The persistence of their regard even after Bobby's entrance suggested to him that the evidence remained secreted, that the officers, under the circumstances, were scarcely interested in his return. He was swept himself into an explosive amazement:

"Carlos! What the deuce are you doing here?"

The Panamanian expelled a cloud of smoke. He smiled.

"Resting after a fatiguing walk."

In his unexpected presence Bobby fancied a demolition of the hope Graham and he had brought back from the city. He couldn't imagine guilt lurking behind that serene manner.

"Where did you come from? What were you up to last night?"

There was no accounting for Paredes's daring, he told himself, no accounting for his easy gesture now as he drew again at his cigarette and tossed it in the fireplace.

"These gentlemen," he said, "have been asking just that question. I'm honoured. I had no idea my movements were of such interest. I've told them that I took a stroll. The night was over. There was no point in going to bed, and all day I had been without exercise."

"Yet," Graham said harshly, "you have had practically no sleep since you came here."

Paredes nodded.

"Very distressing, isn't it?"

"Maybe," Rawlins sneered, "you'll tell us why you went on tiptoe, and I suppose you didn't hear a woman crying in the woods?"

"That's just it," Paredes answered. "I did hear something like that, and it occurred to me to follow such a curious sound. So I went on tiptoe, as you call it."

"Why," Robinson exclaimed angrily, "you walked in the lake to hide your tracks!"

Paredes smiled.

"It was very dark. That was chance. Quite silly of me. My feet got wet."

"I gather," Rawlins said, "it was chance that took you to the deserted house."

Paredes shook his head.

"Don't you think I was as much puzzled as the rest by that strange, disappearing light? It was as good a place to walk as any."

"Where have you been since?" Graham asked.

"When I had got there I was tired," Paredes answered. "Since it wasn't far to the station I thought I'd go on into Smithtown and have a bath and rest. But I assure you I've trudged back from the station just now."

Suddenly he repeated the apparently absurd formula he had used with Howells.

"You know the court seems full of unfriendly things - what the ignorant would call ghosts. I'm Spanish and I know." After a moment he added: "The woods, too. I shouldn't care to wander through them too much after dark."

Robinson stared, but Rawlins brushed the question aside.

"What hotel did you go to in Smithtown?"

"It's called the 'New.' Nothing could be farther from the fact."

"Shall I see if that's straight, sir?"

The district attorney agreed, and Rawlins left the room. Paredes laughed.

"How interesting! I'm under suspicion. It would be something, wouldn't it, to commit crimes with the devilish ingenuity of these? No, no, Mr. District Attorney, look to the ghosts. They alone are sufficiently clever. But I might say, since you take this attitude, that I don't care to answer any more questions until you discover something that might give you the right to ask them."

He lay back on the divan, languidly lighting another cigarette. Graham beckoned Robinson. Bobby followed them out, suspecting Graham's purpose, unwilling that action should be taken too hastily against the Panamanian; for even now guilty knowledge seemed incompatible with Paredes's polished reserve. When he joined the others, indeed, Graham with an aggressive air was demanding the district attorney's intentions.

"If he could elude you so easily last night, it's common sense to put him where you can find him in case of need. He's given you excuse enough."

"The man's got me guessing," Robinson mused, "but there are other elements."

"What's happened since we left?" Graham asked quickly. "Have you got any trace of Howells's evidence?"

Robinson smiled enigmatically, but his failure was apparent.

"I'm like Howells," he said. "I'd risk nearly anything myself to learn how the room was entered, how the crimes were committed, how those poor devils were made to alter their positions."

"So," Bobby said, "you had my rooms in New York searched. You had me followed to-day. It's ridiculous."

Robinson ignored him. He stepped to the front door, opened it, and looked around the court.

"What did the sphinx mean about ghosts in the court?"

They walked out, gazing helplessly at the trampled grass about the fountain, at the melancholy walls, at the partly opened window of the room of mystery.

"He knows something," Robinson mused. "Maybe you're right, Mr. Graham, but I wonder if I oughtn't to go farther and take you all."

Graham smiled uncomfortably, but Bobby knew why the official failed to follow that radical course. Like Howells, he hesitated to remove from the Cedars the person most likely to solve its mystery. As long as a chance remained that Howells had been right about Bobby he would give Silas Blackburn's grandson his head, merely making sure, as he had done this morning, that there should be no escape. He glanced up.

"I wonder if our foreigner's laughing at me now."

Graham made a movement toward the door.

"We might," he said significantly, "find that out without disturbing him."

Robinson nodded and led the way silently back to the house. Such a method was repugnant to Bobby, and he followed at a distance. Then he saw from the movements of the two men ahead that the library had again offered the unexpected, and he entered. Paredes was no longer in the room. Bobby was about to speak, but Robinson shook his head angrily, raising his hand in a gesture of warning. All three strained forward, listening, and Bobby caught the sound that had arrested the others - a stealthy scraping that would have been inaudible except through such a brooding silence as pervaded the old house.

Bobby's interest quickened at this confirmation of Graham's theory. There was a projection of cold fear, moreover, in its sly allusion. It gave to his memory of Paredes, with his tall, graceful figure, his lack of emotion, his inscrutable eyes, and his pointed beard, a suggestion nearly satanic. For the stealthy scraping had come from behind the closed door of the private staircase. Howells had gone up that staircase. None of them could forget for a moment that it led to the private hall outside the room in which the murders had been committed.

It occurred to Bobby that the triumph Graham's face expressed was out of keeping with the man. It disturbed him nearly as thoroughly as Paredes's stealthy presence in that place.

"We've got him," Graham whispered.

Robinson's bulky figure moved cautiously toward the door. He grasped the knob, swung the door open, and stepped back, smiling his satisfaction.

Half way down the staircase Paredes leaned against the wall, one foot raised and outstretched, as though an infinitely quiet descent had been interrupted. The exposure had been too quick for his habit. His face failed to hide its discomfiture. His laugh rang false.

"Hello!"

"I'm afraid we've caught you, Paredes," Graham said, and the triumph blazed now in his voice.

What Paredes did then was more startling, more out of key than any of his recent actions. He came precipitately down. His eyes were dangerous. As Bobby watched the face whose quiet had at last been tempestuously destroyed, he felt that the man was capable of anything under sufficient provocation.

"Got me for what?" he snarled.

"Tell us why you were sneaking up there. In connection with your little excursion before dawn it suggests a guilty knowledge."

Paredes straightened. He shrugged his shoulders. With an admirable effort of the will he smoothed the rage from his face, but for Bobby the satanic suggestion lingered.

"Why do you suppose I'm here?" he said in a restrained voice that scarcely rose above a whisper. "To help Bobby. I was simply looking around for Bobby's sake."

That angered Bobby. He wanted to cry out against the supposed friend who had at last shown his teeth.

"That," Graham laughed, "is why you sneaked, why you didn't make any noise, why you lost your temper when we caught you at it? What about it, Mr. District Attorney?"

Robinson stepped forward.

"Nothing else to do, Mr. Graham. He's too slippery. I'll put him in a safe place."

"You mean," Paredes cried, "that you'll arrest me?"

"You've guessed it. I'll lock you up as a material witness."

Paredes swung on Bobby.

"You'll permit this, Bobby? You'll forget that I am a guest in your house?"

Bobby flushed.

"Why have you stayed? What were you doing up there? Answer those questions. Tell me what you want."

Paredes turned away. He took a cigarette from his pocket and lighted it. His fingers were not steady. For the first time, it became evident to Bobby, Paredes was afraid. Rawlins came back from the telephone. He took in the tableau.

"What's the rumpus?"

"Run this man to Smithtown," Robinson directed. "Lock him up, and tell the judge, when he's arraigned in the morning, that I want him held as a material witness."

"He was at the hotel in Smithtown all right," Rawlins said.

He tapped Paredes's arm.

"You coming on this little joy ride like a lamb or a lion? Say, you'll find the jail about as comfortable as the New Hotel."

Paredes smiled. The evil and dangerous light died in his eyes. He became all at once easy and impervious again.

"Like a lamb. How else?"

"I'm sorry, Carlos," Bobby muttered. "If you'd only say something! If you'd only explain your movements! If you'd only really help!"

Again Paredes shrugged his shoulders.

"Handcuffs?" he asked Rawlins.

Rawlins ran his hands deftly over the Panamanian's clothing.

"No armed neutrality for me," he grinned. "All right. We'll forget the bracelets since you haven't a gun."

Puffing at his cigarette, Paredes got his coat and hat and followed the detective from the house.

Robinson and Graham climbed the private staircase to commence another systematic search of the hall, to discover, if they could, the motive for Paredes's stealthy presence there. Bobby accepted greedily this opportunity to find Katherine, to learn from her, undisturbed, what had happened in the house that morning, the meaning, perhaps, of her despairing gesture. When, in response to his knock, she opened her door and stepped into the corridor he guessed her despair had been an expression of the increased strain, of her helplessness in face of Robinson's harsh determination.

"He questioned me for an hour," she said, "principally about the heel mark in the court. They cling to that, because I don't think they've found anything new at the lake."

"You don't know anything about it, do you, Katherine? You weren't there? You didn't do that for me?"

"I wasn't there, Bobby. I honestly don't know any more about it than you do."

"Carlos was in the court," he mused. "Did you know they'd taken him? We found him creeping down the private stairway."

There was a hard quality about her gratitude.

"I am glad, Bobby. The man makes me shudder, and all morning they seemed more interested in you than in him. They've rummaged every room - even mine."

She laughed feverishly.

"That's why I've been so upset. They seemed -" She broke off. She picked at her handkerchief. After a moment she looked him frankly in the eyes and continued: "They seemed almost as doubtful of me as of you."

He recalled Paredes's suspicion of the girl.

"It's nonsense, Katherine. And I'm to blame for that, too."

She put her finger to her lips. Her smile was wistful.

"Hush! You mustn't blame yourself. You mustn't think of that."

Again her solicitude, their isolation in a darkened place, tempted him, aroused impulses nearly irresistible. Her slender figure, the pretty face, grown familiar and more desirable through all these years, swept him to a harsher revolt than he had conquered in the library. In the face of Graham, in spite of his own intolerable position he knew he couldn't fight that truth eternally. She must have noticed his struggle without grasping its cause, for she touched his hand, and the wistfulness of her expression increased.

"I wish you wouldn't think of me, Bobby. It's you we must all think of."

He accepted with a cold dismay the sisterly anxiety of her attitude. It made his renunciation easier. He walked away.

"Why do you go?" she called after him.

He gestured vaguely, without turning.

He didn't see her again until dinner time. She was as silent then as she had been the night before when Howells had sat with them, his moroseness veiling a sharp interest in the plan that was to lead to his death. Robinson's mood was very different. He talked a great deal, making no effort to hide his irritation. His failure to find any clue in the private staircase after Paredes's arrest had clearly stimulated his interest in Bobby. The sharp little eyes, surrounded by puffy flesh, held a threat for him. Bobby was glad when the meal ended.

Howells's body was taken away that night. It was a relief for all of them to know that the old room was empty again.

"I daresay you won't sleep there," Graham said to Robinson.

Robinson glanced at Bobby.

"Not as things stand," he answered. "The library lounge is plenty good enough for me tonight."

Graham went upstairs with Bobby. There was no question about his purpose. He wouldn't repeat last night's mistake.

"At least," he said, when the door was closed behind them, "I can see if you do get up and wander about in your sleep. I'd bet a good deal that you won't."

"If I did it would be an indication?"

"Granted it's your custom, what is there to tempt you to-night?"

Bobby answered, half jesting:

"You've not forgotten Robinson on the library sofa. The man isn't exactly working for me. Tonight he seems almost as unfriendly as Howells was."

He yawned.

"I ought to sleep now if ever. I've seldom been so tired. Two such nights!"

He hesitated.

"But I am glad you're here, Hartley. I can go to sleep with a more comfortable feeling."

"Don't worry," Graham said. "You'll sleep quietly enough, and we'll all be better for a good rest."

For only a little while they talked of the mystery. While Graham regretted his failure to find any trace of Maria, their voices dwindled sleepily. Bobby recalled his last thought before losing himself last night. He tried to force from his mind now the threat in Robinson's eyes. He told himself again and again that the man wasn't actually unfriendly. Then the blackness encircled him. He slept.

Almost at once, it seemed to him, he was fighting away, demanding drowsily:

"What's the matter? Leave me alone."

He heard Graham's voice, unnaturally subdued and anxious.

"What are you doing, Bobby?"

Then Bobby knew he was no longer in his bed, that he stood instead in a cold place; and the meaning of his position came with a rush of sick terror.

"Get hold of yourself," Graham said. "Come back."

Bobby opened his eyes. He was in the upper hall at the head of the stairs. Unconsciously he had been about to creep quietly down, perhaps to the library. Graham had awakened him. It seemed to offer the answer to everything. It seemed to give outline to a monstrous familiar that drowned his real self in the black pit while it conducted his body to the commission of unspeakable crimes.

He lurched into the bedroom and sat shivering on the bed. Graham entered and quietly closed the door.

"What time is it?" Bobby asked hoarsely.

"Half-past two. I don't think Robinson was aroused."

The damp moon gave an ominous unreality to the room.

"What did I do?" Bobby whispered.

"Got softly out of bed and went to the hall. It was uncanny. You were like an automaton. I didn't wake you at once. You see, I - I thought you might go to the old room."

Bobby shook again. He drew a blanket about his shoulders.

"And you believed I'd show the way in and out, but the room was empty, so I was going downstairs -"

He shuddered.

"Good God! Then it's all true. I did it for the money. I put Howells out to protect myself. I was going after Robinson. It's true. Hartley! Tell me. Do you think it's true?"

Graham turned away.

"Don't ask me to say anything to help you just now," he answered huskily, "for after this I don't dare, Bobby. I don't dare."

CHAPTER VII

THE AMAZING MEETING IN
THE SHADOWS OF THE OLD COURTYARD

Bobby returned to his bed. He lay there still shivering, beneath the heavy blankets. "I don't dare!" He echoed Graham's words. "There's nothing else any one can say. I must decide what to do. I must think it over."

But, as always, thought brought no release. It merely insisted that the case against him was proved. At last he had been seen slipping unconsciously from his room - and at the same hour. All that remained was to learn how he had accomplished the apparent miracles. Then no excuse would remain for not going to Robinson and confessing. The woman at the lake and in the courtyard, the movement of the body and the vanishing of the evidence under his hand, Paredes's odd behaviour, all became in his mind puzzling details that failed to obscure the chief fact. After this something must be done about Paredes's detention.

He hadn't dreamed that his weariness could placate even momentarily such reflections, but at last he slept again. He was aroused by the tramping of men around the house, and strange, harsh voices. He raised himself on his elbow and glanced from the window. It had long been daylight. Two burly fellows in overalls, carrying pick and spade across their shoulders, pushed through the underbrush at the edge of the clearing. He turned. Graham, fully dressed, stood at the side of the bed.

"Those men?" Bobby asked wearily.

"The grave diggers," Graham answered. "They are going to work in the old cemetery to prepare a place for Silas Blackburn with his fathers. That's why I've come to wake you up. The minister's telephoned Katherine. He will be here before noon. Do you know it's after ten o'clock?"

For some time Bobby stared through the window at the desolate, ragged landscape. It was abnormally cold even for the late fall. Dull clouds obscured the sun and furnished an illusion of crowding earthward.

"A funereal day."

The words slipped into his mind. He repeated them.

"When your grandfather's buried," Graham answered softly, "we'll all feel happier."

"Why?" Bobby asked. "It won't lessen the fact of his murder."

"Time," Graham said, "lessens such facts - even for the police."

Bobby glanced at him, flushing.

"You mean you've decided to stand by me after what happened last night?"

Graham smiled.

"I've thought it all over. I slept like a top last night. I heard nothing. I saw nothing."

"Ought I to want you to stand by me?" Bobby said. "Oughtn't I to make a clean breast of it? At least I must do something about Paredes."

Graham frowned.

"It's hard to believe he had any connection with your sleep-walking last night, yet it's as clear as ever that Maria and he are up to some game in which you figure."

"He shouldn't be in jail," Bobby persisted.

"Get up," Graham advised. "Bathe, and have some breakfast, then we can decide. There's no use talking of the other thing. I've forgotten it. As far as possible you must."

Bobby sprang upright.

"How can I forget it? If it was hard to face sleep before, what do you think it is now? Have I any right -"

"Don't," Graham said. "I'll be with you again to-night. If I were satisfied beyond the shadow of a doubt I'd advise you to confess, but I can't be until I know what Maria and Paredes are doing."

When Bobby had bathed and dressed he found, in spite of his mental turmoil, that his sleep had done him good. While he breakfasted Graham urged him to eat, tried to drive from his brain the morbid aftermath of last night's revealing moment.

"The manager took my advice, but Maria's still missing. Her pictures are in most of the papers. There have been reporters here this morning, about the murders."

He strolled over and handed Bobby a number of newspapers.

"Where's Robinson?" Bobby asked.

"I saw him in the court a while ago. I daresay he's wandering around - perhaps watching the men at the grave."

"He learned nothing new last night?"

"I was with him at breakfast. I gather not."

Bobby looked up.

"Isn't that an automobile coming through the woods?" he asked.

"Maybe Rawlins back from Smithtown, or the minister."

The car stopped at the entrance of the court. They heard the remote tinkling of the front door bell. Jenkins passed through. The cold air invading the hall and the dining room told them he had opened the door. His sharp exclamation recalled Howells's report which, at their direction, he had failed to mail. Had his exclamation been drawn by an accuser? Bobby started to rise. Graham moved toward the door. Then Jenkins entered and stood to one side. Bobby shared his astonishment, for Paredes walked in, unbuttoning his overcoat, the former easy-mannered, uncommunicative foreigner. He appeared, moreover, to have slept pleasantly. His eyes showed no weariness, his clothing no disarrangement. He spoke at once, quite as if nothing disagreeable had shadowed his departure.

"Good morning. If I had dreamed of this change in the weather I would have brought a heavier overcoat. I've nearly frozen driving from Smithtown."

Before either man could grope for a suitable greeting he faced Bobby. He felt in his pockets with whimsical discouragement.

"Fact is, Bobby, I left New York too suddenly. I hadn't noticed until a little while ago. You see I spent a good deal in Smithtown yesterday."

Bobby spoke with an obvious confusion:

"What do you mean, Carlos? I thought you were -"

Graham interrupted with a flat demand for an explanation.

"How did you get away?"

Paredes waved his hand.

"Later, Mr. Graham. There is a hack driver outside who is even more suspicious than you. He wants to be paid. I asked Rawlins to drive me back, but he rushed from the courthouse, probably to telephone his rotund superior. Fact is, this fellow wants five dollars - an outrageous rate. I've told him so - but it doesn't do any good. So will you lend me Bobby -"

Bobby handed him a banknote. He didn't miss Graham's meaning glance. Paredes gave the money to the butler.

"Pay him, will you, Jenkins? Thanks."

He surveyed the remains of Bobby's breakfast. He sat down.

"May I? My breakfast was early, and prison food, when you're not in the habit -"

Bobby tried to account for Paredes's friendly manner. That he should have come back at all was sufficiently strange, but it was harder to understand why he should express no resentment for his treatment yesterday, why he should fail to refer to Bobby's questions at the moment of his arrest, or to the openly expressed enmity of Graham. Only one theory promised to fit at all. It was necessary for the Panamanian to return to the Cedars. His purpose, whatever it was, compelled him to remain for the present in the mournful, tragic house. Therefore, he would crush his justifiable anger. He would make it practically impossible for Bobby to refuse his hospitality. And he had asked for money - only a trifling sum, yet Graham would grasp at the fact to support his earlier suspicion.

Paredes's arrival possessed one virtue: It diverted Bobby's thoughts temporarily from his own dilemma, from his inability to chart a course.

Graham, on the other hand, was ill at ease. Beyond a doubt he was disarmed by Paredes's good humour. For him yesterday's incident was not so lightly to be passed over. Eventually his curiosity conquered. The words came, nevertheless, with some difficulty:

"We scarcely expected you back."

His laugh was short and embarrassed.

"We took it for granted you would find it necessary to stay in Smithtown for a while."

Paredes sipped the coffee which Jenkins had poured.

"Splendid coffee! You should have tasted what I had this morning. Simple enough, Mr. Graham. I telephoned as soon as Rawlins got me to the Bastille. I communicated with the lawyer who represents the company for which I once worked. He's a prominent and brilliant man. He planned it with some local fellow. When I was arraigned at the opening of court this morning the judge could hold me only as a material witness. He fixed a pretty stiff bail, but the local lawyer was there with a bondsman, and I came back. My clothes are here. You don't mind, Bobby?"

That moment in the hall when Graham had awakened him urged Bobby to reply with a genuine warmth:

"I don't mind. I'm glad you're out of it. I'm sorry you went as you did. I was tired, at my wits' end. Your presence in the private staircase was the last straw. You will forgive us, Carlos?"

Paredes smiled. He put down his coffee cup and lighted a cigarette. He smoked with a vast contentment.

"That's better. Nothing to forgive, Bobby. Let us call it a misunderstanding."

Graham moved closer.

"Perhaps you'll tell us now what you were doing in the private staircase."

Paredes blew a wreath of smoke. His eyes still smiled, but his voice was harder:

"Bygones are bygones. Isn't that so, Bobby?"

"Since you wish it," Bobby said.

But more important than the knowledge Graham desired, loomed the old question. What was the man's game? What held him here?

Robinson entered. The flesh around his eyes was puffier than it had been yesterday. Worry had increased the incongruous discontent of his round face. Clearly he had slept little.

"I saw you arrive," he said. "Rawlins warned me. But I must say I didn't think you'd use your freedom to come to us."

Paredes laughed.

"Since the law won't hold me at your convenience in Smithtown I keep myself at your service here - if Bobby permits it. Could you ask more?"

Bobby shrank from the man with whom he had idled away so much time and money. That fleeting, satanic impression of yesterday came back, sharper, more alarming. Paredes's clear challenge to the district attorney was the measure of his strength. His mind was subtler than theirs. His reserve and easy daring mastered them all; and always, as now, he laughed at the futility of their efforts to sound his purposes, to limit his freedom of action. Bobby didn't care to meet the uncommunicative eyes whose depths he had never been able to explore. Was there a special power there that could control the destinies of other people, that might make men walk unconsciously to accomplish the ends of an unscrupulous brain?

The district attorney appeared as much at sea as the others.

"Thanks," he said dryly to Paredes.

And glancing at Bobby, he asked with a hollow scorn:

"You've no objection to the gentleman visiting you for the present?"

"If he wishes," Bobby answered, a trifle amused at Robinson's obvious fancy of a collusion between Paredes and himself.

Robinson jerked his head toward the window.

"I've been watching the preparations out there. I guess when he's laid away you'll be thinking about having the will read."

"No hurry," Bobby answered with a quick intake of breath.

"I suppose not," Robinson sneered, "since everybody knows well enough what's in it."

Bobby arose. Robinson still sneered.

"You'll be at the grave - as chief mourner?"

Bobby walked from the room. He hadn't cared to reply. He feared, as it was, that he had let slip his increased self-doubt. He put on his coat and hat and left the house. The raw cold, the year's first omen of winter, made his blood run quicker, forced into his mind a cleansing stimulation. But almost immediately even that prophylactic was denied him. With his direction a matter of indifference, chance led him into the thicket at the side of the house. He had walked some distance. The underbrush had long interposed a veil between him and the Cedars above whose roofs smoke wreathed in the still air like fantastic figures weaving a shroud to lower over the time-stained, melancholy walls. For once he was grateful to the forest because it had forbidden him to glance perpetually back at that dismal and pensive picture. Then he became aware of twigs hastily lopped off, of bushes bent and torn, of the uncovering, through these careless means, of an old path. Simultaneously there reached his ears the scraping of metal implements in the soft soil, the dull thud of earth falling regularly. He paused, listening. The labour of the men was given an uncouth rhythm by their grunting expulsions of breath. Otherwise the nature of their industry and its surroundings had imposed upon them a silence, in itself beast-like and unnatural.

At last a harsh voice came to Bobby. Its brevity pointed the previous dumbness of the speaker:

"Deep enough!"

And Bobby turned and hurried back along the roughly restored path, as if fleeing from an immaterial thing suddenly quickened with the power of accusation.

He could picture the fresh oblong excavation in the soil of the family burial ground. He could see where the men had had to tear bushes from among the graves in order to insert their tools. There was an ironical justice in the condition of the old cemetery. It had received no interment since the death of Katherine's father. Like everything about the Cedars, Silas Blackburn had delivered it to the swift, obliterating fingers of time. If the old man in his selfishness had paused to gaze beyond the inevitable fact of death, Bobby reflected, he would have guarded with a more precious interest the drapings of his final sleep.

This necessary task on which Bobby had stumbled had made the thicket less congenial than the house. As he walked back he forecasted with a keen apprehension his approaching ordeal. It would, doubtless, be more difficult to endure than Howells's experiment over Silas Blackburn's body in the old room. Could he witness the definite imprisonment of his grandfather in a narrow box; could he watch the covering earth fall noisily in that bleak place of silence without displaying for Robinson the guilt that impressed him more and more?

A strange man appeared, walking from the direction of the house. His black clothing, relieved only by narrow edges of white cuffs between the sleeves and the heavy mourning gloves, fitted with solemn harmony into the landscape and Bobby's mood. Such a figure was appropriate to the Cedars. Bobby stepped to one side, placing a screen of dead foliage between himself and the man whose profession it was to mourn. He emerged from the forest and saw again the leisurely weaving of the smoke shroud above the house. Then his eyes were drawn by the restless movements of a pair of horses, standing in the shafts of a black wagon at the court entrance, and his ordeal became like a vast morass which offers no likely path yet whose crossing is the price of salvation.

He was glad to see Graham leave the court and hurry toward him.

"I was coming to hunt you up, Bobby. The minister's arrived. So has Doctor Groom. Everything's about ready."

"Doctor Groom?"

"Yes. He used to see a good deal of your grandfather. It's natural enough he should be here."

Bobby agreed indifferently. They walked slowly back to the house. Graham made it plain that his mind was far from the sad business ahead.

"What do you think of Paredes coming back as if nothing were wrong?" he asked. "He ignores what happened yesterday. He settles himself in the Cedars again."

"I don't know what to think of it," Bobby answered. "This morning Carlos gave me the creeps."

Graham glanced at him curiously. He spoke with pronounced deliberation, startling Bobby; for this friend expressed practically the thought that Paredes's arrival had driven into his own mind.

"Gave me the creeps, too. Makes me surer than ever that he has an abominably deep purpose in using his wits to hang on here. He suggests resources as hard to understand as anything that has happened in the old room. You'll confess, Bobby, he's had a good deal of influence over you - an influence for evil?"

"I've liked to go around with him, if that's what you mean."

"Isn't he the cause of the last two or three months nonsense in New York?"

"I won't blame Carlos for that," Bobby muttered.

"He influenced you against your better judgment," Graham persisted, "to refuse to leave with me the night of your grandfather's death."

"Maria did her share," Bobby said.

He broke off, looking at Graham.

"What are you driving at?"

"I've been asking myself since he came back," Graham answered, "if there's any queer power behind his quiet manner. Maybe he *is* psychic. Maybe he can do things we don't understand. I've wondered if he had, without your knowing it, acquired sufficient influence to direct your body when your mind no longer controlled it. It's a nasty thought, but I've heard of such things."

"You mean Carlos may have made me go to the hall last night, perhaps sent me to the old room those other times?"

Now that another had expressed the idea Bobby fought it with all his might.

"No. I won't believe it. I've been weak, Hartley, but not that weak. And I tell you I did feel Howells's body move under my hand."

"Don't misunderstand me," Graham said gently. "I must consider every possibility. You were excited and imaginative when you went to the old room to take the evidence. It was a shock to have your candle go out. Your own hand, reaching out to Howells, might have moved spasmodically. I mean, you may have been responsible for the thing without realizing it."

"And the disappearance of the evidence?" Bobby defended himself.

"If it had been stolen earlier the coat pocket might have retained its bulging shape. We know now that Paredes is capable of sneaking around the house."

"No, no," Bobby said hotly. "You're trying to take away my one hope. But I was there, and you weren't. I know with my own senses what happened, and you don't. Paredes has no such influence over me. I won't think of it."

"If it's so far-fetched," Graham asked quietly, "why do you revolt from the idea?"

Bobby turned on him.

"And why do you fill my mind with such thoughts? If you think I'm guilty say so. Go tell Robinson so."

He glanced away while the angry colour left his face. He was a little dazed by the realization that he had spoken to Graham as he might have done to an enemy, as he had spoken to Howells in the old bedroom. He felt the touch of Graham's hand on his shoulder.

"I'm only working in your service," Graham said kindly. "I'm sorry if I've troubled you by seeking physical facts in order to escape the ghosts. For Groom has brought the ghosts back with him. Don't make any mistake about that. You want the truth, don't you?"

"Yes," Bobby said, "even if it does for me. But I want it quickly. I can't go on this way indefinitely."

Yet that flash of temper had given him courage to face the ordeal. A lingering resentment at Graham's suggestion lessened the difficulty of his position. Entering the court, he scarcely glanced at the black wagon.

There were more dark-clothed men in the hall. Rawlins had returned. From the rug in front of the fireplace he surveyed the group with a bland curiosity. Robinson sat near by, glowering at Paredes. The Panamanian had changed his clothing. He, too, was sombrely dressed, and, instead of the vivid necktie he had worn from the courthouse, a jet-black scarf was perfectly arranged beneath his collar. He lounged opposite the district attorney, his eyes studying the fire. His fingers on the chair arm were restless.

Doctor Groom stood at the foot of the stairs, talking with the clergyman, a stout and unctuous figure. Bobby noticed that the great stolid form of the doctor was ill at ease. From his thickly bearded face his reddish eyes gleamed forth with a fresh instability.

The clergyman shook hands with Bobby. "We need not delay. Your cousin is upstairs." He included the company in his circling turn of the head.

"Any one who cares to go -"

Bobby forced himself to walk up the staircase, facing the first phase of his ordeal. He saw that the district attorney realized that, too, for he sprang from his chair, and, followed by Rawlins, started upward. The entire company crowded the stairs. At the top Bobby found Paredes at his side.

"Carlos! Why do you come?"

"I would like to be of some comfort," Paredes answered gravely.

His fingers on the banister made that restless, groping movement.

Graham summoned Katherine. One of the black-clothed men opened the door of Silas Blackburn's room. He stepped aside, beckoning. He had an air of a showman craving approbation for the surprise he has arranged.

Bobby went in with the others. Automatically through the dim light he catalogued remembered objects, all intimate to his grandfather, each oddly entangled in his mind with his dislike of the old man. The iron bed; the chest of drawers, scratched and with broken handles; the closed colonial desk; the miserly rag carpet - all seemed mutely asking, as Bobby did, why their owner had deserted them the other night and delivered himself to the ghostly mystery of the old bedroom.

Reluctantly Bobby's glance went to the centre of the floor where the casket rested on trestles. From the chest of drawers two candles, the only light, played wanly over the still figure and the ashen face. So for the second time the living met the dead, and the law watched hopefully.

Robinson stood opposite, but he didn't look at Silas Blackburn who could no longer accuse. He stared instead at Bobby, and Bobby kept repeating to himself:

"I didn't do this thing. I didn't do this thing."

And he searched the face of the dead man for a confirmation. A chill thought, not without excuse under the circumstances and in this vague light, raced along his nerves. Silas Blackburn had moved once since his death. If the power to move and speak should miraculously return to him now! In this house there appeared to be no impossibilities. The cold control of death had been twice broken.

Katherine's entrance swung his thoughts and released him for a moment from Robinson's watchfulness. He found he could turn from the wrinkled face that had fascinated him, that had seemed to question him with a calm and complete knowledge, to the lovely one that was active with a little smile of encouragement. He was grateful for that. It taught him that in the heavy presence of death and from the harsh trappings of mourning the magnetism of youth is unconquerable. So in affection he found an antidote for fear. Even Graham's quick movement to her side couldn't make her presence less helpful to Bobby. He looked at his grandfather again. He glanced at Robinson. As in a dream he heard, the clergyman say:

"The service will be read at the grave."

Almost indifferently he saw the dark-clothed men sidle forward, lift a grotesquely shaped plate of metal from the floor, and fit it in place, hiding from his eyes the closed eyes of the dead man. He nodded and stepped to the hall when Robinson tapped his arm and whispered:

"Make way, Mr. Blackburn."

He watched the sombre men carry their heavy burden across the hall, down the stairs, and into the dull autumn air. He followed at the side of Katherine across the clearing and into the overgrown path. He was aware of the others drifting behind. Katherine slipped her hand in his.

"It is dreadful we shouldn't feel more sorrow, more regret," she said.

"Perhaps we never understood him. That is dreadful, too; for no one understood him. We are the only mourners."

Bobby, as they threaded the path behind the stumbling bearers, found a grim justice in that also. Because of his selfishness Silas Blackburn had lived alone. Because of it he must go to his long rest with no other mourners than these, and their eyes were dry.

Bobby clung to Katherine's hand.

"If I could only know!" he whispered.

She pressed his hand. She did not reply.

Ahead the forest was scarred by a yellow wound. The bearers set their burden down beside it, glancing at each other with relief. Across the heap of earth Bobby saw the waiting excavation. In his ears vibrated the memory of the harsh voice:

"It's deep enough!"

Another voice droned. It was soft and unctuous. It seemed to take a pleasure in the terrible words it loosed to stray eternally through the decaying forest.

Bobby glanced at bent stones, strangled by the underbrush; at other slabs, cracked and brown, which lay prone, half covered by creeping vines. The tones of the clergyman were no longer revolting in his ears. He scarcely heard them. He imagined a fantasy. He pictured the inhabitants of these forgotten, narrow houses straying to the great dwelling where they had lived, punishing this one, bringing him to suffer with them the degradation of their neglect. So Robinson became less important in his mind. Through such fancies the ordeal was made bearable.

A wind sprang up, rattling through the trees and disturbing the vines on the fallen stones. Later, he thought, it would snow, and he shivered for those left helpless to sleep in the sad forest.

The dark-clothed men strained at ropes now. They glanced at Katherine and Bobby as at those most to be impressed by their skill. They lowered Silas Blackburn's grimly shaped casing into the sorrel pit. It passed from Bobby's sight. The two roughly dressed labourers came from the thicket where they had hidden, and with their spades approached the grave. The sound from whose imminence Bobby had shrunk rattled in his ears. The yellow earth cut across the stormy twilight of the cemetery and scattered in the trench. After a time the response lost its metallic petulance.

Katherine pulled at Bobby's hand. He started and glanced up. One of the black-clothed men was speaking to him with a professional gentleness:

"You needn't wait, Mr. Blackburn. Everything is finished."

He saw now that Robinson stood across the grave still staring at him. The professional mourner smiled sympathetically and moved away. Katherine, Robinson, the two grave diggers, and Bobby alone were left of the little company; and Bobby, staring back at the district attorney, took a sombre pride in facing it out until even the men with the spades had gone. The ordeal, he reflected, had lost its poignancy. His mind was intent on the empty trappings he had witnessed. He wondered if there was, after all, no justice against his grandfather in this unkempt burial. The place might have something to tell him. If it could only make him believe that beyond the inevitable fact nothing mattered. If he were sure of that it would offer a way out at the worst; perhaps the happiest exit for Katherine's sake.

Then Doctor Groom returned. His huge hairy figure domina-ted the cemetery. His infused eyes, beneath the thick black brows, were far-seeing. They seemed to penetrate Bobby's thought. Then they glanced at the excavation, appearing to intimate that Silas Blackburn's earthy blanket could hide nothing from the closed eyes it sheltered. At his age he faced the near approach of that inevitable fact, and he didn't hesitate to look beyond. Bobby knew what Graham had meant when he had said that Groom had brought the ghosts back with him. It was as if the cemetery had recalled the old doctor to answer his presumptuous question.

"There's no use your staying here."

The resonance of the deep voice jarred through the woods. The broad shoulders twitched. One of the hairy hands made a half circle.

"I hope you'll clean this up, my boy. You ought to replace the stones and trim the graves. You couldn't blame them, could you, if these old people were restless and tried to go abroad?"

For Bobby, in spite of himself, the man on whose last shelter the earth continued to fall became once more a potent thing, able to appraise the penalty of his own carelessness.

"Come," Katherine whispered.

But Bobby lingered, oddly fascinated, supporting the ordeal to its final moment. The blows of the backs of the spades on the completed mound beat into his brain the end. The workmen wandered off through the woods. From a distance the harsh voice of one of them came back:

"I don't want to dig again in such a place. People don't seem dead there."

Robinson tried to laugh.

"That man's wise," he said to the doctor. "If Paredes spoke of this cemetery as being full of ghosts I could understand him."

The doctor's deep bass answered thoughtfully:

"Paredes is probably right. The man has a special sense, but I have felt it myself. The Cedars and the forest are full of things that seem to whisper, things that one never sees. Such things might have an excuse for evil."

"Let's get out of it," Robinson said gruffly.

Katherine withdrew her hand. Bobby reached for it again, but she seemed not to notice. She walked ahead of him along the path, her shoulders a trifle bent. Bobby caught up with her.

"Katherine!" he said.

"Don't talk to me, Bobby."

He looked closer. He saw that she was crying at last. Tears stained her cheeks. Her lips were strange to him in the distortion of a grief that seeks to control itself. He slackened his pace and let her walk ahead. He followed with a sort of awe that there should have been grief for Silas Blackburn after all. He blamed himself because his own eyes were not moist.

Back of him he heard the murmuring conversation of the doctor and the district attorney. Strangely it made him sorry that Robinson should have been more impressed than Howells by the doctor's beliefs.

They stepped into the clearing. The wind had dissipated the smoke shroud. It was no longer low over the roofs. Against the forest and the darker clouds the house had a stark appearance. It was like a frame from which the flesh has fallen.

The black wagon had gone. The Cedars was left alone to the solution of its mystery.

Paredes, Graham, and Rawlins waited for them in the hall. There was nothing to say. Paredes placed with a delicate accuracy fresh logs upon the fire. He arose, flecking the wood dust from his hands.

"How cold it will be here," he mused, "how impossible of entrance when the house is left as empty as the woods to those who only go unseen!"

Bobby saw Katherine's shoulders shake. She had dried her eyes, but in her face was expressed an aversion for solitude, a desire for any company, even that of the man she disliked and feared.

Robinson took Rawlins to the library for another futile consultation, Bobby guessed. Katherine sat on the arm of a chair, thrusting one foot toward the fresh blaze.

"It will snow," she said. "It is very early for that."

No one answered. The strain tightened. The flames leapt, throwing evanescent pulsations of brilliancy about the dusky hall. They welcomed Jenkins's announcement that luncheon was ready, but they scarcely disturbed the hurriedly prepared dishes, and afterward they gathered again in the hall, silent and depressed, appalled by the long, dreary afternoon, which, however, possessed the single virtue of dividing them from another night.

For long periods the district attorney and the detective were closeted in the library. Now and then they passed upstairs, and they could be heard moving about, but no one, save Graham, seemed to care. Already the officers had had every opportunity to search the house. The old room no longer held an inhabitant to set its fatal machinery in motion. Yet Bobby realized in a dull way that at any moment the two men might come down to him, saying:

"We have found something. You are guilty."

The heavy atmosphere of the house crushed such forecasts, made them seem a little trivial. Bobby fancied it gathering density to cradle new mysteries. The long minutes loitered. Doctor Groom made a movement to go.

"Why should I stay?" he grumbled. "What is there to keep me?"

Yet he sat back in his chair again and appeared to have forgotten his intention.

Graham wandered off. Bobby thought he had joined Rawlins and Robinson in the library.

The only daylight entered the hall through narrow slits of windows on either side of the front door. Bobby, watching these, was, even with the problems night brought to him now, glad when they grew paler.

Paredes, who had been smoking cigarette after cigarette, arose and brought his card table. Drawing it close to him, he arranged the cards in neat piles. The uncertain firelight made it barely possible to identify their numbers. Doctor Groom gestured his disgust. Katherine stooped forward, placing her hands on the table.

"Is it kind," she asked, "so soon after he has left his house?"

Paredes started.

"Wait!" he said softly.

Puzzled, she glanced at him.

"Stay just as you are," he directed. "There has been so much death in this house - who knows?"

Languidly he placed his fingers on the edge of the table opposite hers.

"What are you doing?" Dr. Groom asked hoarsely.

"Wait!" Paredes said again.

Then Bobby, scarcely aware of what was going on, saw the cards glide softly across the face of the table and flutter to the floor. The table had lifted slowly toward the Panamanian. It stood now on two legs.

"What is it?" Katherine said. "It's moving. I can feel it move beneath my fingers."

Her words recalled to Bobby unavoidably his experience in the old room.

"Don't do that!" the doctor cried.

Paredes smiled.

"If," he answered, "the source of these crimes is, as you think, spiritual, why not ask the spirits for a solution? You see how quickly the table responds. It is as I thought. There is something in this hall. Haven't you a feeling that the dead are in this dark hall with us? They may wish to speak. See!"

The table settled softly down without any noise. It commenced to rise again. Katherine lifted her hands with a visible effort, as if the table had tried to hold them against her will. She covered her face and sat trembling.

"I won't! I -"

Paredes shrugged his shoulders, appealing to the doctor. The huge, shaggy head shook determinedly.

"I'm not so sure I don't agree with you. I'm not so sure the dead aren't in this hall. That is why I'll have nothing to do with such dangerous play. It has shown us, at least, that you are psychic, Mr. Paredes."

"I have a gift," Paredes murmured. "It would be useful to speak with them. They see so much more than we do."

He lifted his hands. He waved them dejectedly. He stooped and commenced picking up the cards. The doctor arose.

"I shall go now." He sighed. "I don't know why I have stayed."

Bobby got his coat and hat.

"I'll walk to the stable with you."

He was glad to escape from the dismal hall in which the firelight grew more eccentric. The court was colder and damper, and even beyond the chill was more penetrating than it had been at the grave that noon. Uneven flakes of snow sifted from the swollen sky, heralds of a white invasion.

"No more sleep-walking?" the doctor asked when he had taken the blanket from his horse and climbed into the buggy.

Bobby leaned against the wall of the stable and told how Graham had brought him back the previous night from the stairhead, to which he had gone with a purpose he didn't dare sound. The doctor shook his head.

"You shouldn't tell me that. You shouldn't tell any one. You place yourself too much in my hands, as you are already in Graham's hands. Maybe that is all right. But the district attorney? You're sure he knows nothing of this habit which seems to have commenced the night of the first murder?"

"No, and I think Paredes alone of those who know about that first night would be likely to tell him."

"See that he doesn't," the doctor said shortly. "I've been watching Robinson. If he doesn't make an arrest pretty soon with something back of it he'll lose his mind. He mightn't stop to ask, as I do, as Howells did, about the locked doors and the nature of the wounds."

"How shall I find the courage to sleep to-night?" Bobby asked.

The doctor thought for a moment.

"Suppose I come back?" he said. "I've only one or two unimportant cases to look after. I ought to return before dinner. I'll take Graham's place for to-night. It's time your reactions were better diagnosed. I'll share your room, and you can go to sleep, assured that you'll come to no harm, that harm will come to no one through you. I'll bring some books on the subject. I'll read them while you sleep. Perhaps I can learn the impulse that makes your body active while your mind's a blank."

The idea of the influence of Paredes, which Graham had put into words, slipped back to Bobby. He was, nevertheless, strengthened by the doctor's promise. To an extent the dread of the night fell from him like a smothering garment. This old man, who had always filled him with discomfort, had become a capable support in his difficult hour. He saw him drive away. He studied his watch, computing the time that must elapse before he could return. He wanted him at the Cedars even though the doctor believed more thoroughly than any one else in the spiritual survival of old passions and the power of the dead to project a physical evil.

He didn't care to go back to the hall. It would do him good to walk, to force as far as he could from his mind the memory of the ordeal at the grave, the grim, impending atmosphere of the house. And suppose he should accomplish something useful? Suppose he should succeed where Graham had failed?

So he walked toward the stagnant lake. The flakes of snow fell thicker. Already they had gathered in white patches on the floor of the forest. If this weather continued the woods would cease to be habitable for that dark feminine figure through which they had accounted for the mournful crying after Howells's death, which Graham had tried to identify with the dancer, Maria.

As he passed the neighbourhood of the cemetery; he walked

faster. Many yards of underbrush separated him from the little time-devastated city of the dead, but its mere proximity forced on him, as the old room had done, a feeling of a stealthy and intangible companionship.

He stepped from the fringe of trees about the open space in the centre of which the lake brooded. The water received with a destructive indifference the fluttering caresses of the snow-flakes. Bobby paused with a quick expectancy. He saw nothing of the woman who had startled him that first evening, but he heard from the thicket a sound like muffled sobbing, and he responded again to the sense of a malevolent regard.

He hid himself among the trees, and in their shelter skirted the lake. The sobbing had faded into nothing. For a long time he heard only the whispers of the snow and the grief of the wind. When he had rounded the lake and was some distance beyond it, however, the moaning reached him again, and through the fast-deepening twilight he saw, as indistinctly as he had before, a black feminine figure flitting among the trees in the direction of the lake. Graham's theory lost its value. It was impossible to fancy the brilliant, colourful dancer in this black, shadowy thing. He commenced to run in pursuit, calling out:

"Stop! Who are you? Why do you cry through the woods?"

But the dusk was too thick, the forest too eager. The black figure disappeared. In retrospect it was again as unsubstantial as a phantom. The flakes whispered mockingly. The wind was ironical.

He found his pursuit had led him back to the end of the lake nearest the Cedars. He paused. His triumph was not unmixed with fear. A black figure stood in the open, quite close to him, gazing over the stagnant water that was like a veil for sinister things. He knew now that the woman was flesh and blood, for she did not glide away, and the snow made pallid scars on her black cloak.

He crept carefully forward until he was close behind the black figure.

"Now," he said, "you'll tell me who you are and why you cry about the Cedars."

The woman swung around with a cry. He stepped back, abashed, not knowing what to say, for there was still enough light to disclose to him the troubled face of Katherine, and there were tears in her eyes as if she might recently have expressed an audible grief.

"You frightened me, Bobby."

Without calculation he spoke his swift thought: "Was it you I saw here before? But surely you didn't cry in the house the other night and afterward when we followed Carlos!"

The tranquil beauty of her face was disturbed. When she answered her voice had lost something of its music:

"What do you mean?"

"It was you who cried just now? It was you I saw running through the woods?"

"What do you mean?" she asked again. "I have not run. I - I am not your woman in black, if that's what you think. I happened to pick up this cloak. You've seen it often enough before. And I haven't cried."

She brushed the tears angrily from her eyes.

"At least I haven't cried so any one could hear me. I wanted to walk. I hoped I would find you. I thought you had come this way, so I came, too. Why, Bobby, you're suspecting me of something!"

But the problem of the fugitive figure receded before the more intimate one of his heart. There was a thrill in her desire to find him in the solitude of the forest.

Only the faintest gray survived in the sky above the trees. The shadows were thick about them. The whispering snow urged him to use this moment for his happiness. It wasn't the thought of Graham that held him back. Last night, under an equal temptation, he might have spoken. To-night a new element silenced him and bound his eager hands. His awakening at the head of the stairs raised an obstacle to self-revelation around which there seemed to exist no path.

"I'm sorry. Let us go back," he said.

She looked at him inquiringly.

"What is it, Bobby? You are more afraid to-day than you have ever been before. Has something happened I know nothing of?"

He shook his head. He couldn't increase her own trouble by telling her of that.

The woods seemed to receive an ashy illumination from the passage of the snowflakes. Katherine walked a little faster.

"Don't be discouraged, Bobby," she begged him. "Everything will come out straight. You must keep telling yourself that. You must fight until you believe it."

The nearness of her dusk-clothed, slender figure filled him with a new courage, obscured to an extent his real situation. He burst out impulsively:

"Don't worry. I'll fight. I'll make myself believe. If necessary I'll tell everything I know in order to find the guilty person."

She placed her hand on his arm. Her voice fell to a whisper.

"Don't fight that way. Uncle Silas is dead; Howells has been taken away. The police will find nothing. By and by they will leave. It will all be forgotten. Why should you keep it active and dangerous by trying to find who is guilty?"

"Katherine!" he cried, surprised. "Why do you say that?"

Her hand left his arm. She walked on without answering. Paredes came back to him - Paredes serenely calling attention to the fact that Katherine had alarmed the household and had led it to the discovery of the Cedars's successive mysteries. He shrank from asking her any more.

They left the thicket. In the open space about the house the snow had spread a white mantle. From it the heavy walls rose black and forbidding.

"I don't want to go in," Katherine said.

Their feet lagged as they followed the driveway to the entrance of the court. The curtains of the room of death, they saw, had been raised. A dim, unhealthy light slipped from the small-paned windows across the court, staining the snow. Robinson and Rawlins were probably searching again.

Suddenly Katherine stopped. She pointed.

"What's that?" she asked sharply.

Bobby followed the direction of her glance. He saw a black patch against the wall of the wing opposite the lighted windows.

"It is a shadow," he said.

She relaxed and they walked on. They entered the court. There she turned, and Bobby stopped, too, with a sudden fear. For the thing he had called a shadow was moving. He stared at it with a hypnotic belief that the Cedars was at last disclosing its supernatural secret. He knew it could be no illusion, since Katherine swayed, half-fainting, against him. The moving shadow assumed the shape of a stout figure, slightly bent at the shoulders. A pipe protruded from the bearded mouth. One hand waved a careless welcome.

Bobby's first instinct was to cry out, to command this old man they had seen buried that day to return to his grave. For there wasn't the slightest doubt. The unhealthy candlelight from the room of death shone full on the gray and wrinkled face of Silas Blackburn.

CHAPTER VIII

WHAT HAPPENED AT THE GRAVE

"Hello, Katy! Hello, Bobby! You shown your face at last? I hope you've come sober."

The thin, quarrelsome voice of Silas Blackburn echoed in the mouldy court. The stout, bent figure in the candlelight studied them suspiciously. Katherine clung to Bobby, trembling, startled beyond speech by the apparition. They both stared at the gray face, at the thick figure, which, three days after death, they had seen buried that noon in the overgrown cemetery. Bobby recalled how Doctor Groom had reminded him that an activity like this might emerge from such places. He had suggested that the condition of the family burial ground might be an inspiration to such strayings. Yet why should the spirit of Silas Blackburn have escaped? Why should it have returned forthwith to the Cedars, unless to face his grandson as his murderer?

Afterward Bobby experienced no shame for these reflections. The encounter was a fitting sequel to the moment in the dark room when he had felt Howells move beneath his hand. He had a fleeting faith that the void between the living and the dead had, indeed, been bridged.

Then he wondered that the familiar figure failed to disintegrate, and he noticed smoke curling from the blackened briar pipe. He caught its pungent aroma in the damp air of the court. Moreover, Silas Blackburn had spoken, challenging him as usual with a sneer.

"Let us go past," Katherine whispered.

But Silas Blackburn stepped out, blocking their way. He spoke again. His whining accents held a reproach.

"What's the matter with you two? You might 'a' seen a ghost. Or maybe you're sorry to have me back. Didn't you wonder where I was, Katy? Reckon you hoped I was dead, Bobby."

Bobby answered. He had a fancy of addressing emptiness.

"Why have you come? That is what you are to us - dead."

Silas Blackburn chuckled. He took the pipe from his mouth and tapped the tobacco down with a knotted forefinger.

"I'll show you how dead I am! Trying to be funny, ain't you? I'll make you laugh on the wrong side of your face. It's cold here. I'm going in."

The same voice, the same manner! Yet his presence denied that great fact which during three days had been impressed upon them with a growing fear.

The old man jerked his thumb toward the dimly lighted windows of the wing.

"What you got the old room lighted up for? What's going on there? I tried to sleep there the other night -"

"Uncle!"

Katherine sprang forward. She stretched out her hand to him with a reluctance as pronounced as Graham's when he had touched Howells's body. Her fingers brushed his hand. Her shoulders drooped. She clung to his arm. To Bobby this resolution was more of a shock, less to be explained, than his first assurance of an immaterial visitor. What did it mean to him? Was it an impossible assurance of safety?

The old man patted Katherine's shoulder.

"Why, what you crying for, Katy? Always seems something to scare you lately."

He jerked his thumb again toward the lighted windows.

"You ain't told me yet what's going on in the old room."

Bobby's laugh was dazed, questioning.

"They're trying to account for your murder there."

His grandfather looked at him with blank amazement.

"You out of your head?"

"No," Katherine cried. "We saw you lying there, cold and still. I - I found you."

"You've not forgotten, Katherine," Bobby said breathlessly, "that he moved afterward."

Silas Blackburn took his hand from Katherine's shoulder.

"Trying to scare me? What's the matter with you? Some scheme to get my money?"

"You slept in the old room the other night?" Bobby asked helplessly.

"No, I didn't sleep there," his grandfather whined. "I went in and lay down, but I didn't sleep. I defy anybody to sleep in that room. What you talking about? It's cold here. This court was always damp. I want to go in. Is there a fire in the hall?

We'll light one, while you tell me what's ailin' you."

He turned, and grasped the door knob. They followed him into the hall, shaking the snow from their coats.

Paredes sat alone by the fire, languidly engaged in the solitaire which exerted so potent a fascination for him. He didn't turn at their entrance. It wasn't until Bobby called out that he moved.

"Carlos!"

Bobby's tone must have suggested the abnormal, for Paredes sprang to his feet, knocking over the table. The cards fell lightly to the floor, straying as far as the hearth. His hands caught at the back of his chair. He remained in an awkward position, rigid, white-faced, staring at the newcomer.

"I told you all," he whispered, "that the court was full of ghosts."

Silas Blackburn walked to the fire, and stood with his back to the smouldering logs. In this light he had the pallor of death - the lack of colour Bobby remembered beneath the glass of the coffin. The old man, always so intolerant and authoritative, was no longer sure of himself.

"Why do you talk about ghosts?" he whined. "I - I wish I hadn't waked up."

Paredes sank back in his chair.

"Waked up!" he echoed in an awe-struck voice.

Bobby took a trivial interest, as one will turn to small things during the most vital moments, in the reflection that twice within twenty-four hours the Panamanian had been startled from his cold reserve.

"Waked up!" Paredes repeated.

His voice rose.

"At what time? Do you remember the time?"

"Not exactly. Sometime after noon."

Bobby guessed the object of Paredes's question. He knew it had been about noon when they had seen the coffin covered in the restless, wind-swept cemetery.

Paredes hurried on.

"How long had you been asleep?"

"What makes you ask that?" the other whined. "I don't know."

"It was a long time?"

Blackburn's voice rose complainingly.

"How did you guess that? I never slept so. I dozed nearly three days, but I'm tired now - tired as if I hadn't slept at all."

Paredes made a gesture of surrender. Bobby struggled against the purpose of the man's questions, against the suggestion of his grandfather's unexpected answers.

"Your idea is madness, Carlos," he whispered.

"This house is filled with it," Paredes said. "I wish Groom were here. Groom ought to be here."

"He's coming back," Bobby told him. "He shouldn't be long now. He said before dinner time."

Paredes stirred.

"I wish he would hurry."

The Panamanian said nothing more, as if he realized the futility of pressing the matter before Doctor Groom should return. Necessary questions surged in Bobby's brain. The two that Paredes had put, however, disturbed his logic.

Katherine, who hadn't spoken since entering, kept her eyes fixed on her uncle. Her lips were slightly parted. She had the appearance of one afraid to break a silence covering impossible doubts.

Bobby called on his reason. His grandfather stood before him in flesh. With the old man, in spite of Paredes's ghastly hint, probably lay the solution of the entire mystery and his own safety. He was about to speak when he heard footsteps in the upper hall. His grandfather glanced inquiringly through the stair-well, asking:

"Who's that up there?"

The sharp tone confessed that fear of the Cedars was active in the warped brain.

"The district attorney," Bobby answered, "a detective, probably Hartley Graham."

"What they doing here?"

He indicated Paredes.

"What's this fellow doing here? I never liked him."

Katherine answered:

"They've all come because I thought I saw you dead, lying in the old room."

"We all saw," Bobby cried angrily, and Paredes nodded.

Blackburn shrank away from them.

The three men descended the stairs. Half way down they stopped.

"Who is that?" Robinson cried.

Graham's face whitened. He braced himself against the banister.

"Next time, Mr. District Attorney," Paredes said, "you'll believe me when I say the court is full of ghosts. He walked in from the court. I tell you they found him in the court."

Silas Blackburn's voice rose, shrill and angry:

"What's the matter with you all? Why do you talk of ghosts and my being dead? Haven't I a right to come in my own house? You all act as if you were afraid of me."

Paredes's questions had clearly added to the uncertainty of his manner. Katherine spoke softly:

"We are afraid."

The others came down. Robinson walked close to Silas Blackburn and for some time gazed at the gray face.

"Yes," he said. "You are Silas Blackburn. You came to my office in Smithtown the other day and asked for a detective, because you were afraid of something out here."

"There's no question," Graham cried. "Of course it is Mr. Blackburn, yet it couldn't be."

"What you all talking about? Why are the police in my house? Why do you act like fools and say I was dead?"

They gathered in a group at some distance from him. They

unconsciously ignored this central figure, as if he were, in fact, a ghost. Bobby and Katherine told how they had found the old man, a black shadow against the wall of the wing. Paredes repeated the questions he had asked and their strange answers. Afterward Robinson turned to Silas Blackburn, who waited, trembling.

"Then you did go to the old room to sleep. You lay down on the bed, but you say you didn't stay. You must tell us why not, and how you got out, and where you've been during this prolonged sleep. I want everything that happened from the moment you entered the old bedroom until you wakened."

"That's simple," Silas Blackburn mouthed. "I went there along about ten o'clock, wasn't it, Katy?"

"Nearly half past," she said. "And you frightened me."

"He must tell us why he went, why he was afraid to sleep in his own room," Graham began.

Robinson held up his hand.

"One question at a time, Mr. Graham. The important thing now is to learn what happened in the room. You're not forgetting Howells, are you?"

Silas Blackburn glanced at the floor. He moved his feet restlessly. He fumbled in his pocket for some loose tobacco. With shaking fingers he refilled his pipe.

"Except for Bobby and Katherine," he quavered, "you don't know what that room means to Blackburns; and they only know by hearsay, because I've seen it was kept closed. Don't see how I'm going to tell you -"

"You needn't hesitate," Robinson encouraged him. "We've all experienced something of the peculiarities of the Cedars. Your return alone's enough to keep us from laughter."

"All right," the old man stumbled on. "I was raised on stories of that room - even before my father shot himself there. Later on I saw Katherine's father die in the big bed, and after that I never cared to go near the place unless I had to. The other night, when I made up my mind to sleep there, I tried to tell myself all this talk was tommyrot. I tried to make myself believe I could sleep as comfortably in that bed as anywhere. So I went in and locked the door and raised the window and lay down."

"You're sure you locked the door?" Robinson asked.

"Yes. I remember turning the key in both doors, because I didn't want anything bothering me from outside."

They all looked at each other, unable to forecast anything of Blackburn's experiences; for both doors had been locked when the body had been found. Granted life, how would it have been possible for Silas Blackburn to have left the room to commence his period of drowsiness? An explanation of that should also unveil the criminal's route in and out.

The tensity of the little group increased, but no one interposed the obvious questions. Robinson was right. It would be quicker to let the protagonist of this unbelievable adventure recite its details in his own fashion. Paredes ran his slender fingers gropingly over the faces of several of the cards he had picked up.

"When I got in bed," Silas Blackburn continued, "I thought I'd let the candle burn for company's sake, but there was a wind, and it came in the open window, and it made the queerest black shadows dance all over the walls until I couldn't stand it a minute longer. I blew the candle out and lay back in the dark."

He drew harshly on his cold pipe. He looked at it with an air of surprise, and slipped it in his pocket.

"It was the funniest darkness. I didn't like it. You put your hand out and closed your fingers as if you could feel it. But it wasn't all black, either. Some moonlight came in with the wind between the curtains. It wasn't exactly yellow, and it wasn't white. After a little it seemed alive, and I wouldn't look at it any more. The only way I could stop myself was to shut my eyes, and that was worse, for it made me recollect my father the way I saw him lying there when I was a boy. God grant none of you will ever have to see anything like that. Then I seemed to see Katy's father, too; and I remembered his screams. The room got thick with, things like that - with those two, and with a lot of others come out of the pictures and the stories I've heard about my family."

His experience when he had gone to the room to take the evidence from Howells's body became active in Bobby's memory.

"There I lay with my eyes shut," Silas Blackburn went on in his strange, inquiring voice. "And yet I seemed to see those dead people all around me, and I thought they were in pain again, and were mad at me because I didn't do anything. I guess maybe I must 'a' been dozing a little, for I thought -"

He broke off. He raised his hand slowly and pointed in the direction of the overgrown cemetery where they had seen his coffin covered that noon. His voice was lower and harsher when he continued:

"I - I thought I heard them say that things were all broken out there, and - and awful - so awful they couldn't stay."

His voice became defiant.

"I ain't going to tell you what I dreamed. It was too horrible, but I made up my mind I would do what I could if I ever escaped from that room. I - I was afraid they'd take me back with them underneath those broken stones. And you - you stand there trying to tell me that they did."

He paused again, looking around with a more defiant glare in his bloodshot eyes. He appeared to be surprised not to find them laughing at him.

"What's the matter with you all?" he cried. "Why ain't you making me out a fool? You seen something in that room, too?"

"Go on," Robinson urged. "What happened then? What did you do?"

Blackburn's voice resumed its throaty monotone. As he spoke he glanced about slyly, suspecting, perhaps, the watchfulness of the fancies that had intimidated him.

"I realized I had to get out if they would let me. So I left the bed. I went."

He ceased, intimating that he had told everything.

"I know," Robinson said, "but tell us how you got out of the room, for when you - when the murder was discovered, both doors were locked on the inside, and you know how impossible the windows are."

"I tell you," Katherine said hysterically, "it *was* his body in the bed."

Bobby knew her assurance was justified, but he motioned her to silence.

"Let him answer," Robinson said.

Silas Blackburn ran his knotted fingers through his hair. He shook his head doubtfully.

"That's what I don't understand myself. That's what's been worrying me while these young ones have been talking as if I was dead and buried. I recollect telling myself I must go. I seem to remember leaving the bed all right, but I don't seem to remember walking on the floor or going through the door. You're sure the doors were locked?"

"No doubt about that," Rawlins said.

"Seems to me," Blackburn went on, "that I was in the private staircase, but did I walk downstairs? First thing I see clearly is the road through the woods, not far from the station."

"What did you wear?" Robinson asked.

"I'd had my trousers and jacket on under my dressing-gown," the old man answered, "because I knew the bed wasn't made up. That's what I wore except for the dressing-gown. I reckon I must have left that in the room. I wouldn't have gone back there for anything. My mind was full of those angry people. I wanted to get as far away from the Cedars as possible. I knew the last train from New York would be along about three o'clock, so I thought I'd go on into Smithtown and in the morning see this detective I'd been talking to. I went to Robert Waters's house. I've known him for a long time. I guess you know who he is. He's such a book worm I figured he might be up, and he wouldn't ask a lot of silly questions, being selfish like most people that live all the time with books. He came to the door, and I told him I wanted to spend the night. He offered to shake hands. That's funny, too. I didn't feel like shaking hands with anybody. I recollect that, because I'd felt sort of queer ever since going in the old room, and something told me I'd better not shake hands."

Paredes looked up, wide-eyed. The cards slipped from his fragile, pointed fingers.

"Do you realize, Mr. District Attorney, what this man is saying?"

But Robinson motioned him to silence.

"Let him go on. What happened then?"

"That's all," Blackburn answered, "except this long sleep I can't make out. Old Waters didn't get mad at my not shaking hands. He was too tied up in some book, I guess. I told him I was sleepy and didn't want to be bothered, and he nodded to the spare room off the main hall, and I tumbled into bed and was off almost before I knew it."

Paredes sprang to his feet and commenced to walk about the hall.

"Tell us," he said, "when you first woke up?"

"I guess it was late the next afternoon," Silas Blackburn quavered, fumbling with his pipe again. "But it was only for a minute."

Paredes stopped in front of Robinson.

"When he turned! You see!"

"It was Waters knocking on the door," Blackburn went on. "I guess he wanted to know what was the matter, and he talked about some food, but I didn't want to be bothered, so I called to him through the door to go away, and turned over and went to sleep again."

"He turned over and went to sleep again!" Katherine said breathlessly, "and it was about that time that I heard the turning in the old bedroom."

"Katherine!" Graham called. "What are you talking about? What are you thinking about?"

"What else is there?" she asked.

"She's thinking about the truth," Paredes said tensely. "I've always heard of such things. So have you. You've read of them, if you read at all. India is full of it. It goes back to ancient Egypt - the same person simultaneously in two places - the astral body - whatever you choose to call it. It's the projection of one's self whether consciously or unconsciously; perhaps the projection of something that retains reason after an apparent death. You heard him. He didn't seem to walk. He doesn't remember leaving the room, which was locked on the inside. His descent of the stairs was without motion as we know it. He had gone some distance before his mind consciously directed the movement of this active image of Silas Blackburn, while the double from which it had sprung lay apparently dead in the old room. You notice he shrank from shaking hands, and he slept until we hid away the shell. What disintegration and coming together again has taken place since we buried that shell in the old graveyard? If his friend had shaken hands with him would he have grasped emptiness? Did his normal self come back to him when the shell was put from our sight, and he awakened? These are some of the questions we must answer."

"You've a fine imagination, Mr. Paredes," Robinson said dryly.

His fat face, nevertheless, was bewildered, and in the eyes, surrounded by puffy flesh, smouldered a profound uncertainty.

"I wish Groom were here," Paredes was saying. "He would agree with me. He would know more about it than I."

Robinson threw back his shoulders. He turned to Rawlins with his old authority. The unimaginative detective had stood throughout, releasing no indication of his emotions; but as he raised his hand now to an unnecessary adjustment of his scarf pin, the fingers were not quite steady.

"Telephone this man Waters," Robinson directed. "Then get in communication with the office and put them on that end."

Rawlins walked away. Robinson apologized to Silas Blackburn with an uneasy voice.

"Got to check up what I can. Can't get anywhere with these

things unless you make sure of your first facts. I daresay Waters's story will tally with yours."

Blackburn nodded. Graham cleared his throat.

"Now perhaps we may ask that very important question. The day Mr. Blackburn called at your office in Smithtown he told Howells he was afraid of being murdered. According to Howells, he said: 'My heart's all right. It won't stop yet awhile unless it's made to. So if I'm found cold some fine morning you can be sure I was put out of the way.'"

"I know," Robinson said.

"And that night," Graham continued, "when he went to the old room, he was terrified of something which he wouldn't define for Miss Perrine."

"He warned me not to mention he'd gone there," Katherine put in. "He told me he was afraid - afraid to sleep in his own room any longer."

Robinson turned.

"What about that, Mr. Blackburn?"

For a moment Bobby's curiosity overcame the confusion aroused by his grandfather's apparently occult return. All along they had craved the knowledge he was about to give them, the statement on which Bobby's life had seemed to depend. Blackburn, however, was unwilling. The question seemed to have returned to him something of his normal manner.

"No use," he mumbled, "going into that."

"A good deal of use," Robinson insisted.

Blackburn shifted his feet. He gazed at his pipe doubtfully.

"I don't see why. That didn't come, and seems it wasn't what I ought to have been afraid of after all. All along I ought to have been afraid only of the Cedars and the old room. I've been accused of being unjust. I don't want to do an injustice now."

"Please answer," Robinson said impatiently.

"You must answer," Graham urged.

"I don't see that it makes the slightest difference," Paredes drawled. "What has it got to do with the case as it stands to-night?"

Robinson snapped at him.

"You keep out of it. Don't forget there's a lot you haven't answered yet."

Silas Blackburn looked straight at Bobby. Slowly he raised his hand, pointing an accusing finger at his grandson.

"If you want to know, I was afraid of that young rascal."

Katherine started impulsively forward in an effort to stop him. Blackburn waved her away.

"You trying to scare me, Katy?" he asked suspiciously.

"Evidently," Robinson commented to Graham, "Howells wasn't as dull as we thought him. Go on, Mr. Blackburn. Why were you afraid of your grandson?"

"Maybe he can tell you better than I can," the old man answered. "Don't see any use raking up such things, anyway. Maybe I'd been pretty harsh with him. Anyway, I knew he hated the ground I walked on and would be glad enough to see me drop in my tracks."

"That isn't so," Bobby said.

"You keep quiet now. You always talked too much."

So the old feeling survived.

"Go on," Robinson urged.

"I'd always been a hard worker," Blackburn whined, "and he was a waster. Naturally we didn't get along. I'd decided to make a new will, leaving my money to the Bedford Foundation, and I wrote him that, thinking it would bring him hot foot to make it up with me. I'd been nervous about him before, because I didn't know what might come into his head when he was on these wild parties. So I'd spoken to Howells, thinking I'd trip him if he tried any funny business. When he didn't come that night I got scared. He knew I wouldn't make the new will until morning, and since I couldn't see any man throwing all that money away, I figured he'd guessed he couldn't turn me and wouldn't waste any time talking.

"When you got a lot of money and a grandson who hates you, you have to think of such things. Suppose, I thought, he should come out here drunk when I was sound asleep. I knew he had a latch key, and he might sneak up to my room before I could even get to the telephone. Or I was afraid he might hire somebody. You can buy men for that sort of work in New York. I tell you the more I thought of it the more I was sure he'd do something. You'd understand if you lived in this lonely place with all that money and nobody you wanted to will it to. I nearly sent for Howells right then. But if nothing had happened I'd have looked a fool."

"I wanted you to send for a man," Katherine cried.

Bobby leaned against the wall, repeating to himself the words of Maria's note which accused him of having made the very threat his grandfather had feared.

"So," Blackburn rambled on, "I decided I wouldn't sleep in my room that night, and I picked out the least likely place for anybody to find me. I was more afraid of him than I was of the old room, but, as I've told you, the old room made me forget Master Robert."

Robinson stepped to Bobby's side.

"All along Howells was right. Tell me what you did with that evidence."

Bobby turned away. Katherine tried to laugh. Graham beckoned to Robinson.

"What's the use of bothering with evidence against a suspected murderer when the murdered man stands talking to you?"

Robinson frowned helplessly. Paredes sprang to his feet.

"You're taking too much for granted, Graham. There was a murder. Blackburn was killed. We've as many witnesses to that fact as we have that he's come back. This man who talks with us, accusing Bobby, may not stay. Have you thought of that? I have noticed something that makes me think it possible. I have been afraid to speak of it. But it makes me hesitate to say that this man is alive, as we understand life. We have to learn the nature of the forces we are dealing with, exactly how dangerous they are."

They started at a sharp rap on the front door.

"Now who?" the old man whined. "I wish you wouldn't look at me so. It makes me feel queer. You're all crazy."

"It's probably Doctor Groom," Bobby said, and stepped to the door, opening it.

It was Groom. The huge man walked in, struggling out of his coat. At first the others screened Silas Blackburn from him, but he acknowledged their strained attitudes, the excitement that still animated Paredes's face.

"What's the matter with you?" he asked. "Found something, Mr. District Attorney?"

Robinson moved to one side, jerking his thumb at Silas Blackburn. The coat and hat slipped from Doctor Groom's hand. His mouth opened. His great body crept slowly back until the shoulders rested against the wall. He placed the palms of his hands against the wall as if to push it away in order to assure further retreat. Always the little, infused eyes remained fixed on the man who had been his friend. Such terror was chiefly arresting because of the great figure conquered by it.

Blackburn thrust his pipe in his mouth. He laughed shakily.

"That fellow Groom will have a stroke."

The Doctor's greeting had the difficult quality of a masculine sob.

"Silas Blackburn!"

"Who do you think?" the other whined. "You going to try to frighten me out of my skin, too? These people are trying to say I've been lying dead in the old room. Hoped you'd have enough sense to set them right and tell me what it's all about."

The doctor straightened.

"You did lie dead in the old room."

His harsh, amazed tones held an unqualified conviction.

"I saw you there. I helped the coroner make the examination. You had been dead for many hours. And I saw you bolted in your coffin. I saw you buried in the graveyard you'd let go to pieces."

The others had, as far as possible, recovered from the first shock, had done their best to fathom the mystery, but Groom's fear increased. His reddish eyes grew always more alarmed. Silas Blackburn turned with a quick, frightened gesture, facing the fire. Paredes drew a deep breath.

"Now you'll see," he said.

Doctor Groom shrank against the wall again. After a moment, with the motions of one drawn by an outside will, he approached the figure at the fireplace. Then Bobby saw, and he heard Katherine's choked scream. For now that his grandfather's back was turned there was plainly visible on the white of the collar, near the base of the brain, a scarlet stain. And the hair above it was matted.

"That's what I meant," Paredes whispered.

Graham moved back.

"Good God!"

Robinson stared. The fear had found him, too.

Doctor Groom touched Blackburn's shoulder tentatively.

"What's the matter with the back of your neck?"

Blackburn drew fearfully away. He raised his hand and fumbled at the top of his collar. He held his fingers to the firelight.

"Why," he said blankly, "I been bleeding back there."

To an extent the doctor controlled himself.

"Sit down here, Silas Blackburn," he said. "I want to get the lamplight on your head."

"I ain't badly hurt?" Blackburn whined.

"I don't know," the doctor answered. "Heaven knows."

Blackburn sat down. The light shone full on the stained collar and the dark patch of hair at the base of the brain. Doctor Groom examined the wound minutely. He straightened. He spoke unsteadily:

"It is a healed wound. It was made by something sharp."

Robinson thrust his hands in his pockets.

"You're getting beyond my depths, Doctor. Bring him up to the old bedroom. I want him to see that pillow."

But Blackburn cowered in his chair.

"I won't go to that room again. They don't want me there. I'll have work started in the cemetery to-morrow."

"Mr. Blackburn," Robinson said, "the man we buried in the cemetery to-day, the man these members of your family identify as yourself, died of just such a wound as the doctor says has healed in your head."

Blackburn cowered farther in his chair.

"You're making fun of me," he whimpered. "You're trying to scare an old man."

"No," Robinson said. "How was that wound made?"

The crouched figure wagged its head from side to side.

"I don't know. Nothing's touched me there. I remember I had a headache when I woke up. Why doesn't Groom tell me why I slept so long?"

"I only know," Groom rumbled, "that the wound I examined upstairs must have caused instant death."

Paredes whispered to him. The doctor nodded reluctantly.

"What do you mean?" Blackburn cried. "You trying to tell me I can't stay with you?"

He pointed to Paredes.

"That's what he said - that I might have to go back, but I never heard of such a thing. I'm all right. My neck doesn't hurt. I'm alive. I tell you I'm alive. I'll teach you -"

Rawlins returned from the telephone.

"His story's straight," he said in his crisp manner. "I've been talking to Waters himself. Says Mr. Blackburn turned up about three-thirty, looking queer and acting queer. Wouldn't shake hands, just as he says. He went to the spare room and slept practically all the time until this afternoon. No food. Waters couldn't rouse him. Mr. Blackburn wouldn't answer at all or else seemed half asleep. He'd made up his mind to call in a doctor this afternoon. Then Mr. Blackburn seemed all right again, and started home."

Robinson gazed at the fire.

"What's to be done now, sir?" Rawlins asked.

"Find the answer if we can," Robinson said.

Paredes spoke as softly as he had done the other night while reciting his sensitive reaction to the Cedars's gloomy atmosphere. Only now his voice wasn't groping.

"Call me a dreamer if you want, Mr. District Attorney, but I have given you the only answer. This man's soul has dwelt in two places."

Robinson grinned.

"I'm going slow on calling anybody names, but I haven't forgotten that there's been another crime in this house. Howells was killed in that room, too. I would like to believe he could return as Mr. Blackburn has."

Blackburn looked up.

"What's that? Who's Howells?"

And as Robinson told him of the second crime he sank back in his chair again, whimpering from time to time. His fear was harder to watch.

"Might I suggest," Graham said, "that Howells isn't out of the case yet? It would be worth looking into."

"By all means," Robinson agreed.

Rawlins coughed apologetically.

"I asked them about that at the office. Howells was taken to his home in Boston to-day. The funeral's to be to-morrow."

"Then," Robinson said, "we're confined for the present to this end of the case. The facts I have tell me that two murders have been committed in this house. It is still my first duty to convict the guilty man."

Graham indicated the huddled, frightened figure in the chair.

"You are going against the evidence of your own eyes."

"I shall do what I can," Robinson said sternly. "We buried one of those men this noon. His grandson, his niece, and those who saw him frequently, swear it was this living being who has such a wound as the one that caused the death of that man. There is only one thing to do - see who we buried."

"The permits?" Graham suggested.

"I shall telephone the judge," Robinson answered, "and he can send them out, but I shan't wait for hours doing nothing. I am going to the grave at once."

"A waste of time," Paredes murmured.

"I don't understand," Silas Blackburn whined, "You say the doors were locked. Then how could anybody have got in that room to be murdered? How did I get out?"

Robinson turned on Paredes angrily.

"I'm not through with you yet. Before I am I'll get what I want from you."

He stormed away to the telephone. No one spoke. The doctor's rumpled head was still bent over the back of Silas Blackburn's chair. The infused eyes didn't waver from the crimson stain and the healed wound, and Blackburn remained huddled among the cushions, his shoulders twitching. Paredes commenced gathering up his cards. Katherine watched him out of expressionless eyes. Graham walked to her side. Rawlins, as always phlegmatic, remained motionless, waiting for his superior.

Bobby threw off his recent numbness. He realized the disturbing parallel in the actions of his grandfather and himself. He had come to the Cedars unconsciously, perhaps directed by an evil, external influence, on the night of the first murder. Now, it appeared, the man he was accused of killing had also wandered under an unknown impulse that night. Was the same subtle control responsible in both cases? Was there at the Cedars a force that defied physical laws, moving its inhabitants like puppets for special aims of its own? Yet, he recalled, there was something here friendly to him. After the movement of Howells's body and the disappearance of the evidence, the return of Silas Blackburn stripped Robinson's threats of power and seemed to place the solution beyond the district attorney's trivial reach.

The silence and the delay increased their weight upon the little group. Silas Blackburn, huddled in his chair, was grayer, more haggard than he had been at first. He appeared attentive to an expected summons. He seemed fighting the idea of going back.

The proximity of Graham to Katherine quieted the turmoil of Bobby's thoughts. If he could only have foreseen this return he would have listened to the whispered encouragement of the forest.

Robinson reappeared. Anxiety had replaced the anger in the round face which, one felt, should always have been no more than good-natured.

"Jenkins will have to help," he said.

Silas Blackburn arose unsteadily.

"I'm coming with you. You're not going to leave me here. I won't stay here alone."

"He should come by all means," Paredes said, "in case anything should happen -"

The old man put his hands to his ears.

"You keep quiet. I'm not going back, I tell you."

Bobby didn't want to hear any more. He went to the kitchen and called Jenkins. He let the butler go to the hall ahead of him in order that he might not have to witness this new greeting. But Jenkins's cry came back to him, and when he reached the hall he saw that the man's terror had not diminished.

They went through the court and around the house to the

stable where they found spades and shovels. Their grim purpose holding them silent, they crossed the clearing and entered the pathway that had been freshly blazed that day for the passage of the men in black.

The snow was quite deep. It still drifted down. It filled the woods with a wan, unnatural radiance. Without really illuminating the sooty masses of the trees it made the night white.

Silas Blackburn stumbled in the van with Paredes and Robinson. The doctor and Rawlins followed. Graham was with Katherine behind them. Bobby walked last, fighting an instinct to linger, to avoid whatever they might find beneath the white blanket of the little, intimate burial ground.

Groom turned and spoke to Graham. Katherine waited for Bobby, and the white night closed swiftly about them, whispering until the shuffling of the others became inaudible.

Was she glad of this solitude? Had she sought it? Her extraordinary request in that earlier solitude came to him, and he spoke of it while he tried to control his emotions, while he sought to mould the next few minutes reasonably and justly.

"Why did you tell me to make no attempt to find the guilty person?"

"Because," she answered, "you were too sure it was yourself. Why, Bobby, did you think I was the - the woman in black? That has hurt me."

"I didn't mean to hurt you," he said, "but there is something I must tell you now that may hurt you a little."

And he explained how Graham had awakened him at the head of the stairs.

"You're right," he said. "I was sure then it was myself, in spite of Howells's movement. It followed so neatly on the handkerchief and the footmarks. But now he has come back, and it changes everything. So I can tell you."

He couldn't be sure whether it was the cold, white loneliness through which they paced, or what he had just said that made her tremble.

"Perhaps I shouldn't have told you that."

"I am glad," she answered. "You must never close your confidence to me again. Why have you done it these last few months? I want to know."

Calculation died.

"Then you shall know."

Through the white night his hands reached for her, found her, drew her close. The moment was too masterful for him to mould. He became, instead, plastic in its white and stealthy grasp.

"I couldn't stay," he said, "and see you give yourself to Hartley."

She raised her hands to his shoulders. He barely caught her whisper because of the sly communicativeness of the snow.

"I am glad, but why didn't you say so then?"

The intoxication faded. The enterprise ahead gave to their joy a fugitive quality. Moreover, with her very surrender came to him a great misgiving.

"But you and Hartley? I've watched. It's been forced on me."

"Then you have misunderstood," she answered. "You put me too completely out of your life after our quarrel. That was about Hartley. You were too jealous, but it was my fault."

"Hartley," he asked, "spoke to you about that time?"

"Yes, and I told him he was a very dear friend, and he was kind enough to accept that and not to go away."

His measure of the widening of the rift between them made her more precious because of its affectionate human quality. She had been kinder to Graham, more mysterious about him, to draw Bobby back. Yet ever since his arrival at the Cedars, Graham had assumed toward Katherine an attitude scarcely to be limited by friendship. He had done what he had in Bobby's service clearly enough for her sake. For a long time past, indeed, in speaking of her Graham always seemed to discuss the woman he expected to marry.

"You are quite sure," he asked, puzzled, "that Hartley understood?"

"Why do you ask? He has shown how good a friend he is."

"He has always made me think," Bobby said, "that he had your love. You're sure he guessed that you cared for me?"

In that place, at that moment, there was a tragic colour to her coquetry.

"I think every one must have guessed it except you, Bobby."

He raised her head and touched her lips. Her lips were as cold as the caresses of the drifting snowflakes.

"We must go on," she sighed.

In his memory the chill of her kiss was bitter. In the forest they could speak no more of love.

But Bobby, hand in hand with her as they hurried after the

others, received a new strength. He saw as a condition to their happiness the unveiling of the mystery at the Cedars. He gathered his courage for that task. He would not give way even before the memory of all that he had experienced, even before the return of his grandfather, even before the revelation toward which they walked. And side by side with his determination grew shame for his former weakness. It was comforting to realize that the causes for his weakness and his strength were identical.

The subdued murmur of voices reached them. They saw among the indistinct masses of the trees restless patches of black. Katherine stumbled against one of the fallen stones. They stood with the others in the burial ground, close to the mound that had been made that day.

"They haven't begun," Bobby whispered.

She freed her hand.

A white flame sprang across the mound. The trees from formless masses took on individual shapes. A row of cypresses on which the light gleamed were like sombre sentinels, guarding the dead. The snow patches, clustered on their branches, were like funeral decorations pointing their morbid function. The light gave the overturned stones an illusion of striving to struggle from their white imprisonment. Robinson swung his lamp back to the mound.

"The snow isn't heavy," he said, "and the ground isn't frozen. It oughtn't to take long."

Silas Blackburn commenced to shake.

"It's a desecration of the dead."

"We have to know," Robinson said, "who is buried in that grave."

With a spade Jenkins scraped the snow from the mound. Rawlins joined him. They commenced to throw to one side, staining the white carpet, spadesful of moist, yellow earth. Their labour was rapid. Silas Blackburn watched with an unconquerable fascination. He continued to shake.

"I'm too cold. I'll never be warm again," he whined. "If anything happens to me, Bobby, try to forget I've been hard, and don't let them bury me. Suppose I should be buried alive?"

"Suppose," Paredes said, "you were buried alive to-day?"

He turned to Bobby and Katherine.

"That also is possible. You remember the old theories that have never been disproved of the disintegration of matter into its atoms, of its passage through solid substances, of its reforming in a far place? I wouldn't have to ask an East Indian that."

Jenkins, standing in the excavation, broke into torrential speech.

"Mr. Robinson! I can't work with the light. It makes the stones seem to move. It throws too many shadows. I seem to see people behind you, and I'm afraid to look."

Nothing aggressive survived in Rawlins's voice.

"We can work well enough without it, sir."

Robinson snapped off the light. The darkness descended eagerly upon them. Above the noise of the spades in the soft earth Bobby heard indefinite stirrings. In the graveyard at such an hour the supernatural legend of the Cedars assumed an inescapable probability. Bobby wished for some way to stop the task on which they were engaged. He felt instinctively it would be better not to tamper with the mystery of Silas Blackburn's return.

Bobby grew rigid.

"There it is again," Graham breathed.

A low keening came from the thicket. It increased in power a trifle, then drifted into silence.

It wasn't the wind. It was like the moaning Bobby had heard at the stagnant lake that afternoon, like the cries Graham and he had suffered in the old room. Seeming at first to come from a distance, it achieved a sense of intimacy. It was like an escape of sorrow from the dismantled tombs.

Bobby turned to Katherine. He couldn't see her for the darkness. He reached out. She was not there.

"Katherine," he called softly.

Her hand stole into his. He had been afraid that the forest had taken her. Under the reassurance of her handclasp he tried to make himself believe there was actually a woman near by, if not Maria, some one who had a definite purpose there.

Robinson flashed on his light. Old Blackburn whimpered:

"The Cedars is at its tricks again, and there's nothing we can do."

"It was like a lost soul," Katherine sighed. "It seemed to cry from this place."

"It must be traced," Bobby said.

"Then tell me its direction certainly," Robinson challenged. "We'd flounder in the thicket. A waste of time. Let us get through here. Hurry, Rawlins!"

The light showed Bobby that the detective and Jenkins had nearly finished. He shrank from the first hard sound of metal against metal.

It came. After a moment the light shone on the dull face of the casket which was streaked with dirt.

Jenkins rested on his spade. He groaned. It occurred to Bobby that the man couldn't have worked hard enough in this cold air to have started the perspiration that streamed down his wrinkled face.

"It would be a tough job to lift it out," Rawlins said.

"No need," Robinson answered. "Get the soil away from the edges."

He bent over, passing a screw driver to the detective.

"Take off the top plate. That will let us see all we want."

Jenkins climbed out.

"I shan't look. I don't dare look."

Silas Blackburn touched Bobby's arm timidly.

"I've been a hard man, Bobby -"

He broke off, his bearded lips twitching.

The grating of the screws tore through the silence. Rawlins glanced up.

"Lend a hand, somebody."

Groom spoke hoarsely:

"It isn't too late to let the dead rest."

Robinson gestured him away. Graham, Paredes, and he knelt

in the snow and helped the detective raise the heavy lid. They placed it at the side of the grave.

They all forced themselves to glance downward.

Katherine screamed. Silas Blackburn leaned on Bobby's arm, shaking with gross, impossible sobs. Paredes shrugged his shoulders. The light wavered in Robinson's hand. They continued to stare. There was nothing else to do.

The coffin was empty.

CHAPTER IX

BOBBY'S VIGIL IN THE ABANDONED ROOM

For a long time the little group gathered in the snow-swept cemetery remained silent. The lamp, shaking in the district attorney's hand, illuminated each detail of the casket's interior linings. Bobby tried to realize that, except for these meaningless embellishments, the box was empty. That was what held them all - the void, the unoccupied silken couch in which they had seen Silas Blackburn's body imprisoned. Yet the screws which the detective had removed, and the mass of earth, packed down and covered with snow, must have made escape a dreadful impossibility even if the spark of life had reanimated its occupant. And that occupant stood there, trembling and haggard, sobbing from time to time in an utter abandonment to the terror of what he saw.

To Bobby in that moment the supernatural legend of the Cedars seemed more triumphantly fulfilled than it would have been through the immaterial return of his grandfather. For Silas Blackburn was a reincarnation more difficult to accept than any ghost. Had Paredes, who all along had offered them a spectacle of veiled activity and thought, grasped the truth? At first glance, indeed his gossip of oriental theories concerning the disintegration of matter, its passage through solid substances, its reassembly in far places, seemed thoroughly justified. Yet, granted that, who, in the semblance of Silas Blackburn, had they buried to vanish completely? Who, in the semblance of Silas Blackburn, had drowsed without food for three days in the house at Smithtown?

The old man stretched his shaking hands to Bobby and Katherine.

"Don't let them bury me again. They never buried me. I've not been dead! I tell you I've not been dead!" He mouthed horribly. "I'm alive! Can't you see I'm alive?"

He broke down and covered his face. Jenkins sank on the heap of earth.

"I saw you, Mr. Silas, in that box. And I saw you on the bed. Miss Katherine and I found you. We had to break the door. You looked so peaceful we thought you were asleep. But when we touched you you were cold."

"No, no, no," Blackburn grimaced. "I wasn't cold. I couldn't have been."

"There's no question," Bobby said hoarsely.

"No question," Robinson repeated.

Katherine shrank from her uncle as he had shrunk from her in the library the night of the murder.

"What do you make of it?" the district attorney asked Rawlins.

The detective, who had remained crouched at the side of the grave, arose, brushing the dirt from his hands, shaking his head.

"What is one to make of it, sir?"

Paredes spoke softly to Graham.

"The Cedars wants to be left alone to the dead. We would all be better away from it."

"You won't go yet awhile," Robinson said gruffly. "Don't forget you're still under bond."

The detail no longer seemed of importance to Bobby. The mystery, centreing in the empty grave, was apparently inexplicable. He experienced a great pity for his grandfather; and, recalling that strengthening moment with Katherine, he made up his mind that there was only one course for him. It might be dangerous in itself, yet, on the other hand, he couldn't go to Katherine while his share in the mystery of the Cedars remained so darkly shadowed. He had no right to withhold anything, and he wouldn't ask Graham's advice. He had stepped all at once into the mastery of his own destiny. He would tell Robinson, therefore, everything he knew, from the party with Maria and Paredes in New York, through his unconscious wanderings around the house on the night of the first murder, to the moment when Graham had stopped his somnambulistic excursion down the stairs.

Robinson turned his light away from the grave.

"There's nothing more to do here. Let us go back."

The little party straggled through the snow to the house. The hall fire smouldered as pleasantly as it had done before they had set forth, yet an interminable period seemed to have elapsed. Silas Blackburn went close to the fire. He sank in a chair, trembling.

"I'm so cold," he whined. "I've never been so cold. What is the matter with me? For God's sake tell me what is the matter! Katherine - if - if nothing happens, we'll close the Cedars. We'll go to the city where there are lots of lights."

"If you'd only listened to Bobby and me and gone long ago," she said.

Robinson stared at the fire.

"I'm about beaten," he muttered wearily.

Rawlins, with an air of stealth, walked upstairs. Graham, after a moment's hesitation, followed him. Bobby wondered why they went. He caught Robinson's eye. He indicated he would like to speak to him in the library. As he left the hall he saw Paredes, who had not removed his hat or coat, start for the front door.

"Where are you going?" he heard Robinson demand.

Paredes's reply came glibly.

"Only to walk up and down in the court. The house oppresses me more than ever to-night. I feel with Mr. Blackburn that it is no place to stay."

And while he talked with Robinson in the library Bobby caught at times the crunching of Paredes's feet in the court.

"Why does that court draw him?" Robinson asked. "Why does he keep repeating that it is full of ghosts? He can't be trying to scare us with that now."

But Bobby didn't answer.

"I've come to tell you the truth," he burst out, "everything I know. You may lock me up. Even that would be better than this uncertainty. I must have an answer, if it condemns me; and how could I have had anything to do with what has happened to-night?"

He withheld nothing. Robinson listened with an intent interest. At the end he said not unkindly:

"If the evidence and Howells's report hadn't disappeared I'd have arrested you and considered the case closed before this miracle was thrown at me. You've involved yourself so frankly that I don't believe you're lying about what went on in the old room when you entered to steal those exhibits. Can't say I blame you for trying that, either. You were in a pretty bad position - an unheard-of position. You still are, for that matter. But the case is put on such an extraordinary basis by what has happened to-night that I'd be a fool to lock you up on such a confession. I believe there's a good deal more in what has gone on in that room and in the return of your grandfather than you can account for."

"Thanks," Bobby said. "I hoped you'd take it this way, for, if you will let me help, I have a plan."

He turned restlessly to the door of the private staircase. In his memory Howells's bold figure was outlined there, but now the face with its slow smile seemed sympathetic rather than challenging.

"What's your plan?" Robinson asked.

Bobby forced himself to speak deliberately, steadily:

"To go for the night alone to the old room as Howells did."

Robinson whistled.

"Didn't believe you had that much nerve. Two men have tried that. What good would it do?"

"If the answer's anywhere," Bobby said, "it must be hidden in that room. Howells felt it. I was sure of it when I was prevented from taking the evidence. You've believed it, I think."

"There is something strange and unhealthy about the room," Robinson agreed. "Certainly the secret of the locked doors lies there. But we've had sufficient warning. I'm not ashamed to say I wouldn't take such a chance. I don't know that I ought to let you."

Bobby smiled.

"I've been enough of a coward," he said, "and, Robinson, I've got to know. I shan't go near the bed. I'll watch the bed from a corner. If the danger's at the bed, as we suspect, it probably won't be able to reach me, but just the same it may expose itself. And Rawlins or you can be outside the broken door in the corridor, waiting to enter at the first alarm."

"Howells had no chance to give an alarm," Robinson muttered. "We'll see later."

But Bobby understood that he would agree, and he forced his new courage to face the prospect.

"Maybe something will turn up," Robinson mused. "The case can't grow more mysterious indefinitely."

But his tone held no assurance. He seemed to foresee new and difficult complications.

When they returned to the hall Bobby shrank from the picture of his grandfather still crouched by the fire, his shoulders twitching, his fingers about the black briar pipe shaking. Groom alone had remained with him. Bobby opened the front door. There was no one in the court.

"Paredes," he said, closing the door, "has gone out of the court. Where's Katherine, Doctor?"

"She went to the kitchen," the doctor rumbled. "I'm sure I don't know what for this time of night."

After a little Graham and Rawlins came down the stairs. Graham's face was scarred by fresh trouble. Rawlins drew the district attorney to one side.

"What have you two been doing up there?" Bobby asked Graham.

"Rawlins is hard-headed," Graham answered in a low, worried tone.

He wouldn't meet Bobby's eyes. He seemed to seek an escape.

"Where's Katherine?" he asked.

"Doctor Groom says she went to the back part of the house. Why won't you tell me what you were doing?"

"Only keeping Rawlins from trying to make more mischief," Graham answered.

He wouldn't explain.

"Aren't there enough riddles in this house?" Doctor Groom asked with frank disapproval.

Rawlins and Robinson joined them, sparing Graham a further defence. The district attorney had an air of fresh resolution. He was about to speak when the front door opened quietly, framing the blackness of the court. They started forward, seeing no one.

Silas Blackburn made a slow, shrinking movement, crying out:

"They've opened the door! Don't let them in. Don't let them come near me again."

Although they knew Paredes had been in the court the spell of the Cedars was so heavy upon them that for a moment they didn't know what to expect. They hesitated with a little of the abnormal apprehension Silas Blackburn exposed. Then Rawlins sprang forward, and Bobby called:

"Carlos!"

Paredes stepped from one side. He lingered against the black background of the doorway. It was plain enough something was wrong with him. In the first place, although he had opened the door, he had been unwilling to enter.

"Shut the door," Silas Blackburn moaned.

Paredes, with a quick gesture of surrender, stepped in and obeyed. His face was white. He had lost his immaculate appearance. His clothing showed stains of snow and mould. He held his left hand behind his back.

"What's the matter with you?" Robinson demanded.

The Panamanian's laugh lacked its usual indifference.

"When I said the Cedars was full of ghosts I should have heeded my own warning. I might better have stayed comfortably locked up in Smithtown."

Silas Blackburn spoke in a hoarse whisper:

"What did you see out there? Are they coming?"

"I saw very little," Paredes answered. "It was too dark."

"You saw something," Doctor Groom rumbled.

Paredes nodded. He looked at the floor.

"A - a woman in black."

"By the lake!" Bobby cried.

"Not as far as the lake. It was near the empty grave."

Silas Blackburn commenced to shake again. The doctor's little eyes were wider.

"It was a woman - a flesh-and-blood woman?" Robinson asked.

"If it was a ghost," Paredes answered, "it had the power of attack; but that, as you'll recall, is by no means unusual here. That's why I've come in rather against my will. It seems strange, but I, too, have been struck by a sharp and slender object, and I thought, perhaps, the doctor had better look at the result."

With a motion of repugnance he moved his left hand from behind his back and stretched it to the light. The coat below the elbow was torn. The slender hand was crimson. He tried to smile.

"Luckily it wasn't at the back of my head."

"Sit down," Doctor Groom said, waving Robinson and Rawlins away. "Let me see how badly he's hurt. There'll be plenty of time for questions afterward."

Paredes lay back in one of the chairs and extended his arm. He kept his eyes closed while the doctor stooped, examining the wound. All at once his nearly perpetual sleeplessness since coming to the Cedars had recorded itself in his face. His nerves at last confessed their vulnerability as he fumbled for a cigarette with his good hand, as he placed it awkwardly between his lips.

"Would you mind giving me a light, Bobby?"

Bobby struck a match and held it to the cigarette.

"Thanks," Paredes said. "Are you nearly through, doctor? I daresay it's nothing."

Doctor Groom glanced up.

"Nothing serious with a little luck. It's only torn through a muscle. It might have pierced the large vein."

His forehead beneath the shaggy black hair was deeply lined.

He turned to Robinson doubtfully.

"Maybe you'll tell us," Robinson said, "what made the wound."

"No use shirking facts," the doctor rumbled. "Mr. Paredes has been wounded just as he said, by something sharp and slender."

"You mean," Robinson said, "by an instrument that could have caused death in the case of Howells and - and -"

"I won't have you looking at me that way," Silas Blackburn whined.

"Yes," the doctor answered. "Before we go any farther I want to bind this arm. There must be an antiseptic in the house. Where is Katherine? See if you can find her, Bobby."

As Bobby started to cross the dining room he heard the slight scraping of the door leading to the kitchen. He knew there was someone in the room with him. He touched a cold hand.

"Bobby!" Katherine breathed in his ear.

He understood why the little light from the hall had failed to disclose her when she had come from the kitchen. She wore the black cloak. Against the darkness at the end of the room she had made no silhouette. When he put his arms around her and touched her cheek, he noticed that that, too, was cold; and the shoulders of the cloak were damp as if she had just come in from the falling snow.

"Where have you been?" he asked.

"Looking outside," she answered frankly. "I couldn't sit still. I wondered if the woman in black would be around the house to-night. Then I was afraid, so I came in."

Doctor Groom's voice reached them.

"Have you found her? Is she in the dining room?"

Without any thought of disloyalty Bobby recognized the menace of coincidence.

"Take your cloak off," he whispered. "Leave it here."

"Why?"

While he drew the cloak from her shoulders he raised his voice.

"Carlos has been hurt. The doctor asked me to find you."

His simple strategy was destroyed by the appearance of Rawlins. The detective came directly to them; nor was the coincidence lost on him, and it was his business to advertise rather than to conceal it. Without ceremony he took the cloak from Bobby. He draped it over his arm.

"The doctor," he said to Katherine, "wants a basin of warm water, some old linen, carbolic acid, if you have it."

She nodded and went back to the kitchen while Bobby returned with the detective to the hall. Paredes's eyes remained closed.

"Where did you get the cloak, Rawlins?" Robinson asked.

"The young lady," Rawlins answered with soft satisfaction, "just wore it in. At least it's still wet from the snow."

Paredes opened his eyes. He looked for a moment at the black cloak. He closed his eyes again.

"You could recognize the woman who attacked you?" Rawlins said.

Paredes shook his head.

"You've forgotten how dark it is. Please don't ask me even to swear that it was a woman."

"You're trying to say it wasn't flesh and blood," Blackburn quavered.

Paredes smiled weakly.

"I'm trying to say nothing at all."

"Tell us each detail of the attack," Robinson said.

But Katherine's footsteps reached them from the dining room and Paredes wouldn't answer. Under those conditions Robinson's failure to press the question was as disturbing as the detective's matter-of-fact capture of the cloak.

Paredes glanced at Katherine once. There was no softness in her attitude as she knelt beside his chair. Neither, Bobby felt, was there the slightest uneasiness. With a facile grace she helped the doctor bathe and bandage the slight wound.

"A silk handkerchief for a sling -" the doctor suggested.

"I won't have a sling," Paredes said. "I wouldn't know what to do without the use of both my hands."

"You ought to congratulate yourself that you still keep it," the doctor grumbled.

Bobby took the pan and the bottles from Katherine and rang for Jenkins. It was clear that Robinson had hoped the girl would go out with them herself and so give Paredes an opportunity to speak. This new development made him wonder about Graham's theories as to Paredes. If it was Maria who had struck the man there had either been a quarrel among thieves or else no criminal connection had ever existed between the two. Paredes, however, aping the gestures of an invalid, was less to Bobby's taste than his satanic appearance when he had come from the private staircase.

Rawlins still held the cloak. After Jenkins had removed the doctor's paraphernalia, everyone seemed to wait. It was Silas Blackburn who finally released the strain.

"Katy, where you been with that cloak? What's he doing with it?"

Without answering she took the cloak from Rawlins, and gave the detective and the district attorney the opportunity they craved. She walked up the stairs, turning at the landing. Her farewell seemed pointed at the Panamanian who looked languidly up at her.

"If I'm wanted I shall be in my room."

"Who would want you, Katherine?" Graham blurted out. But it was clear he had caught the coincidence, too, and the trouble he had confessed a little earlier was radically increased.

"That remains to be seen," Robinson sneered as soon as she had gone. "Now, Mr. Paredes."

"I've really told you everything," he said. "I walked toward the graveyard. At a point very close to it I felt the presence of this creature in black. I spoke. I took my courage in my hands. I reached out. I touched nothing." He raised his injured hand. "I got this for my pains."

"What made you go to the graveyard?" Robinson asked suspiciously.

There was no mockery in the Panamanian's answer.

"I have told you the court for me has always been full of ghosts." He pointed to Silas Blackburn. "It frightened me that this man should come back through the court from his grave with all the evidence pointing to an astral magic. I wanted to retrace his journey. I thought at the grave, if I were alone, something might expose itself that had naturally remained hidden in the presence of so many materialistic human beings."

A smile spread over Rawlins's cold, unimaginative features.

"That sounds well, Mr. Paredes, and there is a lot about this case that looks like ghosts, but leave us a few flesh-and-blood clues. This woman in black is one of them, although she's been slippery as an eel. It looks to me as if you went to the grave to meet her alone exactly as you went to the deserted house to talk quietly with her night before last. Maybe she mistook you for one of us snooping in the dark, and let you have it."

"If that is so," Paredes said easily, "the nature of my wound would suggest that she is guilty of the crimes in the old room. Why not go out and arrest her then? She might explain everything except the return to life of Mr. Blackburn. I'm afraid that's rather beyond you in any case. But at least find her."

Robinson joined in Rawlins's laugh.

"Why go outside for that?"

Paredes started.

"You never mean -"

"You bet we do," Rawlins said. "If what I've doped out hadn't been so we'd have caught her long before. We're not blind, and we haven't missed the nerve with which she helped the doctor fix you up. We haven't caught her before because her headquarters have been right in this house all the time. You remember the other night, Mr. Robinson. You'd just questioned her in the court and had threatened to question him, too, when she came in here ahead of us and slipped out the back way. She must have told him to follow because they had to talk, undisturbed by us. They went by different roads to the deserted house where a light had been seen before. We happened to hit his trail first and followed it. I'll guarantee you didn't see her when you first came in."

Robinson shook his head.

"Mr. Graham kept me busy, and I rather waited for your report before pushing things. I didn't see her or question her until after Mr. Graham and Mr. Blackburn had started for New York."

"And she could have sneaked in the back way any time before that," Rawlins said.

"It's utter nonsense!" Graham cried.

Rawlins turned on him.

"See here, Mr. Graham, you've been trying to fight me off this way all afternoon. It won't do."

"Katy's a good girl," Silas Blackburn quavered.

With a growing discomfort Bobby realized that when the woman had cried near the graveyard he had reached out for Katherine and had failed to find her. Moreover, the night Graham and he had heard the crying in the old room she had stood alone in the corridor. It was easily conceivable that the turn of events after Robinson's arrival should have made it necessary for conspirators to consult free from any danger of disturbance. But Katherine, he told himself, was assuredly the victim of coincidence. He couldn't picture her entangled in any of Paredes's purposes. Her dislike of the man was complete and open. But he saw that Rawlins out of the mass of apparently inexplicable clues had extracted this material one and would follow it desperately no matter who was hurt; and

Robinson was behind him. That accounted for their frequent excursions upstairs during the afternoon, for Rawlins's ascent as soon as they had returned from the grave. They had evidently found something to sharpen their suspicions, and Graham probably knew what it was.

Robinson took out his watch.

"We can't put this off too late," he mused.

The detective at his heels, he walked to the library. Bobby started after them. Graham caught him and they crossed the dining room together.

"What do they mean to do?" Bobby asked.

"I have been afraid of it since this afternoon," Graham answered. "I haven't cared to talk about it. I had hoped to hold them off. They intend to search Katherine's room. I think they believe she has something important hidden there. I've been wondering if they've got track of Howells's report which we told Jenkins to hide."

"Why," Bobby asked, "should that involve Katherine?"

"Howells may have written something damaging to her. He knew she was devoted to your interests."

Robinson called to them from the library.

"Won't you please come in, Mr. Blackburn?"

Bobby and Graham continued to the library. They found Rawlins gazing through the door of the private staircase.

"We could go up this way," he was saying, "and across the old room so that she needn't suspect."

"What is he talking about?" Bobby asked Robinson angrily.

"You wanted to help," Robinson answered, "so Rawlins and I are going to give you a chance. We are about to search your cousin's room. We hope to find there an explanation of a part of the mystery - the motive, at least, for Howells's death; perhaps your own exoneration. You'd do anything to have that, wouldn't you? You've said so."

"At her expense!" Bobby cried. "You've no right to go to her room. She's incapable of a share in such crimes. Do you seriously think she could plan an escape from the grave and bring back to life a man three days dead?"

"Give me a human being that caused death," Robinson answered, "and I'll tackle the ghosts later. You're wrong if you think I'm going to quit cold because your grandfather looks like a dead thing that moves about and talks. I shan't give up to that madness until I've done everything in my power. I would be a criminal myself if I failed to do as Rawlins wishes. If your cousin's skirts are clear no harm will be done. I'm acting on the assumption that your confession was honest. I want you to get Miss Perrine out of her room. I want you to see that she stays downstairs while we search."

"You've already searched her room."

"Not since Rawlins -"

Robinson caught himself.

"Never mind that. It is necessary it should be searched to-night. Even you'll acknowledge it's significant that all day when she has been downstairs her door has been locked."

"It's only significant," Bobby flashed, "in view of your treatment of her yesterday."

Robinson grinned.

"That will hardly go down. Rawlins has hesitated to break in.

I've instructed him to do it now, if necessary. For the last time, will you bring your cousin down? Will you go through and unlock the door leading from the old bedroom to the private hall so we can get up?"

"No," Bobby cried, "I wouldn't do it if I believed you were right. And I know you're wrong."

"Prove that we're wrong. Clear your cousin by helping us," Robinson urged.

"Since you're so determined," Graham said quietly, "I'll do it."

"Hartley! What are you thinking of?"

"Of showing them how wrong they are," Graham said. "I'll tell her Doctor Groom wishes to speak to her about Mr. Blackburn. I'll warn him to keep her downstairs for a quarter of an hour. That should give you plenty of time."

Robinson nodded.

"She'll never forgive you," Bobby said. "It's spying."

He wondered that Graham should choose such a course so soon after it had become clear that Katherine had never really loved him.

"It's the best way to satisfy them," Graham said. "I have, perhaps, more faith than you in Katherine."

He left them to carry out Robinson's instructions. They waited at the entrance of the private staircase.

"I may witness this outrage?" Bobby asked.

"I'd rather you didn't speak of it in such harsh terms," Robinson smiled.

Bobby didn't know what to expect. The whole thing might be a trick of Paredes, in line with his hints the night of Howells's death, to involve Katharine. The quiet confidence of the two officials was disturbing. What had Rawlins seen?

After a long time Graham descended the private staircase, carrying a lighted candle. He beckoned and they followed him back through the private hall into the wide and mournful bedroom. It encouraged Bobby to see the district attorney and the detective hurry across it. After all, they were really without confidence of solving its ghostly riddle. What they were about to do, he argued, was a last chance. They would find nothing. They would acknowledge themselves beaten.

When they entered the farther wing he noticed that Katherine's door stood wide.

"You see," he said.

"When I called her," Graham explained, "she thought something had happened to her grandfather. She ran out."

"And forgot all about the door," Robinson grinned. "That's lucky. Now, Rawlins."

Bobby couldn't bring himself to cross the threshold, but from the corridor he could see the interior of the room and all that went on there during the next few moments. A candle burned on the bureau, exposing the feminine neatness and delicacy of the furnishings. The presence of the three men was a desecration; what they were about to do, an unforgivable act of vandalism.

Rawlins went to a work table while Robinson rummaged in the closet. Graham, meantime, bent against the footboard of the bed, watching with anxious eyes. Bobby's anger was increased by this picture. He resisted an impulse to run to the stairs and call Katherine up. That would simply increase Robinson's suspicions. There was nothing she could do, nothing he could do.

Rawlins had clearly been unsuccessful at the work table. He glided to the bureau. One after the other he opened the drawers, fumbling within, lifting the contents out, replacing them with a rough haste while Bobby's futile rage increased.

Suddenly he saw Graham's attitude alter. Rawlins's back stiffened. He pulled the bottom drawer altogether from the bureau and thrust it to one side. He gazed in the opening.

"Come here, Mr. Robinson," he said softly.

Robinson left the closet and stooped beside the detective. He exclaimed. Graham went closer looking over their backs.

"You'd better see, Bobby," he said without turning.

"Yes," Robinson said. "Let me show you how wrong you were, Mr. Blackburn. Let me ask if you knew you were wrong."

Bobby entered with a quicker pulse. He, too, stooped and looked in the opening. Abruptly everything altered for him. He wondered that his physical surroundings should remain the same, that the eager faces beside him should retain their familiar lines.

Against the back-board of the bureau, where it would fit neatly when the drawer was in place, lay a plaster cast of a footmark. Near by was a rumpled handkerchief that Bobby recognized as his own, and the envelope, containing Howells's report which they had told Jenkins to hide.

"Well?" Robinson grinned.

"I swear I didn't know they were there," Bobby answered. "You'll never make me believe that Katherine knows it."

"I've guessed," Rawlins said, "that the stuff was hidden here ever since this afternoon when I saw a small bundle sneaked in."

"Who brought it?" Bobby took him up.

Robinson's grin expanded.

"Leave us one or two surprises to spring in court."

"Then," Bobby said, "my cousin wasn't in the room when this evidence was brought here."

"I'll admit that," Rawlins answered, "but she wasn't far away, and she got here before I could investigate, and she's kept the door locked ever since until just now."

He lifted the exhibits out. The shape of the cast, the monogram on the handkerchief cried out their testimony.

Robinson grasped Howells's report and glanced over the fine handwriting. After a time he looked up.

"There's the case against you, Mr. Blackburn, and at the least your cousin's an accessory. But why the devil did you come to me and make a clean breast of it?"

"Because," Bobby cried, "I didn't know anything about these things being here. Can't you see that?"

"That's the trouble," Robinson answered uncertainly, "I think I do see it."

"Besides," Graham said, "you're still without the instrument that caused death."

"I expect to land it in this room," Rawlins answered grimly.

He replaced the drawer and continued to fumble among the clothing it contained. All at once he called out and raised his hand. On the forefinger a tiny red stain showed.

"How did you do that?" Robinson asked.

"Something pricked me," the detective answered. "Maybe it was only a pin, but it might have been -"

Excitedly he resumed his search. He took the clothing from the drawer and threw it to one side. Nothing remained in the drawer.

"I guess it must have been a pin," Robinson said, disappointed.

But Rawlins took up each article of clothing and examined it minutely. His face brightened.

"Here's something stiff. By gad, I believe I've got it!"

Concealed in a woollen sack, with the slender shaft thrust through and through the folds, was a peculiarly long, stout, and sharp hat pin. Rawlins drew it out. He held it up triumphantly.

"Now maybe we're not getting somewheres! That's the boy that did the trick in both cases, and it's what scratched Mr. Paredes. Maybe you noticed how quickly she came upstairs to hide this when she got in."

"Good work, Rawlins," Robinson said.

He glanced at Bobby and Graham.

"Have either of you seen this deadly thing before?"

Bobby wouldn't answer, but after a moment's hesitation Graham spoke:

"There's no point in lying, Bobby. Katherine knows nothing of this. I disagree with Rawlins. If she had been working with

Paredes, which is unthinkable, she'd never have made such a mistake. She wouldn't have struck him. I have seen her wear such a pin."

"If she didn't cut him with it," Rawlins reasoned, "who else could have got it out of here and put it back to-night when she kept her door locked?"

"There's no getting around it," Robinson said. "Take charge of these things, Rawlins. Put them in a safe place."

"What are you going to do?" Bobby asked.

"I'm afraid there's only one thing to do," Robinson answered. "I'll have to arrest you both. One of you used this pin in the old room. It doesn't make much difference which one. You've been working together, and we'll find out about Paredes later."

"You're making a terrible mistake," Bobby muttered. "You don't know Katherine or you couldn't suspect her of any share in such crimes. Give me until morning to prove how wrong you are."

"What would be the use?" Robinson asked.

"If you'll do that, I will get the truth for you - the whole truth, how the room was entered, everything. I swear it, Robinson. Only a few hours. Let me carry out my plan. Let me offer myself to the dangers of the old room as Howells and my grandfather did. Your case is no good unless you can explain the miracle to-night. Give us this chance. Then in the morning, if nothing happens and you still think I'm guilty, lock me up, but for God's sake, Robinson, leave her out of it."

Graham walked to the window and flung it open. A violent gust of wind swept in, carrying a multitude of icy flakes.

"The storm is worse," he said. "No one is likely to try to escape from this house to-night."

Bobby stretched out his hand.

"You can't expose her to that."

Rawlins hadn't forgotten the sense of fellowship sprung from the pursuit of Paredes through the forest.

"He's right, Mr. Robinson. You could lock up a dozen people. You might send them to the chair without uncovering the real mystery of the Cedars. Maybe he might find something, and he'd be as safe in that room as in any jail I know of. I mean one of us would be in the library and the other in the corridor outside the broken door. How could he reasonably get out? If there was an attempt to repeat the trick we'd be ready. As for the girl, it's simple enough to safeguard against her getting away before morning. As Mr. Graham says, no one's likely to run far in this storm, anyway."

Robinson considered.

"I don't want to be hard," he said finally, "and I don't want to miss any chance of cleaning up where poor Howells failed."

He glanced at the extraordinary array of evidence. The good nature which, one felt, should always have been in his face, shone at last.

"I don't believe you're guilty. As far as you're concerned it's likely enough a put-up job. I don't know about the girl. Go ahead, anyway, and tell us, if you can, how the locked room was entered. Explain the mystery of that old man who looks as if he were dead, but who moves around and talks with us."

"The answer, if it's anywhere," Bobby said, "is in the old room."

Robinson nodded.

"Under the conditions it seems worth while. Go on then and

clear your cousin and yourself if you can. You have until daylight to-morrow."

Bobby's gratitude was sufficiently eloquent in his eyes, but he said nothing. He hurried from the room to find Katherine. As soon as he had stepped in the corridor he saw her figure against the wall.

"Katherine!" he breathed.

"I've heard everything," she said.

He led her to the main hall where the greedy ears in her bedroom couldn't overhear them.

"Then you suspected what they were about?" he asked her.

"Uncle Silas," she answered, "seemed just as he had been when I went upstairs, so I wondered, and I remembered I had left my door unlocked."

"Then you knew those things were there?"

Her face was white. She trembled. Her words came jerkily:

"Of course I didn't. I only kept my door locked because they had searched so thoroughly before. It was an humiliation I couldn't bear to face again."

"You don't know," he asked, "who took that stuff from Howells; who hid it in your bureau?"

The trembling of her slender body became more pronounced. She spoke through chattering teeth:

"Bobby! Why do you ask such things? You believe I am guilty as you thought I was the woman in black. You think now, because those things were in my bureau -"

"Stop, Katherine! You won't answer me?"

"No," she said, backing away from him. "But you are going to answer me. We have come to that point already. Just an hour or two of trust, and then this! It's the Cedars forcing us apart as it did when we had our quarrel. Only this time it is definite. Do you think I'm guilty of these atrocious crimes, or don't you? Everything for us depends on your answer, and I'll know whether you are telling me the truth."

"Then," he said, "why should I answer?"

And he took her in his arms and held her close.

She didn't cry, but for a moment she ceased trembling, and her teeth no longer chattered.

"My dear," he said, "even if you had hidden that evidence I'd have known it was to protect me."

Then she cried a little, and for a moment, even in the unmerciful grasp of their trouble, they were nearly happy. The footsteps of the others in the corridor recalled them. Katherine leaned against the table, drying her eyes. Graham, Robinson, and Rawlins walked into the hall.

"Hello!" Robinson said, "I suppose that isn't an unfair advantage, Mr. Blackburn. Still, I'd rather she hadn't been told."

"He's told me nothing," Katherine answered. "I came back to the corridor; I heard everything you said."

"Maybe it's as well," Robinson reflected. "It certainly is if what you heard has shown you the wisdom of giving up the whole thing."

She stared at him without replying.

"Come now," he wheedled. "You might tell us at least why you stole and secreted the evidence."

"I'll answer nothing."

"That's wiser, Katherine," Graham put in.

She turned on him with a complete and unexpected fury. The colour rushed back to her face. Her eyes blazed. Bobby had never guessed her capable of such anger. His wonder grew that her outburst should be directed against Graham.

"Keep quiet!" she cried hysterically. "Don't speak to me again. I hate you! Do you understand?"

Graham drew back.

"Why, Katherine -"

"Don't," she said. "Don't call me that."

The officers glanced at Graham with frank bewilderment. Rawlins's materialistic mind didn't hesitate to express its first thought:

"Must say, I always thought you were sweet on the lady."

"Hartley!" Bobby said. "You have been fair to us?"

"I don't know why she attacks me," Graham muttered.

His face recorded a genuine pain. His words, Bobby felt, overcame a barrier of emotion.

They heard Paredes and Doctor Groom on the stairs.

"What's this?" the doctor rumbled as he came up.

"I - I'm sorry I forgot myself," Katherine said through her

chattering teeth. She turned to Robinson. "I am going to my room. You needn't be afraid. I shan't leave it until you come to take me."

"Truly I hope it won't be necessary," the district attorney answered.

She hurried away. Rawlins grinned at Paredes.

"I'm wondering what the devil you know."

Robinson made no secret of what had happened. In reply to the questions of Paredes and the doctor he told of the discovery of the evidence and of the stout hat-pin that had, unquestionably, caused death. The man made it clear enough, however, that he didn't care to have Paredes know of Bobby's plan to spend the night in the old room, and Rawlins, Bobby, and Graham indicated that they understood.

"It's quite absurd that any one should think Katherine guilty," the doctor said to Robinson. "This evidence and its presence in her room are details that don't approach the heart of the mystery. That's to be found only in the old room, and I don't think any one wants to tempt it again. In fact, I'm not sure one can learn the truth there and live. You know what happened to Howells when he tried. Silas Blackburn went there, and none of us can understand the change that's taken place. I have been watching him closely. So has Mr. Paredes. We have seen him become grayer. We have seen his eyes alter. He sits shaking in his chair. Since we came back from the grave the man - if we can call him a man - seems to have - shrunk."

"Yes," Paredes said. "Perhaps we shouldn't have left him alone. Let us go back. Let us see if he is all right."

Rawlins laughed skeptically.

"You're not afraid he'll melt away!"

"I'm not so sure he won't," Paredes answered.

They followed him downstairs. Because of the position of Blackburn's chair they could be sure of nothing until they had reached the lower floor and approached the fireplace. Then they saw. It was as if Paredes's far-fetched fear had been realized. Blackburn was not in his chair, nor was he to be found in the hall. Even then, with the exception of Paredes, they wouldn't take the thing seriously. Since the old man wasn't in the hall; since he couldn't have gone upstairs, unobserved by them, he must be either in the library, the dining room, or the rear part of the house. There was no one in the library or the dining room; and Jenkins, who sat in the kitchen, still shaken by the discovery at the grave, said he hadn't moved for the last half hour, was entirely sure no one had come through from the front part of the house.

They returned to the hall and stood in a half circle about the empty chair, where a little while ago Silas Blackburn had cowered, mouthing snatches of his fear - "I'm not dead! I tell you I'm not dead! They can't make me go back -"

The echoes of that fear still shocked their ears.

There was a hypnotic power about the vacancy as there had been about the emptiness in the burial ground. Paredes spoke gropingly.

"What would we find," he whispered, "if we went to the cemetery and looked again in the coffin?"

"Why should he have come back at all?" Groom mused.

Robinson opened the front door.

"You know he might have gone this way."

But already the snow had obliterated the signs of their own passage in and out. It showed no fresh marks.

"Silas Blackburn has not gone that way in the body," Doctor Groom rumbled.

The storm was more violent. It discouraged the idea of examining the graveyard again before morning.

Robinson glanced at his watch. He led Bobby and the detective to the library.

"Then try your scheme if you want," he said, "but understand I assume no responsibility. Honestly, I doubt if it amounts to anything. You'll shout out if you are attacked, or the moment you suspect any real cause for fear. Rawlins will be in the corridor, and I'll be in the library or wandering about the house - always within call. Rawlins will guard the broken door, but be sure and lock the other one."

The two officers went upstairs with Bobby. Graham followed.

"You understand," Robinson said. "I'd rather Paredes and the doctor didn't suspect what you are going to do. Change your mind before it's too late, if you want."

Bobby walked on without replying.

"You can't dissuade him," Graham said, "because of what will happen to-morrow unless the truth is discovered to-night."

In the upper hall they found Katherine waiting. Her endeavours were hard to face.

"You shan't go there for me, Bobby," she said.

"Isn't it clear I must go in my own service?" he said, trying to smile.

He wouldn't speak to her again. He wouldn't look at her. Her anxiety and the affection in her eyes weakened him, and he needed all his strength, for at the entrance of the dark, narrow corridor the fear met him.

Rawlins brought a candle and guided him down the corridor. Graham came, too. The detective locked the door leading to the private hall and slipped the key in his pocket.

"Nobody will get through there any more than they will through the other door which I'll watch."

With Graham's help he made a quick inspection of the room, searching the closets and glancing beneath the bed and behind the furniture.

"There's no one," he said, preparing to depart. "I tell you there's no chance of a physical attack."

His unimaginative mind cried out.

"I tell you you'll find nothing, learn nothing, for there's nothing here to find, nothing to learn."

"Just the same," Graham urged, "you'll call out, won't you, Bobby, at the first sign of anything out of the way? For God's sake take no foolish chances."

"I don't want the light," Bobby forced himself to say. "My grandfather and Howells both put their candles out. I want everything as it was when they were attacked."

Rawlins nodded and, followed by Graham, carried the candle from the room and closed the broken door.

The sudden solitude and the darkness crushed Bobby, taking his breath. Yellow flames, the response of his eyes to the disappearance of the candle, tore across the blackness, confusing him. He felt his way to the wall near the open window. He sat down there, facing the bed.

At first he couldn't see the bed. He saw only the projections of his fancy, stimulated by Silas Blackburn's story, against the black screen of the night. He understood at last what the old man had meant. The darkness did appear to possess a physical resistance, and as the minutes lengthened it seemed to encase all the suffering the room had ever harboured. But he wouldn't close his eyes as his grandfather had done. It was a defence to keep them on the spot where the bed stood while his mind, in spite of his will, pictured, lying there, still forms with bandaged heads. He wouldn't close his eyes even when those fancied shapes commenced to struggle in grotesque and impotent motion, like ants whose hill has been demolished. Nor could he drive from his ears the echoes of delirium that seemed to have lingered in the old room. He continued to watch the darkness until the outlines of the room and of its furniture dimly detached themselves from the black pall. The snow apparently caught what feeble light the moon forced through, reflecting it with a disconsolate inefficiency. He could see after a time the pallid frames of the windows, the pillow on the bed, and the wall above it. He fancied the dark stain, the depression in the mattress where the two bodies had rested. Those physical objects forced on him the probability of his guilt. Then he recalled that both men, dead for many hours, had moved apparently of their own volition; and his grandfather had come back from the grave and then had disappeared, leaving no trace; and he comforted himself with the thought that the explanation, if it came at all, must arise from a force outside himself, whether of the living or the dead.

Because of that very assurance his fear of the room was incited. Could any subtle change overcome him here as it evidently had the others? Could there be repeated in his case a return and a disappearance like his grandfather's? There was, as Rawlins had said, no way in or out for an attack. Therefore the danger must emerge from the dead, and he was helpless before their incomprehensible campaign.

The whole illogical, abominable course of events warned him to bring his vigil to an end before it should be too late; urged him to escape from the restless revolt of the dead who had dwelt in this room. And he wanted to respond. He wanted to go to the corridor and confess to Rawlins and Robinson that he was beaten. Yet he had begged so hard for this chance! That course, moreover, meant the arrest of Katherine and himself in the morning. For a few hours he could suffer here for her sake. Daylight, if he could persist until then, would bring release, and surely it couldn't be long now.

He shrank back. Steadily it had grown colder in the old room. He shivered. He drew his coat closer about him. What temerity to invade the domain of death, as Paredes had called it, to seek the secrets of unquiet souls!

He ceased shivering. He waited, tensely quiet. Without calculation he realized that the moment for which he had hoped was at hand. The old room was about to disclose its secret, but would it permit him to depart with his knowledge? He forgot to call. He waited, helpless and terrified, against the wall. He heard a moaning cry, faint and distant - the voice they had heard in the forest and at the grave. But it was more than that that held him. He knew now what Katherine had heard across the court, heralding each tragedy and mystery. He caught a formless stirring. Yet on the bed there was no one. Fortunately he had not gone there.

He tried to call out, realizing that the danger could find him if it chose, but his throat was tight and it permitted no response.

His glance hadn't wavered from the wall above the stained pillow. There was movement there. Then he saw. A hand protruded from the blackness of the panelling where they had sounded and measured without success. In the ashen, unnatural light from the snow the long fingers of the hand were like the feelers of a gigantic reptile. They wavered feebly, and he became convinced that the hand was immaterial, that it was unattached to any body. If that was so it couldn't be the hand of Katherine. At least he had proved that Robinson and Rawlins had been wrong about her. That sense of victory stripped him of his paralyzing fear. It loosed the tight band about his throat. He called. He could prove the immaterial nature of the repulsive hand wavering from the wall.

Crying out, he sprang to his feet. He flung himself across the bed. With both of his own hands he grasped the slender, inquisitive fingers which wavered above the stained pillow, and once more his throat tightened. He couldn't cry out again.

CHAPTER X

THE CEDARS IS LEFT TO ITS SHADOWS

Straightway Bobby repented the alarm he had, perhaps too impulsively, given. For the hand protruding from the wall was, indeed, flesh and blood, and with the knowledge came back his fear for Katherine, conquering his first relief. A sick revulsion swept him. He remembered the evidence found in Katherine's room, and her refusal to answer questions. Could Paredes and the officers have been right? Was it conceivably her hand struggling weakly in his grasp?

The door from the corridor crashed open. Rawlins burst through. Graham ran after him. From the private stairway arose the sound of the district attorney's hurrying footsteps.

"What is it? What have you got?" Rawlins shouted.

Graham cried out:

"You're all right, Bobby?"

The candle which the detective carried gleamed on the slender fingers, showing Bobby that they had been inserted through an opening in the wall. He couldn't understand, for time after time each one of the panels had been sounded and examined. Beyond, he could see dimly the dark clothing of the person who, with a stealth in itself suggestive of abnormal crime, had made use of such a device. As Rawlins hurried up he wondered if it wouldn't be the better course to free his prisoner, to cry out, urging an escape.

Already it was too late. The detective and Graham had seen, and clearly they had no doubt that he held the one responsible for two brutal murders and for the confusing mysteries that had capped them.

"Looks like a lady's hand," Rawlins called. "Don't let go, young fellow."

He unlocked the door to the private hallway. Graham and he dashed out. In Bobby's uncertain grasp the hand twitched.

Robinson's voice reached him through the opening.

"Let go, Mr. Blackburn. You've done your share, the Lord knows. You've caught the beast with the goods."

Bobby released the slender fingers. He saw them vanish through the opening. He left the bed and reluctantly approached the door to the private hall. Excited phrases roared in his ears. He scarcely dared listen because of their possible confirmation of his doubt. The fingers, he repeated to himself, had been too slender. The moment that had freed him from fear of his own guilt had constructed in its place an uncertainty harder to face. Yet there was nothing to be gained by waiting. Sooner or later he must learn whether Katherine had hidden the evidence, whether she had used the stout and deadly hatpin, whether she struggled now in the grasp of vindictive men.

A voice from the corridor arrested him.

"Bobby!"

With a glad cry he swung around. Katherine stood in the opposite doorway. Her presence there, beyond a doubt, was her exculpation. He crossed the sombre room. He grasped her hands. He smiled happily. After all, the hand he had held was not as slender as hers.

"Thank heavens you're here."

In a word he recited the result of his vigil.

"It clears you," she said. "Quick! We must see who it is."

But he lingered, for he wanted that ugly fear done with once for all.

"You can tell me now how the evidence got in your room."

"I can't," she said. "I don't know."

The truth of her reply impressed him. He looked at her and wondered that she should be fully dressed.

"Why are you dressed?" he asked.

She was puzzled.

"Why not? I don't think any one had gone to bed."

"But it must be very late. I supposed it was the same time - half-past two."

She started to cross the room. She laughed nervously.

"It isn't eleven."

He recalled his interminable anticipation among the shadows of the old room.

"I've watched there only a little more than an hour!"

"Not much more than that, Bobby."

"What a coward! I'd have sworn it was nearly daylight."

She pressed his hand.

"No. Very brave," she whispered. "Let us see if it was worth it."

They stepped through the doorway. Half way down the hall Robinson, Graham, and Rawlins held a fourth, who had ceased struggling. Bobby paused, yet, since seeing Katherine step from the corridor, his reason had taught him to expect just this.

The fourth man was Paredes, nearly effeminate, slender-fingered.

"Carlos!" Bobby cried. "You can't have done these unspeakable things!"

The Panamanian stared without answering. Evidently he had had time to control his chagrin, to smother his revolt from the future; for the thin face was bare of emotion. The depths of the eyes as usual turned back scrutiny. The man disclosed neither guilt nor the outrage of an assumed innocence; neither confession nor denial. He simply stared, straining a trifle against the eager hands of his captors.

Rawlins grinned joyously.

"You ought to have a medal for getting away with this, young fellow. Things didn't look so happy for you an hour or so ago."

"And I had half a mind," Robinson confessed, "to refuse you the chance. Glad I didn't. Glad as I can be you made good."

With the egotism any man is likely to draw from his efforts in the detection of crime he added easily:

"Of course I've suspected this spigotty all along. I don't have to remind you of that."

"Sure," Rawlins said. "And didn't I put it up to him strong enough to-night?"

Paredes laughed lightly.

"All credit where it is due. You also put it up to Miss Perrine."

"The details will straighten all that out," Robinson said. "I don't pretend to have them yet."

"I gather not," Paredes mused, "with old Blackburn's ghost still in the offing."

"That talk," Rawlins said, "won't go down from you any more. I daresay you've got most of the details in your head."

"I daresay," Paredes answered dryly.

He fought farther back against the detaining hands.

"Is there any necessity for this exhibition of brute strength? You must find it very exhausting. You may think me dangerous, and I thank you; but I have no gun, and I'm no match for four men and a woman. Besides, you hurt my arm. Bobby was none too tender with that. I ought to have used my good arm. You'll get no details from me unless you take your hands off."

Robinson's hesitation was easily comprehensible. If Paredes were responsible for the abnormalities they had experienced at the Cedars he might find it simple enough to trick them now, but the man's mocking smile brought the anger to Robinson's face.

"Of course he can't get away. See if there's anything on his clothes, Rawlins. He ought to have the hatpin. Then let him go."

The detective, however, failed to find the hatpin or any other weapon.

"You see," Paredes smiled. "That's something in my favour."

He stepped back, brushing his clothing with his uninjured hand. He lighted a cigarette. He drew back the coat sleeve of his left arm and readjusted the bandage. He glanced up as heavy footsteps heralded Doctor Groom.

"Hello, Doctor," he called cheerily. "I was afraid you'd nap through the show. It seems the bloodhounds of the law left us out of their confidence."

"What's all this?" the doctor rumbled.

Paredes waved his hand.

"I am a prisoner."

The doctor gaped.

"You mean you -"

"Young Blackburn caught him," Robinson explained. "He was in a position to finish him just as he did Howells."

"Except that I had no hatpin," Paredes yawned.

The doctor's uneasy glance sought the opening in the wall.

"I thought you had examined all these walls," he grumbled. "How did you miss this?"

Robinson ran his fingers through his hair.

"That's what I've been asking myself," he said. "I went over that panelling a dozen times myself."

Bobby and Katherine went closer. Bobby had been from the first puzzled by Paredes's easy manner. He had a quick hope. He saw the man watch with an amused tolerance while the district attorney bent over, examining the face of the panel.

"An entire section," Robinson said - "the thickness of the wall - has been shifted to one side. No wonder we didn't see any joints or get a hollow sound from this panel any more than from the others. But why didn't we stumble on the mechanism? Maybe you'll tell us that, Paredes."

The Panamanian blew a wreath of smoke against the ancient wall.

"Gladly, but you will find it humiliating. I have experienced humility in this hall myself. The reason you didn't find any mechanism is that there wasn't any. You looked for something most cautiously concealed, not realizing that the best concealment is no concealment at all. It's fundamental. I don't know how it slipped my own mind. No grooves show because the door is an entire panel. There isn't even a latch. You merely push hard against its face. Such arrangements are common enough in colonial houses, and there was more than the nature of the crimes to tell you there was some such thing here. I mean if you will examine the farther door closer than you have done you will find that it has fewer coats of paint than the one leading to the corridor, that its frame is of newer wood. In other words, it was cut through after the wing was built. This panel was the original door, designed, with the private stairway and the hall, for the exclusive use of the master of the house. Try it."

Robinson braced himself and shoved against the panel. It moved in its grooves with a vibrant stirring.

"Rusty," he said.

Katherine started.

"That's what I heard each time," she cried.

Above his heavy black beard the doctor's cheeks whitened. Robinson made a gesture of revulsion.

"That gives the nasty game away."

"Naturally," Paredes said, "and you must admit the game is as beautifully simple as the panel. The instrument of death wasn't inserted through the bedding as you thought inevitable, Doctor. Suppose you were lying in that bed, asleep, or half asleep, and you were aroused by such a sound as that in the wall behind you? What would you do? What would any man do first of all?"

Robinson nodded.

"I see what you mean. I'd get up on my elbow. I'd look around as quickly as I could to see what it was. I'd expose myself to a clean thrust. I'd drop back on the bed, more thoroughly out of it than though I'd been struck through the heart."

"Exactly," Paredes said, with the familiar shrug of his shoulders.

"You're sensible to give up this way," Robinson said. "It's the best plan for you. What about Mr. Blackburn?"

Graham interfered.

"After all," he said thoughtfully. "I'm a lawyer, and it isn't fair, Robinson. It's only decent to tell him that anything he says may be used against him."

"Keep your mouth shut," Robinson shouted.

But Paredes smiled at Graham.

"It's very good of you, but I agree with the district attorney. There's no point in being a clam now."

"Can you account for Silas Blackburn's return?" the doctor asked eagerly.

"That's right, Doctor," Paredes said. "Stick to the ghosts. I fancy there are plenty in this house. I'm afraid we must look on Silas Blackburn as dead."

"You don't mean we've been talking to a dead man?" Katherine whispered.

"Before I answer," Paredes said, "I want to have one or two things straight. These men, Bobby, I really believe, think me capable of the crimes in this house. I want to know if you accept such a theory. Do you think I had any idea of killing you?"

Bobby studied the reserved face which even now was without emotion.

"I can't think anything of the kind," he said softly.

"That's very nice," Paredes said. "If you had answered differently I'd have let these clever policemen lay their own ghosts."

He turned to Robinson.

"Even you must begin to see that I'm not guilty. Your common sense will tell you so. If I had been planning to kill Bobby, why didn't I bring the weapon? Why did I put my hand through the opening before I was ready to strike? Why did I use my left hand - my injured hand? I was like Howells. I couldn't consider the case finished until I had solved the mystery of the locked doors. I supposed the room was empty. When I found the secret to-night, I reached through to see how far my hand would be from the pillow."

Bobby's assurance of Paredes's innocence clouded his own situation; made it, in a sense, more dangerous than it had ever been. His wanderings about the Cedars remained unexplained, and they knew now it had never been necessary for the murderer to enter the room, Katherine, too, evidently realized the menace.

"Do you think I -" she began.

Paredes bowed.

"You dislike me, Miss Katherine, but don't be afraid for yourself or Bobby. I think I can tell you how the evidence got in your room. I can answer nearly everything. There's one point -"

He broke off, glancing at his watch.

"Extraordinary courage!" he mused enigmatically. "I scarcely understand it."

Rawlins looked at him suspiciously.

"All this explaining may be a trick, Mr. Robinson. The man's slippery."

"I've had to be slippery to work under your noses," Paredes laughed. "By the way, Bobby, did you hear a woman crying about the time I opened this door?"

"Yes. It sounded like the voice we heard at the grave."

"I thought I heard it from the library," Robinson put in. "Then the rumpus up here started, and I forgot about it."

"The woman in black is very brave," Paredes mused. "We should have had a visit from her long before this."

"Do you know who she is?" Robinson asked. "And as Rawlins

says, no tricks. We haven't let you go yet."

"I thought," Paredes mocked, "that you had identified the woman in black as Miss Katherine. She hasn't had anything to do with the mystery directly. Neither has Bobby. Neither have I."

"Then what the devil have you been doing here?" Robinson snapped.

"Seeing your job through," Paredes answered, "for Bobby's sake."

With a warm gratitude Bobby knew that Paredes had told the truth. Then he had told it in the library yesterday when they had caught him prowling in the private staircase. All along he had told it while they had tried to convict him of underhanded and unfriendly intentions.

"I saw," Paredes was saying, "that Howells wouldn't succeed, and it was obvious you and Rawlins would do worse, while Graham's blundering from the start left no hope. Somebody had to rescue Bobby."

"Then why did you give us the impression," Graham asked, "that you were not a friend?"

Paredes held up his hand.

"That's going rather far, Mr. Graham. Never once have I given such an impression. I have time after time stated the fact that I was here in Bobby's service. That has been the trouble with all of you. As most detectives do, you have denied facts, searching always for something more subtle. You have asked for impossibilities while you blustered that they couldn't exist. Still every one is prone to do that when he fancies himself in the presence of the supernatural. The facts of this case have been within your reach as well as mine. The motive has been an easy one to understand. Money! And you have consistently turned your back."

Robinson spread his hands.

"All right. Prove that I'm a fool and I'll acknowledge it."

Doctor Groom interrupted sharply.

"What was that?"

They bent forward, listening. Even with Paredes offering them a physical explanation they shrank from the keening that barely survived the heavy atmosphere of the old house.

"You see the woman in black isn't Miss Perrine," Paredes said.

He ran down the stairs. They followed, responding to an excited sense of imminence. Even in the private staircase the pounding that had followed the cry reached them with harsh reverberations. Its echoes filled the house as they dashed across the library and the dining room. In the hall they realized that it came from the front door. It had attained a feverish, a desperate insistence.

Paredes walked to the fireplace.

"Open the door," he directed Rawlins.

Rawlins stepped to the door, unlocked it, and flung it wide.

"The woman!" Katherine breathed.

A feminine figure, white with snow, stumbled in, as if she had stood braced against the door. Rawlins caught her and held her upright. The flakes whirled from the court in vicious pursuit. Bobby slammed the door shut.

"Maria!" he cried. "You were right, Hartley!"

Yet at first he could scarcely accept this pitiful creature as the brilliant and exotic dancer with whom he had dined the night of the first murder. As he stared at her, her features twisted. She burst into retching sobs. She staggered toward Paredes. As she went the snow melted from her hat and cloak. She became a black figure again. With an appearance of having been immersed in water she sank on the hearth, swaying back and forth, reaching blindly for Paredes's hand.

"Do what you please with me, Carlos," she whimpered with her slight accent from which all the music had fled. "I couldn't stand it another minute. I couldn't get to the station, and I - I wanted to know which - which -"

Paredes watched her curiously.

"Get Jenkins," he said softly to Rawlins.

He faced Maria again.

"I could have told you, I think, when you fought me away out there. No one wants to arrest you. Jenkins will verify my own knowledge."

"This is dangerous," the doctor rumbled. "This woman shouldn't wait here. She should have dry clothing at once."

Maria shrank from him. For the first time her wet skirt exposed her feet, encased in torn stockings. The dancer wore no shoes, and Bobby guessed why she had been so elusive, why she had left so few traces.

"I won't go," she cried, "until he tells me."

Katherine got a cloak and threw it across the woman's shoulders. Maria looked up at her with a dumb gratitude. Then Rawlins came back with Jenkins. The butler was bent and haggard. His surrender to fear was more pronounced than it had been at the grave or when they had last seen him in the kitchen. He grasped a chair and, breathing heavily, looked from one to the other, moistening his lips.

Paredes faced the man, completely master of the situation. Through the old butler, it became clear, he would make his revelation and announce that simple fact they all had missed.

"It was Mr. Silas, of course, who came back?"

"Oh my God!" the butler moaned, "What do you mean?"

"I know everything, Jenkins," Paredes said evenly.

The butler collapsed against the chair. Paredes grasped his arm.

"Pull yourself together, man. They won't want you as more than an accessory."

Maria started to rise. She shrank back again, shivering close to the fire.

"Is your master hiding," Paredes asked, "or has he left the house?"

Jenkins's answer came through trembling lips.

"He's gone! Mr. Silas is gone! How did you find out? My God! How did you find out?"

"He said nothing to you?" Paredes asked.

Jenkins shook his head.

"Tell me how he was dressed."

The old servant covered his face.

"Mr. Silas stumbled through the kitchen," he answered hoarsely. "I tried to stop him, but he pushed me away and ran out." His voice rose. "I tell you he ran without a coat or a hat into the storm."

Paredes sighed.

"The Cedars's final tragedy, yet it was the most graceful exit he could have made."

Maria struggled to her feet. Her eyes were the eyes of a person without reason. That familiar, hysterical quality which they had heard before at a distance vibrated in her voice.

"Then he was the one! I wanted to kill him, I couldn't kill him because I never was sure."

"Did you see him go out an hour or so ago?" Paredes asked.

"I saw him," she cried feverishly, "run from the back of the house and down the path to the lake. I - I tried to catch him, but my feet were frozen, and the snow was slippery, and I couldn't find my shoes. But I called and he wouldn't stop. I had to know, because I wanted to kill him if it was Silas Blackburn. And I saw him run to the lake and splash in until the water was over his head."

She flung her clenched hands out. Her voice became a scream, shot with all her suffering, all her doubt, all her fury.

"You don't understand. He can't be punished. I tell you he's at the bottom of the lake with the man he murdered. And I can't pay him. I tried to go after him, but it - it was too cold."

She sank in one of the chairs, shaking and sobbing.

"Unless we want another tragedy," the doctor said, "this woman must be put to bed and taken care of. She has been terribly exposed. You've heard her. She's delirious."

"Not so delirious that she hasn't told the truth," Paredes said.

The doctor lifted her in his arms and with Rawlins's help carried her upstairs. Katherine went with them. Almost immediately the doctor and Rawlins hurried down.

"I have told Katherine what to do," Doctor Groom said. "The woman may be all right in the morning. What's she been up to here?"

"Then," Bobby cried, "there was a connection between the dinner party and the murders. But what about my coming here unconscious? What about my handkerchief?"

"I can see no answer yet," Graham said.

Paredes smiled.

"Not when you've had the answer to everything? I have shown you that Silas Blackburn was the murderer. The fact stared you in the face. Everything that has happened at the Cedars has pointed to his guilt."

"Except," the doctor said, "his own apparent murder which made his guilt seem impossible. And I'm not sure you're right now, for there is no other Blackburn he could have murdered, and Blackburns look alike. You wouldn't mistake another man for one of them."

"This house," Paredes smiled, "has all along been full of the presence of the other Blackburn. There has been evidence enough for you all to have known he was here."

He stretched himself in an easy chair. He lighted a cigarette and blew the smoke toward the ceiling.

"I shall tell you the simple facts, if only to save my skin from this blood-thirsty district attorney."

"Rub it in," Robinson grinned. "I'll take my medicine."

They gathered closer about the Panamanian. Jenkins sidled to the back of his chair.

"I don't see how you found it out," he muttered.

"I had only one advantage over you or the police, Graham," Paredes began, "and you were in a position to overcome that. Maria did telephone me the afternoon of that ghastly dinner. She asked me to get hold of Bobby. She was plainly anxious to keep him in New York that night, and, to be frank, I was glad enough to help her when you turned up, trying to impress us with your puritan watchfulness. Even you guessed that she had drugged Bobby. I suspected it when I saw him go to pieces in the cafe. He gave me the slip, as I told you, in the coat room when I was trying to get him home, so I went back and asked Maria what her idea was. She laughed in my face, denying everything. I, too, suspected the stranger, but I've convinced myself that he simply happened along by chance.

"Now here's the first significant point: Maria by drugging Bobby defeated her own purpose. He had been drinking more than the Band of Hope would approve of, and on top of that he got an overdose of a powerful drug. The doctor can tell you better than I of the likely effect of such a combination."

"What I told you in the court, Bobby," the doctor answered, "much the same symptoms as genuine aphasia. Your brain was unquestionably dulled by an overdose on top of all that alcohol, while your mechanical reflexes were stimulated. Automatically you followed your ruling impulse. Automatically at the last minute you revolted from exposing yourself in such a condition to your cousin and your grandfather. Your lucid period in the woods just before you reached the deserted house and went to sleep showed that your exercise was overcoming the effect of the drug. That moment, you'll remember, was coloured by the fanciful ideas such a drug would induce."

"So, Bobby," Paredes said, "although you were asleep when the body moved and when Howells was murdered, you can be sure you weren't anywhere near the old room."

"But I walked in my sleep last night," Bobby reminded him.

The doctor slapped his knee.

"I understand. It was only when we thought that was your habit that it frightened us. It's plain. This sleep-walking had been suggested to you and you had brooded upon the suggestion until you were bound to respond. Graham's presence in your room, watching for just that reaction, was a perpetual, an unescapable stimulation. It would have been a miracle in itself if your brain had failed to carry it out."

Bobby made a swift gesture of distaste.

"If you hadn't come, Carlos, where would I have been?"

"Why did you come?" Graham asked.

"Bobby was my friend," the Panamanian answered. "He had been very good to me. When I read of his grandfather's death I wondered why Maria had drugged him to keep him in New York. In the coincidence lurked an element of trouble for him. At first I suspected some kind of an understanding between her and old Blackburn - perhaps she had engaged to keep Bobby away from the Cedars until the new will had been made. But here was Blackburn murdered, and it was manifest she hadn't tried to throw suspicion on Bobby, and the points that made Howells's case incomplete assured me of his innocence. Who, then, had killed his grandfather? Not Maria, for I had dropped her at her apartment that night too late for her to get out here by the hour of the murder. Still, as you suspected, Maria was the key, and I began to speculate about her.

"She had told me something of her history. You might have had as much from her press agent. Although she had lived in Spain since she was a child, she was born in Panama, my own country, of a Spanish mother and an American father. Right away I wondered if Blackburn had ever been in Panama or Spain. I began to seek the inception of the possible understanding between them. Since I found no illuminating documents about Blackburn's past in the library, I concluded, if such papers existed, they would be locked up in the desk in his room. I searched there a number of times, giving you every excuse I could think of to get upstairs. The other night, after I had suspected her of knowing something, Miss Katherine nearly caught me. But I found what I wanted - a carefully hidden packet of accounts and letters and newspaper clippings. They're at your service, Mr. District Attorney. They told me that Silas Blackburn had been in Panama. They proved that Maria, instead of ever having been his accomplice, was his enemy. They explained the source of his wealth and the foundation of that enmity. Certainly you remember the doctor told us Silas Blackburn started life with nothing; and hadn't you ever wondered why with all his money he buried himself in this lonely hole?"

"He returned from South America, rich, more than twenty-five years ago," the doctor said. "Why should we bother about his money?"

"I wish you had bothered about several things besides your ghosts," Paredes said. "You'd have found it significant that Blackburn laid the foundation of his fortune in Panama during the hideous scandals of the old French canal company. We knew he was a selfish tyrant. That discovery showed me how selfish, how merciless he was, for to succeed in Panama during those days required an utter contempt for all the standards of law and decency. The men who got along held life cheaper than a handful of coppers. That's what I meant when I walked around the hall talking of the ghosts of Panama. For I was beginning to see. Silas Blackburn's fear, his trip to Smithtown, were the first indications of the presence of the other Blackburn. The papers outlined him more clearly. Why had it been forgotten here, Doctor, that Silas Blackburn had a brother - his partner in those wretched and profitable contract scandals?"

"You mean," the doctor answered, "Robert Blackburn. He was a year younger than Silas. This boy was named in memory of him. Why should any one have remembered? He died in South America more than a quarter of a century ago, before these children were born."

"That's what Silas Blackburn told you when he came back," Paredes said. "He may have believed it at first or he may not have. I daresay he wanted to, for he came back with his brother's money as well as his own - the cash and the easily convertible securities that were all men would handle in that hell. But he never forgot that his brother's wife was alive, and when he ran from Panama he knew she was about to become a mother.

"That brings me to the other feature that made me wander around here like a restless spirit myself that night. You had just told your story about the woman crying. If there was a strange woman around here it was almost certainly Maria. As Rawlins deduced, she must either be hysterical or signalling some one. Why should she come unless something had gone wrong the night she drugged Bobby to keep him in New York? She wasn't his enemy, because that very night she did him a good turn by trampling out his tracks in the court."

Bobby took Maria's letter from his pocket and handed it to Paredes.

"Then how would you account for this?"

The Panamanian read the letter.

"Her way of covering herself," he explained, "in case you suspected she had made you drink too much or had drugged you. She really wanted you to come to tea that afternoon. It was after writing that that she found out what had gone wrong. In other words, she read in the paper of Silas Blackburn's death, and in a panic she put on plain clothes and hurried out to see what had happened. The fact that she forgot her managers, her professional reputation, everything, testified to her anxiety, and I began to sense the truth. She had been born in Panama of a Spanish mother and an American father. She had some stealthy interest in the Cedars and the Blackburns. She was about the right age. Ten to one she was Silas Blackburn's niece. So for me, many hours before Silas Blackburn walked in here, the presence of the other Blackburn about the Cedars became a tragic and threatening inevitability. Had Silas Blackburn been murdered or had his brother? Where was the survivor who had committed that brutal murder? Maria had come here hysterically to answer those questions. She might know. The light in the deserted house! She might be hiding him and taking food to him there. But her crying suggested a signal which he never answered. At any rate, I had to find Maria. So I slipped out. I thought I heard her at the lake. She wasn't there. I was sure I would trap her at the deserted house, for the diffused glow of the light we had seen proved that it had come through the cobwebbed windows of the cellar, which are set in little wells below the level of the ground. The cellar explained also how she had turned her flashlight off and slipped through the hall and out while we searched the rooms. She hadn't gone back. I couldn't find her. So I went on into Smithtown and sent a costly cable to my father. His answer came to-night just before Silas Blackburn walked in. He had talked with several of the survivors of those evil days. He gave me a confirmation of everything I had gathered from the papers. The Blackburns had quarrelled over a contract. Robert had been struck over the head. He wandered about the isthmus, half-witted, forgetting his name, nursing one idea. Someone had robbed him, and he wanted his money back or a different kind of payment, but he couldn't remember who, and he took it out in angry talk. Then he disappeared, and people said he had gone to Spain. Of course his wife suspected a good deal. In Blackburn's desk are pitiful and threatening letters from her which he ignored. Then she died, and Blackburn thought he was safe. But he took no chances. Some survivor of those days might turn up and try blackmail. It was safer to bury himself here."

"Then," Bobby said, "Maria must have brought her father with her when she came from Spain last summer."

"Brought him or sent for him," Paredes answered. "She's made most of her money on this side, you know. And she's as loyal and generous as she is impulsive. Undoubtedly she had the doctors do what they could for her father, and when she got track of Silas Blackburn through you, Bobby, she nursed in the warped brain that dominant idea with her own Latin desire for justice and payment."

"Then," Graham said, "that's what Silas Blackburn was afraid of instead of Bobby, as he tried to convince us to-night to cover himself."

"One minute, Mr. Paredes," Robinson broke in. "Why did you maintain this extraordinary secrecy? Nobody would have hurt you if you had put us on the right track and asked for a little help. Why did you throw sand in our eyes? Why did you talk all the time about ghosts?"

"I had to go on tiptoe," Paredes smiled. "I suspected there was at least one spy in the house. So I gave the doctor's ghost talk all the impetus I could. I was like Howells, as I've told you, in believing the case couldn't be complete without the discovery of the secret entrance of the room of death. My belief in the existence of such a thing made me lean from the first to Silas Blackburn rather than Robert. It's a tradition in many families to hand such things down to the head of each generation. Silas Blackburn was the one most likely to know. Such a secret door had never been mentioned to you, had it, Bobby?"

Bobby shook his head. Paredes turned and smiled at the haggard butler.

"I'm right so far, am I not, Jenkins?"

Jenkins bobbed his head jerkily.

"Then," Paredes went on, "you might answer one or two questions. When did the first letter that frightened your master come?"

"The day he went to Smithtown and talked to the detective," the butler quavered.

"You can understand his reflections," Paredes mused. "Money was his god. He distrusted and hated his own flesh and blood because he thought they coveted it. He was prepared to punish them by leaving it to a public charity. Now arises this apparition from the past with no claim in a court of law, with an intention simply to ask, and, in case of a refusal, to punish. The conclusion reached by that selfish and merciless mind was inevitable. He probably knew nothing whatever about Maria. If all the world thought his brother dead, his brother's murder now wouldn't alter anything. I'll wager, Doctor, that at that time he talked over wounds at the base of the brain with you."

The doctor moved restlessly.

"Yes. But he was very superstitious. We talked about it in connection with his ancestors who had died of such wounds in that room."

"Everything was ready when he made the rendezvous here," Paredes went on. "He expected to have Bobby at hand in case his plan failed and he had to defend himself. But Maria had made sure that there should be no help for him. When the man came did you take him upstairs, Jenkins?"

"No, sir. I watched that Miss Katherine didn't leave the library, but I think she must have caught Mr. Silas in the upper hall after he had pretended to give up and had persuaded his brother to spend the night."

Paredes smiled whimsically. He took two faded photographs from his pocket. They were of young men, after the fashion of Blackburns, remarkably alike even without the gray, obliterating marks of old age.

"I found these in the family album," he said.

"We should have known the difference just the same," the doctor grumbled. "Why didn't we know the difference?"

"I've complained often enough," Paredes smiled, "of the necessity of using candles in this house. There was never more than one candle in the old bedroom. There were only two when we looked at the murdered man in his coffin. And in death there are no familiar facial expressions, no eccentricities of speech. So you can imagine my feelings when I tried to picture the drama that had gone on in that room. You can imagine poor Maria's. Which one? And Maria didn't know about the panel, or the use of Miss Katherine's hat-pin, or the handkerchief. All of those details indicated Silas Blackburn."

"How could my handkerchief indicate anything of the kind?" Bobby asked, "How did it come there?"

"What," Paredes said, "is the commonest form of borrowing in the world, particularly in a climate where people have frequent colds? I found a number of your handkerchiefs in your grandfather's bureau. The handkerchief furnished me with an important clue. It explains, I think, Jenkins will tell you, the moving of the body. It was obviously the cause of Howells's death."

"Yes, sir," Jenkins quavered. "Mr. Silas thought he had dropped his own handkerchief in the room with the body. I don't know how you've found these things out."

"By adding two and two," Paredes laughed. "In the first place, you must all realize that we might have had no mystery at all if it hadn't been for Miss Katherine. For I don't know that Maria could have done much in a legal way. Silas Blackburn had intended to dispose of the body immediately, but Miss Katherine heard the panel move and ran to the corridor. She made Jenkins break down the door, and she sent for the police. Silas Blackburn was helpless. He was beaten at that moment, but he did the best he could. He went to Waters, hoping, at the worst, to establish an alibi through the book-worm who probably wouldn't remember the exact hour of his arrival. Waters's house offered him, too, a strategic advantage. You heard him say the spare room was on the ground floor. You heard him add that he refused to open his door, either asking to be left alone or failing to answer at all. And he had to return to the Cedars the next day, for he missed his handkerchief, and he pictured himself, since he thought it was his own, in the electric chair. I'm right, Jenkins?"

"Yes, sir. I kept him hidden and gave him his chance along in the afternoon. He wanted me to try to find the handkerchief, but I didn't have the courage. He couldn't find it. He searched through the panel all about the body and the bed."

"That was when Katherine heard," Bobby said, "when we found the body had been moved."

"It put him in a dreadful way," Jenkins mumbled, "for no one had bothered to tell me it was young Mr. Robert the detective suspected, and when Mr. Silas heard the detective boast that he knew everything and would make an arrest in the morning, he thought about the handkerchief and knew he was done for unless he took Howells up. And the man did ask for trouble, sir. Well! Mr. Silas gave it to him to save himself."

"I've never been able to understand," Paredes said, "why he didn't take the evidence when he killed Howells."

"Didn't you know you prevented that, sir?" Jenkins asked. "I heard you come in from the court. I thought you'd been listening. I signalled Mr. Silas there was danger and to get out of the private stairway before you could trap him. And I couldn't give him another chance for a long time. Some of you were in the room after that, or Miss Katherine and Mr. Graham were sitting in the corridor watching the body until just before Mr. Robert tried to get the evidence for himself. Mr. Silas had to act then. It was his last chance, for he thought Mr. Robert would be glad enough to turn him over to the law."

"Why did you ever hide that stuff in Miss Katherine's room?" Bobby asked.

Jenkins flung up his hands.

"Oh, he was angry, sir, when he knew the truth and learned what a mistake he'd made. Howells didn't give me that report I showed you. It was in his pocket with the other things. We got it open without tearing the envelope and Mr. Silas read it. He wouldn't destroy anything. He never dreamed of anybody's suspecting Miss Katherine, so he told me to hide the things in her bureau. I think he figured on using the evidence to put the blame on Mr. Robert in case it was the only way to save himself."

"Why did you show the report to me?" Bobby asked.

"I - I was afraid to take all that responsibility," the butler quavered. "I figured if you were partly to blame it might go easier with me."

Paredes shrugged his shoulders.

"You were a good mate for Silas Blackburn," he sneered.

"Even now I don't see how that old scoundrel had the courage to show himself to-night," Rawlins said.

"That's the beautiful justice of the whole thing," Paredes answered, "for there was nothing else whatever for him to do. There never had been anything else for him to do since Miss Katherine had spoiled his scheme, since you all believed that it was he who had been murdered. He had to hide the truth or face the electric chair. If he disappeared he was infinitely worse off than though he had settled with his brother - a man without a home, without a name, without a penny."

Jenkins nodded.

"He had to come back," he said slowly, "and he knew how scared you were of the old room."

"The funeral and the snow," Paredes said, "gave him his chance. Jenkins will doubtless tell you how they uncovered the grave late this afternoon, took that poor devil's body, and threw it in the lake, then fastened the coffin and covered it again. Of course the snow effaced every one of their tracks. He came in, naturally scared to death, and told us that story based on the legends of the Cedars and the doctor's supernatural theories. And you must admit that he might, as you call it, have got away with it. He did create a mystification. The body of the murdered man had disappeared. There was no murdered Blackburn as far as you could tell. Heaven knows how long you might have struggled with the case of Howells."

He glanced up.

"Here is Miss Katherine."

She stood at the head of the stairs.

"I think she's all right," she said to the doctor. "She's asleep. She went to sleep crying. May I come down?"

The doctor nodded. She walked down, glancing from one to the other questioningly.

"Poor Maria!" Paredes mused. "She's the one I pity most. She's been at times, I think, what Rawlins suspected - an insane woman, wandering and crying through the woods. Assuredly she was out of her head to-night, when I found her finally at the grave. I tried to tell her that her father was dead. I begged her to come in. I told her we were friends. But she fought. She wouldn't answer my questions. She struck me finally when I tried to force her to come out of the storm. Robinson, I want you to listen to me for a moment. I honestly believe, for everybody's sake, I did a good thing when I asked Silas Blackburn just before he disappeared why he had thrown his brother's body in the lake. I'd hoped it would simply make him run for it. I prayed that we would never hear from him again, and that Miss Katherine and Bobby could be spared the ugly scandal. Doesn't this do as well? Can't we get along without much publicity?"

"You've about earned the right to dictate," Robinson said gruffly.

"Thanks."

"For everybody's sake!" Bobby echoed. "You're right, Carlos. Maria must be considered now. She shall have what was taken from her father, with interest. I know Katherine will agree."

Katherine nodded.

"I doubt if Maria will want it or take it," Paredes said simply. "She has plenty of her own. It isn't fair to think it was greed that urged her. You must understand that it was a bigger impulse than greed. It was a thing of which we of Spanish blood are rather proud - a desire for justice, for something that has no softer name than revenge."

Suddenly Rawlins stooped and took the Panamanian's hand.

"Say! We've been giving you the raw end of a lot of snap judgments. We've never got acquainted until to-night."

"Glad to meet you, too," Robinson grinned.

Rawlins patted the Panamanian's shoulder.

"At that, you'd make a first-class detective."

Paredes yawned.

"I disagree with you thoroughly. I have no equipment beyond my eyes and my common sense."

He yawned again. He arranged the card table in front of the fire. He got the cards and piled them in neat packs on the green cloth. He placed a box of cigarettes convenient to his right hand. He smoked.

"I'm very sleepy, but I've been so stupid over this solitaire since I've been at the Cedars that I must solve it in the interest of my self-respect before I go to bed."

Bobby went to him impulsively.

"I'm ashamed, Carlos. I don't know what to say. How can I say anything? How can I begin to thank you?"

"If you ever tell me I saved your life," Paredes yawned, "I shall have to disappear because then you'd have a claim on me."

Katherine touched his hand. There were tears in her eyes. It wasn't necessary for her to speak. Paredes indicated two chairs.

"If you aren't too tired, sit here and help me for a while. Perhaps between us we'll get somewhere. I wonder why I have been so stupid with the thing."

After a time, as he manipulated the cards, he laughed lightly.

"The same thing - the thing I've been scolding you all for. With a perfectly simple play staring me in the face I nearly made the mistake of choosing a difficult one. That would have got me in trouble while the simple one gives me the game. Why are people like that?"

As he moved the cards with a deft assurance to their desired combination he smiled drolly at Graham, Rawlins, and Robinson.

"I guess it must be human nature. Don't you think so, Mr. District Attorney?"

*   *   *   *   *

The condition Paredes had more than once foreseen was about to shroud the Cedars in loneliness and abandonment. After the hasty double burial in the old graveyard the few things Bobby and Katherine wanted from the house had been packed and taken to the station. At Katherine's suggestion they had decided to leave last of all and to walk. Paredes with a tender solicitude had helped Maria to the waiting automobile. He came back, trying to colour his good-bye with cheerfulness.

"After all, you may open the place again and let me visit you."

"You will visit us perpetually," Bobby said, while Katherine pressed the Panamanian's hand, "but never here again. We will leave it to its ghosts, as you have often prophesied."

"I am not sure," Paredes said thoughtfully, "that the ghosts aren't here."

It was evident that Graham wished to speak to Bobby and Katherine alone, so the Panamanian strolled back to the automobile. Graham's embarrassment made them all uncomfortable.

"You have not said much to me, Katherine," he began. "Is it because I practically lied to Bobby, trying to keep you apart?"

She tried to smile.

"I, too, must ask forgiveness. I shouldn't have spoken to you as I did the other night in the hall, but I thought, because you saw Bobby and I had come together, that you had spied on me, had deliberately tricked me, knowing the evidence was in my room. Of course you did try to help Bobby."

"Yes," he said, "and I tried to help you that night. I was sure you were innocent. I believed the best way to prove it to them was to let them search. The two of you have nothing worse than jealousy to reproach me with."

In a sense it pleased Bobby that Graham, who had always made him feel unworthy in Katherine's presence, should confess himself not beyond reproach.

"Come, Hartley," he cried, "I was beginning to think you were perfect. We'll get along all the better, the three of us, for having had it out."

Graham murmured his thanks. He joined Paredes and Maria in the automobile. As they drove off Paredes turned. His face, as he waved a languid farewell, was quite without expression.

Bobby and Katherine were left alone to the thicket and the old house. After a time they walked through the court and from the shadow of the time-stained, melancholy walls. At the curve of the driveway they paused and looked back. The shroud of loneliness and abandonment descending upon the Cedars became for them nearly ponderable. So they turned from that brooding picture, and hand in hand walked out of the forest into the friendly and welcoming sunlight.

Choose from Thousands of 1stWorldLibrary Classics By

A. M. Barnard
Ada Leverson
Adolphus William Ward
Aesop
Agatha Christie
Alexander Aaronsohn
Alexander Kielland
Alexandre Dumas
Alfred Gatty
Alfred Ollivant
Alice Duer Miller
Alice Turner Curtis
Alice Dunbar
Ambrose Bierce
Amelia E. Barr
Amory H. Bradford
Andrew Lang
Andrew McFarland Davis
Andy Adams
Anna Sewell
Annie Besant
Annie Hamilton Donnell
Annie Payson Call
Annonaymous
Anton Chekhov
Arnold Bennett
Arthur Conan Doyle
Arthur M. Winfield
Arthur Ransome
Atticus
B.H. Baden-Powell
B. M. Bower
Baroness Emmuska Orczy
Baroness Orczy
Basil King
Bayard Taylor
Ben Macomber
Bertha Muzzy Bower
Bjornstjerne Bjornson
Booth Tarkington
Boyd Cable
Bram Stoker
C. Collodi
C. E. Orr
C. M. Ingleby
Carolyn Wells
Catherine Parr Traill
Charles A. Eastman
Charles Dickens

Charles Dudley Warner
Charles Farrar Browne
Charles Ives
Charles Kingsley
Charles Klein
Charles Amory Beach
Charles Hanson Towne
Charles Lathrop Pack
Charles Whibley
Charles Willing Beale
Charlotte M. Braeme
Charlotte M. Yonge
Charlotte Perkins Stetson
Clair W. Hayes
Clarence Day Jr.
Clarence E. Mulford
Clemence Housman
Confucius
Cornelis DeWitt Wilcox
Cyril Burleigh
D. H. Lawrence
Daniel Defoe
David Garnett
Dinah Craik
Don Carlos Janes
Donald Keyhoe
Dorothy Kilner
Dougan Clark
Douglas Fairbanks
E. Nesbit
E.P.Roe
E. Phillips Oppenheim
Earl Barnes
Edgar Rice Burroughs
Edith Van Dyne
Edith Wharton
Edward J. O'Biren
Edward S. Ellis
Edwin L. Arnold
Eleanor Atkins
Eliot Gregory
Elizabeth Gaskell
Elizabeth McCracken
Elizabeth Von Arnim
Ellem Key
Emerson Hough
Emilie F. Carlen
Emily Dickinson
Enid Bagnold

Enilor Macartney Lane
Erasmus W. Jones
Ernie Howard Pie
Ethel Turner
Ethel Watts Mumford
Eugenie Foa
Eugene Wood
Eustace Hale Ball
Evelyn Everett-green
Everard Cotes
F. H. Cheley
F. J. Cross
Federick Austin Ogg
Ferdinand Ossendowski
Francis Bacon
Francis Darwin
Frances Hodgson Burnett
Frances Parkinson Keyes
Frank Gee Patchin
Frank Harris
Frank Jewett Mather
Frank L. Packard
Frank V. Webster
Frederic Stewart Isham
Frederick Trevor Hill
Frederick Winslow Taylor
Friedrich Kerst
Friedrich Nietzsche
Fyodor Dostoyevsky
G.A. Henty
G.K. Chesterton
Gabrielle E. Jackson
Garrett P. Serviss
Gaston Leroux
George A. Warren
George Ade
Geroge Bernard Shaw
George Durston
George Ebers
George Eliot
George Gissing
George MacDonald
George Meredith
George Orwell
George Sylvester Viereck
George Tucker
George W. Cable
George Wharton James
Gertrude Atherton

Grace E. King	J. Henri Fabre	Katherine Stokes
Grace Gallatin	J. M. Barrie	L. A. Abbot
Grant Allen	J. Macdonald Oxley	L. T. Meade
Guillermo A. Sherwell	J. S. Fletcher	L. Frank Baum
Gulielma Zollinger	J. S. Knowles	Latta Griswold
Gustav Flaubert	J. Storer Clouston	Laura Lee Hope
H. A. Cody	Jack London	Laurence Housman
H. B. Irving	Jacob Abbott	Lawrence Beasley
H.C. Bailey	James Allen	Leo Tolstoy
H. G. Wells	James Andrews	Leonid Andreyev
H. H. Munro	James Baldwin	Lewis Carroll
H. Irving Hancock	James DeMille	Lewis Sperry Chafer
H. Rider Haggard	James Joyce	Lilian Bell
H. W. C. Davis	James Lane Allen	Lloyd Osbourne
Hamilton Wright Mabie	James Lane Allen	Louis Hughes
Hans Christian Andersen	James Oliver Curwood	Louis Tracy
Harold Avery	James Oppenheim	Louisa May Alcott
Harold McGrath	James Otis	Lucy Fitch Perkins
Harriet Beecher Stowe	James R. Driscoll	Lucy Maud Montgomery
Harry Houidini	Jane Austen	Lydia Miller Middleton
Helent Hunt Jackson	Janet Aldridge	Lyndon Orr
Helen Nicolay	Jens Peter Jacobsen	M. Corvus
Hendrik Conscience	Jerome K. Jerome	M. H. Adams
Hendy David Thoreau	John Burroughs	Margaret E. Sangster
Henri Barbusse	John Cournos	Margaret Vandercook
Henrik Ibsen	John F. Kennedy	Margret Penrose
Henry Adams	John Gay	Maria Edgeworth
Henry Ford	John Glasworthy	Maria Thompson Daviess
Henry Frost	John Habberton	Mariano Azuela
Henry James	John Joy Bell	Marion Polk Angellotti
Henry Jones Ford	John Kendrick Bangs	Mark Overton
Henry Seton Merriman	John Milton	Mark Twain
Henry W Longfellow	John Philip Sousa	Mary Austin
Herbert A. Giles	Jonas Lauritz Idemil Lie	Mary Catherine Crowley
Herbert N. Casson	Jonathan Swift	Mary Cole
Herman Hesse	Joseph A. Altsheler	Mary Hastings Bradley
Homer	Joseph Carey	Mary Roberts Rinehart
Honore De Balzac	Joseph Conrad	Mary Rowlandson
Horace Walpole	Joseph E. Badger Jr	M. Wollstonecraft Shelley
Horatio Alger Jr.	Joseph Hergesheimer	Maud Lindsay
Howard Pyle	Joseph Jacobs	Max Beerbohm
Howard R. Garis	Jules Vernes	Myra Kelly
Hugh Lofting	Julian Hawthrone	Nathaniel Hawthrone
Hugh Walpole	Julie A Lippmann	Nicolo Machiavelli
Humphry Ward	Justin Huntly McCarthy	O. F. Walton
Ian Maclaren	Kakuzo Okakura	Oscar Wilde
Inez Haynes Gillmore	Kenneth Grahame	Owen Johnson
Irving Bacheller	Kenneth McGaffey	P.G. Wodehouse
Israel Abrahams	Kate Langley Bosher	Paul and Mabel Thorne
Ivan Turgenev	Kate Langley Bosher	Paul G. Tomlinson
J.G.Austin	Katherine Cecil Thurston	Paul Severing

Percy Brebner
Peter B. Kyne
Plato
R. Derby Holmes
R. L. Stevenson
R. S. Ball
Rabindranath Tagore
Rahul Alvares
Ralph Bonehill
Ralph Henry Barbour
Ralph Victor
Ralph Waldo Emmerson
Rene Descartes
Rex Beach
Rex E. Beach
Richard Harding Davis
Richard Jefferies
Richard Le Gallienne
Robert Barr
Robert Frost
Robert Gordon Anderson
Robert L. Drake
Robert Lansing
Robert Lynd
Robert Michael Ballantyne
Robert W. Chambers
Rosa Nouchette Carey
Rudyard Kipling
Samuel B. Allison

Samuel Hopkins Adams
Sarah Bernhardt
Sarah C. Hallowell
Selma Lagerlof
Sherwood Anderson
Sigmund Freud
Standish O'Grady
Stanley Weyman
Stella Benson
Stephen Crane
Stewart Edward White
Stijn Streuvels
Swami Abhedananda
Swami Parmananda
T. S. Ackland
T. S. Arthur
The Princess Der Ling
Thomas A. Janvier
Thomas A Kempis
Thomas Anderton
Thomas Bailey Aldrich
Thomas Bulfinch
Thomas De Quincey
Thomas H. Huxley
Thomas Hardy
Thomas More
Thornton W. Burgess
U. S. Grant
Valentine Williams

Various Authors
Vaughan Kester
Victor Appleton
Virginia Woolf
Walter Camp
Walter Scott
Washington Irving
Wilbur Lawton
Wilkie Collins
Willa Cather
Willard F. Baker
William Dean Howells
William le Queux
W. Makepeace Thackeray
William W. Walter
Winston Churchill
Yei Theodora Ozaki
Yogi Ramacharaka
Young E. Allison
Zane Grey